Can't Hide Love

Can't Hide Love

Love

CHERIS HODGES

www.kensingtonbooks.com

First Printing: June 2022
ISBN: 978-1-4967-3193-7

ISBN: 978-1-4967-3194-4 (ebook)

10 9 8 7 6 5 4 3 2 1

Printed in the United States of America

This book is dedicated to my champion, my father, Freddie Hodges, Jr. Sunrise, July 1947, Sunset May 2021. I couldn't have asked for a better #GirlDad. My dad was my biggest fan, my biggest supporter, and my best friend. I wouldn't have a writing career if it hadn't been for him believing in his little girl's big dream.

Daddy, you will always be my North Star, my guiding light, and the missing piece of my heart. Thank you for loving me and believing in my dreams.

CHAPTER ONE

Alexandria Richardson was finally in a hospital without thinking about death. She was about to become an auntie. She paced the floor outside her sister's room waiting to hear something. Cries from the baby, Yolanda screaming dramatically or something. But Alex had to give her sister credit. Yolanda Richardson-Morris wasn't being the stereotypical mother-to-be Alex had expected. Yolanda had been in labor for more than three hours and she hadn't screamed once.

Maybe it helped that their brother-in-law, Dr. Logan Baptiste, was assisting in the delivery of Baby Morris. Alex glanced over her shoulder at her two other sisters, Nina and Robin. She wasn't surprised that they were looking back at her, laughing.

"What?" Alex snapped.

"How about sitting down?" Nina said. "You're making me nervous."

Alex sighed and joined her sisters in the plush chairs they'd been sitting on. "Is giving birth supposed to take this long?"

"Labor and delivery don't work on your schedule," Robin said with a laugh. "I'm glad she decided to have our niece . . ."

"Or nephew," Nina interjected.

"Here in Charleston," Robin said with an eye roll.

"Niece or nephew, I just hope the baby is healthy," Alex said as she fingered her bun. "I can't believe Yolanda is having a kid."

"I really thought Nina would be first," Robin said with a giggle.

Alex wondered how Robin was really feeling after her fertility issues. Robin had a life-saving surgery after a bout with cancer and was left unable to have children, which had been a longtime dream of hers. Robin didn't talk about it much and Alex wasn't going to bring it up today.

"Where's Daddy?" Alex asked. Just then, the elevator dinged and Sheldon Richardson, owner of Charleston, South Carolina's historic Richardson Bed and Breakfast, stepped off carrying a teddy bear and balloons in one hand and a bag of food in the other.

"Hey, girls, I figured y'all would be hungry. And I know Yolanda will be."

Alex crossed over to her father and took the food from his hand. "Thanks, Daddy."

"Any word on my grandbaby yet?"

"Still waiting," Nina said as Sheldon sat beside her and gave her a kiss on the cheek and then did the same to

Robin. "And this one," Nina pointed at Alex, "is trying to say it's taking too long."

Sheldon laughed. "First babies are either early or late. Nora was in labor with Alex for fourteen hours."

"Dear God," Robin said. "This is going to be a long day."

He patted Robin's knee. "Relax, we're all here together for a celebration of life." Sheldon beamed as he looked at his daughters. "Now, I got enough shrimp and grits for all of us."

"Daddy, you're amazing," Nina said as she reached for one of the boxes.

"So," Robin began as she took a fork from Nina. "Are you going to be Granddad, Pop-Pop, or Papa?"

Just as he was about to answer, the door to Yolanda's room opened and Charles Morris, Yolanda's husband, known affectionately as Chuck, walked out of the room. The Richardsons stood up and Chuck smiled at them.

"It's a boy and a girl," he said.

Nina and Robin screamed, then hugged. "Twins! This is so awesome," Nina exclaimed. "I can't believe she didn't tell us she was having twins!"

Charles laughed. "You know my wife likes to keep secrets, and she has a flair for the dramatic."

"You got that right." Robin laughed. "Two babies. I can't believe it. Auntie squared."

"How is Yolanda?" Alex asked.

"When can we see her?" Sheldon asked. "And congratulations."

Chuck held up his hands. "Yolanda and the babies are fine. She's tired, and right now they're stitching her up."

"Stitching her up?" Robin asked. "What happened?"

"Um, she popped out two babies," Nina said. "It's normal, right?"

"Yes," Chuck said. "That's what Dr. Logan told me to tell y'all."

Robin expelled a relieved sigh. "Twins, though?"

"My sisters are twins, and I guess it was my turn to add multiples to the family," he said with a shrug.

"Will your family be coming to Charleston?" Alex asked.

"Probably at the end of the month. I think they've just accepted the fact that I'm really married."

Alex always wondered about Chuck's family, and how they could go so many months without speaking and visiting one another. But she couldn't deny how much he loved her sister.

Logan walked out of the room and crossed over to Robin. "Hey, Auntie."

"Oh stop." She stood on her tiptoes and kissed him on the nose. "Thank you for taking care of my sister."

He hugged her tightly. "She's my sister, too. You're all right?"

Robin nodded.

"So, when can I go see my daughter and my grand-babies?" Sheldon asked Logan.

"In about ten minutes," Logan said as two nurses pushed the babies out of the room. "They have to go to the nursery and . . ."

"Chuck!" Yolanda called out. "Where is my food?"

Sheldon pointed to one of the boxes of shrimp and grits, "If you give her hospital food, you're going to hear about it for the rest of your life."

Chuck grabbed a box. "Thanks. Let me feed her."

"I have to call Clinton and tell him!" Nina said as she reached for her phone. "And I need to know if he has twins in his family."

As everyone gushed over the twins and waited to see Yolanda, Alex's smartphone vibrated.

Three days until you hit the high seas.

She was supposed to go on vacation, but she couldn't leave now. Yolanda was going to need a nursey set up for two babies, and she was going to have to make sure her room at the bed-and-breakfast was set up for the twins as well. And there was still the summer season she needed to prepare for.

"Whatever is on that phone can wait," Robin said when she approached Alex.

"It was just a reminder about my cruise. I think I'm going to cancel it. There's so much that has to be done here for Yolanda and . . ."

"You *are not* canceling your vacation. Alex, we got this. And Chuck probably has so many things prepared and we aren't even going to be able to see the babies without a fingerprint and an eye scan."

Charles Morris was a personal security expert and he'd met Yolanda after Sheldon hired him to protect his daughter after she'd witnessed a murder in Richmond, Virginia. Then she'd started getting death threats.

In between protecting Yolanda and finding out the truth about the man who wanted her dead, they fell in love. Only Yolanda could make that happen, Alex always thought, when she saw the over-six-foot man and her five-foot-five sister together.

Alex shook her head. "You're right, but I don't want to miss time with the babies."

"Newborns sleep a lot. Alex, you know you don't have

to take care of everybody. It's time for you to do something nice for yourself."

"Robin, I just . . . fine, I'll go."

Robin took Alex's phone and confirmed her reservation. "Now your credit card has been charged and you have to go."

"You make me sick."

"That's why I'm your favorite," she replied with a smile.

About thirty minutes later, Alex, Nina, Robin, and Sheldon were surrounding Yolanda and her babies.

"What are you and Chuck going to name the Morris twins?" Nina asked as she stroked her sister's hair. "I like Mercury for my nephew."

"Don't do that," Yolanda said. "I'm not naming my son after a football player. Especially not that one. One day some other team is going to break that record."

"I just knew you weren't going to catch that." Nina laughed. "And let Mercury be great. I don't think another team will do what the '72 Dolphins did."

Yolanda rolled her eyes. "Chuck has been a Morris his whole life; we've discussed this. And before you ask, there will not be a Chuck Morris Jr."

Nina glanced down at the babies and smiled. "They look like little dolls," she said.

"Want to hold them?" Yolanda asked.

Nina took a step back. "Um, no. Not yet."

Robin gently pushed Nina out of the way. "Let me hold our babies," she said as she took her nephew into her arms. He whined a little before closing his eyes. Robin held his tiny hand and smiled. Then she reached for her niece, who was wide awake. She had eyes like her dad, big and emerald-colored. "She's going to be a heart-breaker."

"Let's just hope she doesn't have a mouth like her mama," Alex quipped.

"Why are you even here?" Yolanda asked. "Aren't you supposed to be on vacation?"

Alex stood beside her sister and stroked her forehead. "This was a day I wasn't going to miss. I'm proud of you, Yolanda."

Yolanda blinked and looked up at her big sister. "Who are you? And what have you done with Alexandria the Great?"

Alex pinched Yolanda's forearm. "See, this is why I can't be nice to you."

"You just assaulted me after I had two babies," Yolanda joked. "And I sent you a package to the bed-and-breakfast."

Alex shook her head. "Do I even want to know?"

"Vacation clothes."

Alex turned toward Robin and reached for one of the babies. She took her nephew in her arms and stroked his cherublike cheek. "These babies are so precious," she said as she walked over to the armchair in the corner next to the sofa, where Sheldon and Chuck were talking.

"What's up, Grandpa and Daddy?" Alex asked.

"Give me that baby," Sheldon said as he stood up and took his grandson from Alex's arms. The little boy opened his eyes and seemed to smile at his grandfather. Chuck watched his in-laws and smiled.

"Have you two come up with names for the babies yet?" Alex asked as Nina and Robin joined them in the corner.

"Yolanda is knocked out," Robin said. Chuck reached for his daughter and stood beside Sheldon.

"Well, since all of you are here now," Chuck began, "we wanted to name the twins Bradford and Nora."

Tears shone in Sheldon's eyes. His middle name was Bradford. "I couldn't be prouder that you want to name these babies after me and Nora."

Robin didn't try to hide her tears. "That's just beautiful. I love it."

"Bradford and Nora Morris," Nina said with a sweet sigh. "No one is going to make up a funny nickname about these kids."

Alex shook her head. "Only you would think something like that," she said.

"No, Yolanda was on the same page." Chuck laughed. "She said we weren't going to have baby Chuck Morris. I had to agree with her. If I wasn't athletic and into martial arts, life would've been hell growing up. I wouldn't want to put that on my son."

"We should let you and the babies rest, too," Alex said. "And I need to . . ."

"Get ready for your vacation?" Chuck said. "Yolanda said our babies aren't an excuse for you to cancel."

"How was she thinking about me when she was giving birth?" Alex shook her head.

When the nurses came in to examine Yolanda and the babies, the Richardsons left, and Alex did just what her sisters thought she would do: head to the office at the bed-and-breakfast. Yes, she was still going on vacation, but she needed to tie up a few things. Including the meeting with an architect from Prescott Architects. The bed-and-breakfast was expanding and Sheldon wanted the new wing to reflect the history of the property. Alex had been on board with the idea, but she wanted and hoped her father would agree to adding a few modern touches to the new wing as well. She hadn't had a chance to talk to him about it since Yolanda's pregnancy had taken their attention from the business. Alex smiled as she sat down at her desk and thought about her sister and the twins. She was happy to be an auntie and couldn't wait to see the changes that motherhood would make in Yolanda.

"Hey," Clinton Jefferson, the bed-and-breakfast's marketing director and Nina's husband, said as he stuck his head in Alex's office. "How is Yolanda?"

"Resting. Nina told you she had twins, right?"

Clinton nodded. "My wife said the pressure is off now." He laughed. "I know Pops is excited."

"We all are."

"Nina and I are going to see the babies tomorrow, so I'll be a little late."

"Take your time, Uncle Clint," Alex replied with a smile.

"Are you all right? Because you're usually not about anyone missing the morning meeting."

"It's canceled," Alex said. Her relationship with Clinton had started out rocky because before he'd started working for the company, he'd been employed by Randall Birmingham, an underhanded property owner who wanted to buy the bed-and-breakfast. The first time Clinton had come to the Richardson Bed and Breakfast, he had been offering to buy the place. The next time he was in Sheldon's office he was asking for a job, and Alex wasn't having it. As much as she tried to act as if she was in charge, Sheldon was the king of his castle and hired Clinton. Then he and Nina met. When he'd started dating her, Alex had been sure he was trying to use her sister. Thankfully, she had been wrong and the love was real.

"So, you're really going on vacation?" Clinton asked.

"I'm getting tired of y'all asking me that. And thanks to Robin, my cruise is paid for. They have a strict no-cancellation policy, so I'm going."

"Alex, you do need to relax. I've never seen anyone as nonstop as you. Whether it's business or family. It's time to do something for yourself."

She shrugged. "You're right."

"Oh, and I have a box for you," he said, then crossed back to his office. When he returned to Alex's office with a huge box, she could only shake her head.

"Is this from Yolanda?"

"It is."

"How long does she think I'm going to be gone?" Alex asked as Clinton set the box on the floor.

After Clinton left Alex took the box to her room and checked the time. It was still early enough for her to decompress at her favorite place, the Alice Davis Dance Studio. There were a few things Alex did for herself; ballroom dancing was the main one. It was great exercise, and that was one place where she didn't think about business or legacies.

She changed into her navy-blue leotard and headed to the Savannah Highway studio.

When she arrived, her favorite instructor, Alan Kelly, greeted her at the door. "Miss Alex," he said excitedly, then gave her a peck on the cheek. "Where have you been? I know you aren't cheating on me with that new dance studio downtown."

Alex slapped her hand on her hip. "Absolutely not. I've just been busy at work, becoming an auntie, and getting ready for vacation."

Alan clasped his smooth, cinnamon hands together. "Where are you off to?"

Alex walked over to the mirrored wall and began warming up. "A little singles cruise my sister rudely confirmed for me today."

"I don't understand how a stunner like you is single in this city," Alan said.

"All the good men have married my sisters," she quipped.

"Whatever, Miss Alex. I know there's that special guy out there for you."

Alex shrugged. "Not worrying about some man. Let's dance."

"All right, but remember, I lead the tango, all right?"

"Okay," she said as she got in the ready position. The tango shifted into the foxtrot, where Alex showed her skill by dropping down and kicking her leg up like she'd seen Eartha Kitt do in an old video.

Alan clapped. "Wow, see, it's moves like that . . . Why aren't you entering the ballroom dancing state competition?"

"Because I do this for me and to keep in shape." Alex shook her head. "I don't want to be judged."

"Listen, you are what this studio needs to get statewide cred. Think about it," he said as he clasped his hands together.

"I'd tell you that I'd think about it, but I don't want to lie to you."

"Now, Miss Alex, you know you're one of the best

dancers I've seen in a long time. You're in here channel-
ing Ms. Eartha Kitt and I have dancers who can't make a
move on the one and two. Come on, you have to do it."

"Alan, I'm sorry, but that just isn't who I am," she
said. "But I'll put your studio on the bed-and-breakfast's
list of go-to places in Charleston."

"That's nice and all. Alex! I want a trophy! I need you
to make that happen."

Alex wiped the sweat from her brow. "What if I help
you find someone else who can do what I do?"

Alan smacked his lips. "You know no one else can do
what you do. And you can work out anywhere. The way
you dance, you should be on somebody's stage."

Inwardly, she beamed under his compliments, but
Alexandria Richardson wasn't getting on anyone's stage.

CHAPTER TWO

Wesley Prescott wasn't a man who believed in all work and no play. Even though he was the principal architect and owner of Prescott Architects, Wesley played as hard as he worked. He never allowed himself to be the face of PA, which was a world-renowned firm. Wesley had created structures across the globe for business and royalty. But he never made himself the focus of the company. It was all about the team. Wes liked flying under the radar when it came to showing up in trade magazines. Media coverage led to questions about one's personal life, and that was nobody's business. He didn't have time to fight off rumors and he made sure any woman he played with felt the same way. Hell, his ex-wife had disappeared from his life quietly.

This upcoming vacation was just what he needed before assigning one of PA's most important projects of the year. While he planned to oversee the designing of the new wing at the historic bed-and-breakfast in Charleston, he was planning on going to Las Vegas to work on designs for a new casino. Work and play at the same time made him happy. But nothing was as exciting to him at the moment as his third cruise of the year. An exclusive singles cruise to the Cayman Islands. He'd taken cruises like this one before and they were always so much fun. For the most part, the women he'd met on those cruises stuck around for a good time and not a long time.

The intercom on his desk phone buzzed.

"Yes, Karen," he said to his receptionist.

"Your brother is here."

Wes smiled. Johnathan was going to be in charge while he was on vacation. Johnathan needed plans to go over plans. It didn't matter that he knew as much about the company as Wes did. That was one of the reasons why Wes made him co-CEO. But he hated that his brother was so much like their father and thought every minute of the day had to be consumed by work.

"Send him in, and you can take the rest of the day off."

"But—it's only eleven."

"With pay, Karen."

"All right, I'm out of here."

Seconds later, Johnathan walked through the door with a scowl on his face. "How are the phones going to get answered now?"

"There's this super great invention called voice mail and people can leave a message. The 1950s are over, J. People don't expect some woman to be sitting by the phone waiting for them to call."

Johnathan shook his head. "Where are you running off to now?"

"The Caymans."

"Haven't you been on vacation enough for three people this year?"

Wes nodded, then kicked his feet up on his desk as Johnathan took a seat across from him. "You've seen the financial reports, right? My vacations aren't hurting anyone."

"And if you took things a little more seriously, we would be doing ten times better."

"I'm not Dad and I'm not working myself to death. You might want to try to take a break yourself. I'd hate to find you at your desk dead one day."

"And then who's going to make sure this business is going to stay in the black?"

"You need to stop taking yourself so seriously."

"Then let me go on the cruise and you stay here and meet with the people in Charleston. I don't want to go down South."

"You're not. Kyle is taking the meeting and overseeing the project. You can keep your corny ass in Brooklyn."

"Thank God. I mean, good looking out."

Wes shook his head and laughed. "You have issues with the South you should work out in therapy," he said as he dropped his feet.

"Whatever. When do you head off to the Caymans?"

"Two more days," Wes said with a satisfied sigh. "How about when I come back, you go on a trip somewhere?"

Johnathan rolled his eyes. "How long am I going to have before you decide to take another trip?"

"Bruh, if you actually go on a trip, I'll stay put for a year. Now, what do you want?"

Johnathan sighed and began asking Wes about upcoming projects and what he needed to know for the next two weeks. Things they had discussed a month ago and hadn't changed. Wes couldn't be happier to be leaving in forty-eight hours.

Alex was hoping she was alone in the family wing of the bed-and-breakfast as she tried on some of the clothes Yolanda had put together for her. She had to admit that her fashionista sister had made some good decisions, like the sundresses. They were classic and tasteful. Alex loved that they reached her ankles. With her height, it was always difficult to find dresses that fit her frame and didn't end up looking like minidresses. The black-and-white sundress with the white sequins on the neckline was a definite keeper. And clearly Yolanda had been listening when Alex said how much she loved the rainbow dress Diana Ross wore in *Mahogany.* Yolanda had packed a dress that was very similar to the dress from that movie, only it was strapless. The jury was still out on that one. She picked up the dress again and held it against her body. Fine, she'd take it.

Just as Alex pulled on the pink-and-yellow bathing suit that was in the box there was a knock at her door. *Damn!*

"Hold on," Alex said as she scrambled to find her robe. When she opened the door, Robin was standing there with a bottle of wine. "What are you doing here?"

"Logan has rounds at the hospital tonight and Yolanda told me to make sure you were actually packing the clothes she sent you."

Alex stepped aside and allowed her sister to walk in.

"Let me guess, Nina's going to pop out of the corner next?"

"No, she and Clinton were still at the hospital when I left. I want to see what Yolanda sent you."

"There are a few nice things here. I don't know about the strapless dress, but . . ."

"Why not? Your boobs are amazing, even if you always try to hide them behind double-breasted suits."

"Shut up."

Robin walked over to the pile of clothes and started looking through them. "Ooh," she said as she held up a yellow romper. "You have to wear this."

"I don't wear shorts," Alex said.

"You're going to the Caymans, it's going to be hot. Take it and thank me later. Where's the bathing suit?"

Alex shrugged. "What bathing suit? I'm just going to wear a sundress by the pool."

Robin tilted her head to the side. "What's under the robe?"

"Nothing. I'm naked."

"Liar. Let me see it."

"No. I'm not wearing this revealing bathing suit."

"Open the robe."

Alex sighed and opened her robe.

"Oh my God, Alex! You look amazing. I forgot you had a body."

"This is why y'all get on my nerves," Alex said as she closed her robe. "You'd think I dressed like one of the Golden Girls."

"Well, you do. And not Blanche." Robin laughed. "Alex, can you have fun on this vacation? Do something you wouldn't do if you were in Charleston, where you feel like you have to be Alexandria the Great?"

Alex shot her sister a questioning look. "Really?"

"If we've learned anything in the last two years, we've learned that nothing is promised, and you never do a thing for Alex. It's always about the family or the bed-and-breakfast. For the next two weeks, you don't have a family or a job. You can be a whole new person."

"You're starting to sound like Yolanda, and that's a little scary."

"Just so you know, your very pregnant sister took her time putting those clothes together, and there may be an original design or ten in there."

"I appreciate the effort you all are putting into my vacation plans," Alex quipped.

Robin rolled her eyes. "Shit, we're just trying to make sure you go."

"There you go. I'm going on this trip since you paid for it," Alex sniped.

"Let me see the bathing suit again," Robin said as Alex held her robe together.

"Why? I mean, this isn't the kind of . . ."

"Drop the robe!"

Alex knew Robin wasn't going away, so she opened her robe and showed off the bathing suit. "Just because I tried it on doesn't mean I'm taking it with me."

"But you should. Alex, go out there and have some fun. After all, we have to live vicariously through you now, since you're the only single one. And you need to do something exciting to make us feel like we're missing out."

Alex rolled her eyes and opened her robe again. "You all should grab some books by Farrah Rochon if your lives are that boring. She has some scenes that . . ."

"Your life is boring," Robin said.

"My life isn't boring to me. And clearly you all have been able to take advantage of me always being here."

Robin rolled her eyes. "That's what you think."

Alex sighed. "What about what I think?"

Robin shrugged. "We're not really concerned with that. Just that you actually take the trip and have some fun."

"Please stop acting as if I don't know how to have fun."

"Once upon a time you did, but that was a long time ago."

"Get out of my room," Alex snapped.

Robin shrugged and stood up. "Take that bathing suit with you."

"Out."

Once she was alone, Alex looked at her reflection in the mirror. She looked good in that suit. Obviously, Yolanda had put a lot of thought into the design of the bathing suit. There was a time when Alex thought her legs were too long. But now, since she had a leg day every week, her legs were shapely like Tina Turner's, at least in her mind. But it wasn't as if she showed off her figure or her legs to anyone.

Alex was all business because she had to be. She never wanted to be known as the pretty one when it came to the bed-and-breakfast. Alex wore more pantsuits than the law should allow to downplay her figure. And her signature hairdo, a tight bun, was just to show off that she was serious.

But she didn't have to be serious on her vacation. Maybe there was another outlandish outfit in the box she'd never wear in Charleston that she could take on the cruise. And there it was, Alex thought as she pulled out a white cotton

romper. It was shorts, just like the yellow one. Alex wasn't
into shorts. Still, it was put together with such great stitching, and it seemed as if Yolanda had put some of the
things she knew Alex would like into it. The lace around
the bodice and the color. But in true Yolanda fashion,
she'd made the shorts look like hot pants from the seventies, as if she was daring Alex to wear them. When Alex
tried on the suit, she laughed because it hugged her body
so well. However, Yolanda could've added more material
to the legs or even made it a skirt.

Alex decided to take it with her anyway. Not that she
planned to wear it, but she could at least shock her sister
with a fake story about it. She made a mental note to
make sure she went to Charlotte to see what Yolanda
had for a business casual look when she returned from
her cruise. Yolanda and Charles split their time between
Charleston and Charlotte. His security business was based
out of Charleston and Yolanda's thriving boutique was in
uptown Charlotte.

*All right, I'm really doing this and I'm going to have a
good time,* she thought as she finished packing. Alex took
a quick shower, pulled on her PJ's, and called Yolanda,
hoping that she wasn't waking her sister.

"Hey, Alex," she said when she answered the phone.

"Yo-Yo, how are you doing?"

"Um, I'm okay, I guess. Your nephew has latched on
to my breast, but little Ms. Nora acts like her Auntie Alex.
She has to have her milk pumped and put in a bottle.
Treating me like I'm a red Solo cup." Yolanda laughed.

"I'm not going to keep you long, because you have
two babies, but thank you for the clothes."

"See, and you thought I was going to load you up with
some crazy clothes you wouldn't want," Yolanda said.

"Shh, shh. Nora wants all of my attention now that Bradford is sleeping."

"Then give it to her. I'll stop by to see you all before I
leave."

"Good night, Alex."

When she hung up with her sister, Alex smiled. Maybe
Robin had a point. She didn't have to feel so responsible
for her younger sisters anymore. She could see what that
selfish life was all about. Alex always felt as if she had to
do what she could to make up for her mother's absence.
Sure, Nina and Yolanda didn't like it, but Alex wanted to
help her father as much as she could. Taking responsibility for her youngest sisters and working for the B&B had
been what she thought she had to do. Now, she didn't
have to, and if she was honest, she didn't know how to
handle that.

CHAPTER THREE

Wes glanced at his watch as he ran on the treadmill at Absolute Power Fitness. He had about twenty minutes left in his workout and he was ready to go. Wes knew that once he got on the ship, the only exercise he was going to get would come from the pool or in the bed of one of the willing singles he was sure to meet.

Though it was a singles cruise, he was under no illusion that he'd meet Miss Right. He wasn't even trying. He figured this cruise was just a Tinder live-action event, and when he swiped right, there would be a quick replacement in real life. Wes knew that his serial dating was just another way he had fun. But he was mostly honest with the women he dated. He let them know he was here for a good time and not a long time. But he never told them that he was Wesley Prescott, a multimillionaire. He didn't want the headache of some woman cozying up to him for a piece of the pie. He'd given enough to his ex-wife and was in no hurry to do that again. But it was fun to date without expectations of anything further than a few nights of passion and a couple of nice steak dinners. Although most of the women he met these days were vegan or vegetarian. That was a life he wasn't ever going to be about.

Just as he ended his cardio workout, his phone rang. Wes shook his head when he saw his ex-wife's face on the screen.

"Jasmine," he said after tapping his earbuds. "To what do I owe the pleasure of this call?"

"You always act as if I'm bothering you when I call."

"I gave you a Chick-fil-A greeting and that's how you feel?"

"Anyway," she said in her brand-new British accent, "I heard you're going to be working on the Richardson Bed and Breakfast in Charleston. How exciting."

"It's just another job. Why do you think it's exciting?"

"Because that place is historic. My grandparents spent summers there. I figured you would've researched the place before taking the job."

"That's Johnathan's thing, not mine. How are you doing?"

"Great, and very happy that things are going so well at the company. I got my quarterly check and I'm probably going to get an Aston Martin next week."

"Hey, I'm working to make sure that divorce settlement stays in place. You married a prince yet?"

"Nope. Somebody beat me to it. But seriously, Wesley. The Richardson Bed and Breakfast is Black royalty in the States. I know you Brooklyn-born men have issues with the South, but I was born and raised there."

"Still, you ended up in the big city."

"Shut up. You should be thankful I went to NYU and became the best public relations director you've ever met."

She did have a point, he thought as he chuckled at her humble brag. "And that's all I should be thankful for?"

"Well, the fact that I'm the best ex-wife you'll ever have."

"The *only* ex-wife I'll ever have. Won't be doing the marriage thing ever again."

"Yes, you want the party and not the work," she quipped.

"And you want to work yourself to death," he replied.

"Speaking of work, I still think it's time you take Prescott international."

Wes rolled his eyes, even though Jasmine couldn't see him. She had been harping on expanding the company since he gave her a seat on the board in the divorce. Johnathan had been in his ear about the same thing, but he hadn't been open to doing it. Not if he had to lay the groundwork and be the one doing the meetings and pretending that he needed more money. And while Johnathan was fully capable of leading the international build, he was boring and didn't want to do it. And anyone waiting for Wes to put a stamp on his passport to create something he had no interest in would be waiting for a long damn time.

"You're breaking up, I'm going to let you go." Wes ended the call, then wiped his face with the towel he kept tucked in the back pocket of his gray sweatpants. And he wore them because he enjoyed the way women checked him out in those pants.

Heading to his car, he decided to head to his office and take a shower. Then he'd go have a quiet dinner with his favorite aunt in Harlem, Rita Prescott. She was his dad's youngest sister and the one who taught him to work hard and play harder, much to Leon Prescott's dismay.

Wes's father was about working harder than the next man and being better than everyone in the room. He knew that was how Leon was brought up and thought that was the only way to get ahead, but watching his father taught Wes how to work smarter, not harder. Wes started his workdays at five a.m. And he ended them at three p.m. Like his auntie always said, there was a time for work and a time to live. Wes combined what he loved and made it his career. He'd always liked to draw and build things. At one point he'd thought about being an artist, but Leon was not having a "starving artist son to take care of."

Thinking about his father made him happy and sad at the same time. Leon wanted to build wealth for his family because he never had that growing up. He also wanted to make sure his sons knew nothing was given to them freely. But he worked so hard and so much that his heart gave out.

Of all the many lessons he'd taken from his father, that had always been the main one. He would never work himself to death, but he would make Leon proud.

Shaking his head, Wes turned his focus to the packing he needed to do when he returned to his Harlem brownstone. Tomorrow he'd be on a luxury cruise ship soaking up the sun and ignoring all phone calls from Johnathan.

Alex promised herself that she was only going to look over a couple of files in her office before heading to the

Charleston Harbor to take her cruise. Her plan had been to spend fifteen minutes in the office and . . .

"Told you she'd be up here," she heard Nina say.

Alex looked up at the top of the stairs and saw Clinton and Nina standing outside his office. "I left something on my desk," she said.

"You're not even going in there to get it," Nina said. "If you forgot it, it wasn't that important to begin with. Let's go. I'm driving you to the harbor."

"I don't think so," Alex said. "You drive like a maniac."

"She's going to take my car and she still has trouble with the clutch," Clinton said, then gave Nina a kiss on the cheek.

"I don't, and just for the record, I have an appointment with Thomas at the Ford dealership later." She pulled Clinton's keys from his pocket. "Come on, Alex. And where are your bags?"

"Downstairs on a luggage cart. Like I said, I'd only came up here to . . ."

"Let's go. You know you have never been a good liar."

Alex rolled her eyes at her sister. "Just drive like you have some damned sense."

Nina shrugged. "I make no promises. Because little does my husband know, I have mastered the clutch."

"Lord help me," she whispered as they headed down the stairs.

"Are you excited?" Nina asked once they reached the lobby. "Sun, sea, and great food."

"I'll tell you how excited I am once I get out of the car with you."

"You know, you taught me how to drive, so if you don't like how I do it, it's your fault," Nina said.

"Whatever. The last thing I taught you was to be a speed demon," Alex said as she crossed over to the luggage cart and grabbed her bags. "Let's go."

Nina bounded out the door and Alex followed her to the classic Mustang. She shook her head as Nina unlocked the trunk. "What are you and Clinton going to do when you have a family of your own?"

"Bite your tongue. We aren't even trying to go there yet," Nina said as she unlocked the doors of the car. "We're just going to spoil Yolanda's kids for a while. And speaking of doing things, are you going to have a good time on this vacation?"

"Why do you all think that I'm going to have a problem with relaxing and having a good time?"

"I've never seen it happen," Nina said as they climbed into the car.

"Stop listening to your sisters," Alex snapped.

"I'm serious. My whole life you have been acting as if you had to take care of everything and everyone around you. But I've never seen you doing anything for yourself."

"Here we go. I don't want to have this conversation again."

"Fine," Nina said. "But I hope you don't have a laptop packed in your luggage."

"I don't," Alex said, not telling her sister she was taking her iPad with her.

"Robin told me to check, but I'm going to take your word for it."

Alex hitched a brow at Nina. "I can't even with y'all."

"We know you, Alex. Do I need to check?"

"You need to crank up the car and drive, unless you want to be the one responsible for me missing the boat."

Without another word, Nina started the car and headed quickly for the Charleston Harbor. Alex held her seat belt as her sister drove. Being that it was a short trip, Nina didn't hit high speeds, but she was definitely driving like a maniac in Alex's opinion.

"Does Clinton know you treat his car this way?" Alex asked once Nina parked at the harbor.

"Treat his car like what? Please show me one person who has a Mustang to drive the speed limit. And how do you think Clinton gets to work on time every day? He drives just like me."

"That's scary."

The sisters hopped out of the car and unloaded the trunk. Nina gave Alex a hug before she headed for the security line. "Now remember, no one has to know that you're Alexandria the Great when you get on that boat," Nina said.

"I'm not even going there with you today. Send me pictures of the twins."

"Nope, you are on the no-text list unless it is an absolute emergency."

Alex shook her head. "You all are the worst," she said. "See you in two weeks."

"Have fun," Nina sang to Alex's retreating figure.

Alex hadn't expected the port to be so busy at eight a.m., but she was happy that the security line moved efficiently and quickly. The porters took her bags to her stateroom and then she was led over to the breakfast area. Alex opted for a plate of fruit and a cup of coffee to get started. She took a seat at an empty table and looked out over the water. Soon enough she'd be out of Charleston in search of that good time everyone was telling her to have. Okay, she was wound tightly, but it was because she always felt as if she had to be.

You don't have a son to carry on your legacy.

Alex never forgot those words from Mr. Eldridge, one of her father's oldest friends. The man was a relic and she knew that. But when she was ten years old, dealing with the loss of her mother and realizing that she had to help her daddy more than ever, that statement stung like a swarm of bees. Just because she wasn't a boy it didn't mean she couldn't carry on the Richardson legacy.

She'd hoped her sisters would feel the same way, but they didn't. And she wanted to prove Mr. Eldridge wrong. And above all else, she wanted her father to be proud of her. Maybe her sisters were right. These next two weeks were about being relaxed and not trying to prove anything to anybody.

She took a small bite of her pineapple slice and smiled. Maybe she could be silly and pretend she was a whole new person while wearing clothes she wouldn't let anyone see her in if she was on the beach in Charleston. Looking down at her fruit, Alex decided she was going to start right now. She headed back to the bar and grabbed two cinnamon rolls.

Wes spent the night in Miami, dancing all night and kissing a few pretty girls. When he woke up at nine-thirty he didn't have much time to get to the port and get on the cruise ship for the Caymans. Thank goodness he was already packed. He made it to the port with minutes to spare before the ship sailed away. One thing he loved about being a frequent sailor was that everyone knew him, and he got through security like a breeze. Better than anything else, he didn't have to wait to get to his state- room, and he needed at least two hours of sleep before heading out to the pool and soaking up some sun and watching the single ladies in next to nothing. The thought of women in bikinis almost made him reconsider his nap, but his body had other ideas as he almost fell asleep in the line for coffee.

"Excuse me," a sweet voice said before his coffee cup overflowed. Wes turned around and was sure he'd seen an angel.

"Sorry," he said as he took a seat at an empty table near the coffee bar. She snorted and fixed her cup of java. Before he could tell her that she was beautiful, Wes had leaned back in his chair and drifted off to sleep. Moments later he felt a hand on his shoulder. "Mr. Prescott? Is everything all right?"

Wes opened his eyes and nodded. "My body just in- formed me that I'm not as young as they thought I was in Miami last night." His laugh rippled through the empty room.

"Well, you'll get a lot more rest in your stateroom."

He yawned and rose to his feet. "And that's just what I'm going to do."

CHAPTER FOUR

Alex had only checked her work e-mail once since the ship stopped in Florida. She had to blame it on the soothing motion of the ocean. She'd napped, she'd snacked, and she'd watched the waves and sun from the window of her stateroom, and then she'd napped some more. When she woke up as the sun was about to set, Alex decided to go on the deck and take in the warm breezes. She opened her suitcase and glanced at the bathing suit Yolanda had made for her. She wasn't ready to show off that much. It was just the first day and she was going to read the Kwana Jackson novel Robin insisted she needed to take with her—the actual book, not the e-book. Alex grabbed a white sundress and slipped into it. Then she slid her feet into a pair of nude flats. After grabbing a towel and her book, she headed for the deck.

Even though she was happy to be an auntie, Alex was glad she hadn't taken a family cruise. It was nice to be around a pool and not have to worry about children running and splashing water. She took a seat in a lounge chair that gave her a perfect view of the ocean. Alex kicked off her shoes and leaned back in the chair. She took a deep breath of the salty air and opened her book. She was about to start reading when she heard someone shout, "Cannonball."

"What the—?" Alex exclaimed as water splashed on her, soaking her dress, book, and shoes. "Are you freaking kidding me!" She leaped to her feet, unaware of how her dress was sticking to her frame. That was until two men across the way saluted her.

"I'm so sorry," the diver said as he emerged from the pool. Somehow, water dripping from his body didn't look as ridiculous as she felt standing there in a wet sundress.

"You ruined my book."

He shook his head and smiled. "Usually when people hear *cannonball* they move out of the way."

"And usually grown people don't act like children in a pool area," Alex snapped.

He smiled, and Alex wanted to push him in the pool. When she locked eyes with another man who had been snapping pictures of her, she did push him in the pool. "Grow up," she snapped before grabbing her towel and wrapping it around her body. This was not how she thought she was going to start her vacation, but here she was. When was the fun going to start?

This woman was either a model or taught supermodels how to put their looks together, Wes thought until she pushed him into the pool. That had been just rude. But he deserved it. When he'd been on the diving board, he'd seen the leggy beauty below him and been intrigued. Surely she hadn't booked a singles cruise to read books for two weeks. And he couldn't help but wonder why she was in a sundress and not a bathing suit like all the other women roaming around the pool. When Wes saw there wasn't anyone in the pool, he'd decided to act like an eight-year-old and pull a cannonball.

He'd wanted to get her wet, but he didn't think he'd soak her and reveal her braless silhouette. Wes wasn't sure if she had been embarrassed or truly pissed at him for ruining her book. It was a good thing it wasn't a tablet, he thought as he grabbed a towel of his own and wrapped it around his waist.

Who is she? he thought as he headed back to his stateroom.

"Is that *the* Wesley Prescott?" a voice said from behind him. Turning around, Wes almost smiled until he recognized the woman behind the silky voice.

"Elizabeth," he said, as if he'd swallowed sour milk. "Hasn't been long enough, has it?"

She snorted and tossed her bleached blond hair over her bare shoulder. Wes saw that she'd added another cup of silicone to her chest. He wasn't impressed, but he could tell some of the people passing them were.

"Don't be so mean. We can still be friends, right?"

"Friends don't stalk friends," he said. "Let's just keep in mind that we are both on vacation and there's no need to get the authorities involved."

Elizabeth rolled her eyes. "Whatever. I was just saying hello. But since you want to be like that, fuck you, Wesley."

"There she is, Unstable Liz. Just stay away from me."

"You think it's really cute to play with a woman's emotions. One day you're going to pay, and . . ."

"I paid in divorce court. It's not my fault you heard what you wanted to hear, Liz. I never wanted anything serious with you and I didn't know she was your sister." Wes headed down the hall, ignoring Liz's swearing.

Glancing at his watch, Wes decided he needed to take a quick shower and head to dinner. Part of him hoped the supermodel would be there with a better attitude and no bra. His goal was to make her nipples harden again, this time without splashing her.

After his shower Wes tried to decide what he wanted to wear to dinner. His tuxedo seemed a little pretentious for a singles cruise, but he did want to stand out and possibly find the supermodel who'd pushed him in the pool. Even if he didn't find her, he didn't plan to spend his first night on this cruise alone or searching for that woman. That fine woman.

There are other women on this cruise, he thought as he dressed.

Alex wanted to call Robin and tell her about the pool incident, but her sisters weren't taking her calls and she didn't have her cell phone anyway. She'd taken a shower hoping the massaging shower head would calm her down. It hadn't.

And she knew why she was masking her feelings with anger. That man was gorgeous. A big child, but he was something else. Something she would have to avoid for the rest of the time on this ship.

And why would you do something like that? Alex almost expected to see Yolanda standing beside her. She shook her head, crossed over to the closet, and tried to figure out if she wanted to wear the jumpsuit or the gown Yolanda had designed for her. It was an emerald, floor-length gown with a slit on the side. Shrugging, she reached for the gown and the gold belt that went with it. Now she needed shoes. Part of her wanted to go for a pair of flats, but she knew that dress deserved the gold heels Yolanda had sent her.

"Do something different," she muttered as she picked up the shoes. Alex dressed and then brushed her hair back behind her ears. No bun tonight. Taking in her reflection, Alex smiled. Okay, Yolanda was a damned good designer, and green was her color. Grabbing her clutch and her cruise pass, Alex headed for the door, ready to take her sisters' advice and be someone else.

The energy in the dining room sizzled. There were so many beautiful people, everyone dressed to the nines. Alex appreciated the looks she was getting from some of the men in their well-fitting suits.

"Good evening," one of the hostesses said to Alex. "Would you like a glass of champagne before heading to your table?"

"No thank—You know what, yes, I do want champagne."

The hostess smiled. "It's okay to relax, and you look amazing in that dress."

Alex smiled. "Thank you." A waiter walked over with a tray of bubbly. She took a glass and then followed the hostess to her table. She was surprised she had gotten a seat at the captain's table, but then she remembered that Robin had upgraded her package. That chick was going to pay her back when she returned to Charleston. Tonight she would just enjoy the view. Alex took a dainty sip of her drink and glanced out over the ocean. The view was like a painting she wanted to hang in the bed and breakfast.

"Well, tonight must be my lucky night. I was hoping to see you."

It. Was. Him. Alex sighed and shook her head. "I hope you have better table manners than you have poolside ones."

"You know, I'm sorry about that. And being the gentleman I am, I want to make it up to you in any and every way I can." He winked at her, then took the empty seat next to her. "I'm Wes."

Alex blinked at his hand as he captured hers in his and brought it to his lips. This man was flirting with her and she didn't know what to do.

Wes half expected his mystery lady to slap him when he reached for her hand. And when he almost kissed her hand like in a Noir Alley movie, he *knew* she was going to slap him. Instead she snatched her hand away.

"You're extremely presumptuous."

"I thought I was charming," he quipped.

She rolled her eyes, but he saw a slight grin on her lips. "That's not what I think at all. Besides, charm is a tool of serial killers and psychopaths."

"You can't write me off yet; you haven't even told me your name."

"Ever think I don't want to?" She leaned back in her seat and folded her arms across her chest. Her chest. Water. Those perky nipples. *Look in her eyes, look in her eyes.*

She met his gaze at her chest and narrowed her eyes at him. "You're disgusting."

"I was admiring the dress. You look like a very expensive emerald."

"Let me guess, you're one of those guys who takes this cruise every year just hoping to meet the most desperate woman on the ship and pretends that these two weeks mean something, promises to keep in touch, but ghosts her as soon as the ship returns to the States? Not interested, buddy."

"You got me all wrong, sweetheart."

The way she broke out laughing gave him pause. "Am I missing something?"

She brought her hand to her chest. Damn it, he followed her hand. "The women in my family don't like the term *sweetheart*. If my little sister was here, you'd be the one all wet now."

"What's wrong with *sweetheart*?"

"The fact that you have to ask is further proof that we don't need to play with each other. I'm here to relax."

"And that is my superpower. I can make beautiful women relax."

The look she gave him nearly made his blood run cold. If his goal had been to impress her, he'd failed. "Listen, Wes. Since we have to sit here for dinner, let's at least be cordial. My name is Alexandria."

"Very regal. Suits you."

She drained the rest of her champagne, and Wes wondered what brought Alexandria on this cruise. Celebrating a divorce? Was she one of those single women who traveled alone because she could and she liked it?

"Thank you," she replied.

Wes waved for a waiter, then turned to Alexandria.

"So, is champagne your drink of choice or . . ."

"Bourbon would be great," she said.

"Okay, color me impressed."

"Bourbon impresses you? You don't get out much, huh?"

Wes smiled. Alexandria was going to be a handful and he was intrigued. "Have you ever been on a runway in Paris? It just seems as if I know you from somewhere."

"I'm not a model, but that is a cute pickup line."

"Alexandria, I'm not trying to pick you up, but give me at least a day to revise your first impression of me."

She seemed to be studying him; maybe she was considering his offer. A few beats passed, and two other people joined the table, nodding hello to them.

"I'll think about it and choose the day," she finally said. Her voice was like velvet, smooth. He wondered how it would sound with her lips close to his ear moaning his name.

"I guess I could agree to that," Wes said. "As long as tomorrow is the day."

"That's not how this works," she replied. "And tomorrow doesn't work for me. I have a full spa day planned."

"Massages and whatnot? You know, I'm good with my hands."

"Be better with your hands and keep them to yourself. Again, you just have this air about you that can be a bit creepy. You just learned my name and now you want to touch my body?"

Wes shrugged. "If we're being honest here, I wanted to towel-dry you poolside."

"I would've held your head underneath that water had you touched me," Alexandria snapped.

He threw up his hands. "I got that. When you pushed

me in the pool that was unexpected. I think you should apologize to me also."

She laughed. "You must be out of your damned mind."

"Some people think so. But what if I couldn't swim?"

"Then I think you wouldn't have been up on the diving board," Alexandria retorted.

"Facts. You got me there. You're just as smart as you are beautiful."

He could've sworn that he saw a flash of anger contort her face. She folded her arms across her chest and glared at him. "Why do you men think that it's hard to be both, and that it's a compliment when you find that a woman who looks as good as I do isn't a vapid bag of flesh?"

Okay, that wasn't what he'd expected. And he didn't deserve that smoke. "On behalf of all of the men who have ever underestimated you, I apologize."

"Ugh, shut up."

"Wait, did I mess up that bad?"

"Yeah, you did, and I'm not sure I want to continue this conversation. This isn't relaxing." Alex rose to her feet and Wes followed her lead.

"Fine, let's not talk. Let's dance." He held out his hand to her as the band played a version of Michael Jackson's "Human Nature."

Alex looked down at Wes's hand. Was he serious? She'd just told that man that she didn't want to talk to him; now he expected her to allow him to take her in his arms and dance with him? She wanted to, but . . . What the hell? Dancing was her secret kryptonite. After all, she'd spent so many nights at the studio practicing for a night like this. Did it matter that she didn't like her partner?

"Okay," she said. Wes's face seemed frozen with shock. When he didn't move she hitched her right brow. "You want me to change my mind?"

"Oh hell no." He led her to the dance floor and pulled her close to his chest. Alex had to admit he felt good. Strong. And he smelled like vanilla and ocean breezes. That clicked something between her thighs. She took a deep breath as she leaned closer to him. Wes placed his hand on the small of her back as they swayed. Alex couldn't remember the last time she'd been eye level with a man while in heels.

"How tall are you?" she whispered.

"Where did that come from?"

She took a half step back from him. He had to be about six-three. And those three inches mattered. "Just wondering," she said as he drew her back into his arms.

Wes spun her around and dipped her as if they were auditioning for *Dancing with the Stars*. Alex went with it and kicked her leg up, silently thanking Robin for telling her that ballroom dancing was great exercise all those years ago.

When the song ended they didn't immediately go back to the table; they stood on the edge of the dance floor swaying. "We should probably go eat," she said.

"If you want to follow the rules, that's fine. But I'd like to keep dancing with you and just have breakfast."

Alex pressed her hand against his chest and pushed back from him. "Don't be that guy. I was just about to say I was having a good time with you."

"Let's keep this energy going, then."

"Nothing's going to keep going if I don't get my meal," Alex quipped.

"Then let's eat and dance off the dessert later."

"If you're using *dance* as a euphemism for anything other than dancing, you're going to be really disappointed with yourself."

Wes grinned as he led her to the table. "I bet you're some kind of vegan who believes carrot slices taste like bacon if you fry them."

Alex snorted. "You got the wrong sister. I'm looking forward to a nice surf-and-turf meal."

"The more I talk to you, the more impressed I get."

"Sadly, the feeling isn't mutual."

"You're kind of mean, huh?"

"That's usually what people who don't know me think," she replied as they took their seats.

"Then I'd better get to know you better so I can see that softer side."

She shrugged and smiled as the waiter brought them a couple of menus. "Good evening," he said to Alex's cleavage.

She cleared her throat. "Hello."

"Yes, um, do you need some time to look over the menu?" His cheeks turned red as he looked at Wes, whose face was wound tight.

"You know what?" Wes began. "This woman likes moonlight and stars. We're going to eat on deck. I'm sure there's a *waitress* who can take our orders out there."

Alex started to tell him that she wasn't leaving the captain's table, which she'd been hoodwinked into paying for, but she wasn't totally opposed to heading outside and dining under the stars.

"Sure, let me get a table for you, Mr. . . . ."

"Wes," he said as he stood up and held out his hand to Alex. "Are you all right with heading outside?"

"Sounds like a good plan," she replied as she took his

hand. Was this an act? she wondered. Did he think the perfect gentleman role would get her to lower her inhibitions and fall under his alluring spell? She wasn't ready to admit that it was working, but it was. There was something about interacting with a man who didn't want to talk about business or get closer to her father or wasn't slimy-ass Randall Birmingham. Another reason Alex wanted to get away from Charleston was because she hated running into that underhanded son of a bitch after he tried to make her think her brother-in-law, Clinton Jefferson, had been working with him to steal the bed-and-breakfast from the family. Alex had made it easy for him to play that cruel game because she hadn't trusted Clinton when he started working at the Richardson Bed and Breakfast and she hadn't wanted him dating her sister at all. Thankfully, she'd been wrong. But she still hated being thought of as a fool. When she'd see Birmingham in passing, his slick sneer made her feel like she was everything old man El-dridge said: *You don't have a son to carry on your legacy.*

But she didn't have to worry about the legacy tonight or for the next two weeks. "Make sure we get a table away from the pool area. I don't want to get wet again."

CHAPTER FIVE

Why did she say *wet*? Wes glanced at her hips as she walked over to an empty table. She might claim she wasn't a model, but she sauntered as if everywhere she walked was her personal runway. And those long legs. He was a leg man and she had him weak. He prayed that she had a dress like the one she was wearing for every day of the week. He didn't want to sound like a cliché and ask her why she was single. Hell, he didn't care if she had a husband at home, she was going to be his for the remainder of this cruise.

"You don't like the table?" Alexandria asked, misunderstanding why he was silent.

"Oh no, this is fine." He pulled out her chair for her, then took his seat across from her. They were away from the pool and other guests. The table was perfect.

Alexandria leaned back in her chair and turned toward

the ocean. "It's so beautiful out here. I can't wait to see the sunrise over the ocean."

"You live in a city far away from the ocean or something?"

She shook her head. "I actually live on a beach, but this is different. Just peaceful."

"You have to make peace everywhere you go. That's how I keep sane. Work hard and play harder."

She propped up her chin on her fist. "You mean you're not some trust fund baby who travels the world splashing people from diving boards?"

Wes chuckled. "No. But I do travel the world because all work and no vacations isn't a life I want to live. What about you, Alexandria?"

"According to my sisters, I am all work and no play. But someone has to . . . wait. I'm going to try something new. No talk about business."

"You won't get an argument from me," he said with a smile. "Where are you from?"

"South Carolina. And you?"

"Brooklyn."

"I should've known."

Wes folded his arms across his chest. "And what does that mean?"

Before she could reply a waitress walked over to their table to bring them champagne and menus. After giving the waitress their drink and dinner orders, Wes speared Alexandria with a questioning look. "So, what were you saying about Brooklyn?"

"Oh, so you're a Spike Lee Brooklynite, I see," Alexandria said with a laugh. "BK all day, right? There is no place in the world like Brooklyn and the rest of us could never understand how amazing that place is. Yeah, you have that arrogant Brooklyn vibe."

Wes ran his hand across his face. "Sounds like you're jealous."

"Ha! You remind me of someone I used to know and that isn't a compliment," she said as she crossed her legs. Whatever smart response he had floated out of his mind as he looked at her firm thighs. Alexandria snapped her fingers. "Eyes up."

"Sorry. Your legs are . . ."

She pulled the fabric of the dress across her leg. "Whatever."

"Is it yoga or running?" he asked.

"What?"

"To keep those legs in tip-top shape, running or yoga? I'm trying to learn something."

Alexandria laughed and picked up her glass of champagne. "Both. And karate. So, if you keep looking at me like that, I'm going to practice the roundhouse kick I learned last week on you."

Wes threw up his hands. "No disrespect. Maybe we can hit the gym together in the morning. You know, if you've decided tomorrow is the day you're going to give me my do-over."

"You don't stop, huh? I said I was going to pick the day and you keep forcing tomorrow down my throat."

He leaned across the table. "I figure the sooner I get my second chance to make a first impression, the sooner I can kiss you."

Alex could count on one hand when she'd been speechless. Today was that day. Did he just say he wanted to kiss her? And why was she so excited? *Stop it*, she thought as she stroked her chin. Now she couldn't stop looking at his lips. Was he inching closer to her or had she been hoping he would? When she felt his hand brush against her cheek, it was coming, and she was powerless to stop it. He brushed his lips across hers, and Alex closed her eyes expecting something hotter and deeper. But Wes pulled back. "I'm not a guy who takes things he isn't offered or hasn't earned."

She expelled a sigh as he leaned back in his chair. "That is an admirable trait, but you should've gone in for the kiss."

"I won't make that mistake again," he said with grin. Alex was about to say something saucy when the waitress returned to the table with their drinks.

"You may never have the chance again," she said once the waitress left.

"Not saying I can see into the future, but I'll have another chance because you're not going to miss your chance to kiss me. And you can do it anytime you want."

Alex took a sip of her Jim Beam and cola and smiled at Wes. "You know, I bet you'll be begging for a kiss before I do."

"What do you want to lose?"

She ran her tongue across her bottom lip. "Mmm, I don't plan to lose at all."

Wes leaned forward again and stared into Alex's eyes. She clamped her thighs together as she felt a wave of desire take hold of her. He lifted her chin and inched closer to her. Alex's eyes fell on his lips. She drank in the thickness of his bottom lip. She wondered if his lips were as soft as they looked. And if he was a good kisser. Where else would his lips feel good? On her neck, between her thighs?

Just how much had she had to drink? These thoughts, this yearning, this wasn't who she was.

Be someone else, Yolanda's voice played in her head. Her eyes locked with Wes's and then she pressed her lips against his. Soft. His lips were soft and his tongue was hot and sweet. Alex couldn't remember the last time her mouth had been treasured. Wes was doing that as he nibbled her bottom lip and brushed his tongue across it as if she was a succulent piece of chocolate, nearly making her explode.

She pulled away from his lips. "Whoa," she muttered as Wes smiled.

"More like wow," he replied. "Didn't expect that."

"So, what were you expecting when you kissed me?"

Wes chuckled. "When I kissed you? You're mistaken, Alexandria, because you kissed me."

"That couldn't be further from the truth because you know you kissed me and you liked it."

"Yes, I liked it, but my favorite part was when you kissed me."

She shook her head. "Just because I enjoyed one kiss doesn't mean I started it."

"Why don't we try it again?"

"Once you admit that you kissed me first I'd be glad to."

Wes stroked her cheek. "You're a woman who doesn't like to be wrong, huh?"

"I'm a woman who's never wrong." She placed her hand on top of his and smiled. Wes pulled her closer.

"I believe it. But you kissed me first." Before she could protest, Wes captured her mouth and kissed her again. Hotter and wetter than before. Alex moaned and pulled back from him.

"We should probably stop doing this. I'm sure people are watching," she said breathlessly.

"And? Two adults having a good time needs to be broadcast for everyone to see and—" Wes said as he waved his hand toward the other people eating outside. "No one is paying us any attention."

Alex closed her eyes and smiled. "Good," she replied when she opened her eyes and crossed over to Wes's seat. Alex sat on his lap and whispered in his ear, "Let's take our dinner somewhere even more private and beautiful."

"And where would that be?"

"The balcony in my stateroom," she said. "Just me, you, and the moon."

"I knew you were some kind of a goddess." Wes waved at the waitress who was walking over to their table. "Can we have dinner sent up to a room?"

"Three-one-nine," Alex said.

The woman nodded and shot Alex a thumbs-up with her free hand. Alex turned away from the woman and what the hell she was getting into.

Hadn't she been the one telling her sisters—Yolanda in particular—that she wasn't going to have a vacation fling? *No one has to know*, she thought as Wes took her hand in his.

They moved quickly through the dining room and arrived at Alex's stateroom just as a waiter rolled a dinner cart to the door. "Perfect timing," the man said as Alex opened her door.

"Yes, it is," Wes said as he reached into his jacket pocket and handed the man a twenty-dollar bill. "I can take it from here."

The waiter nodded. "Yes, sir. Have a good night."

Wes closed the door as Alex took off her heels. "Damn, is every part of you beautiful?"

She glanced down at her feet and shook her head. "The last thing my feet feel like right now are beautiful."

He crossed over to her and took her left foot in his hand. As he massaged her foot, Alex was sure this was what heaven must feel like. She almost leaned back on the bed and allowed him to touch her all over, but there was no way she could allow that to happen.

They were just going to eat dinner, kiss a little more, and then he could go back to whatever cabin he was assigned to. Yeah. That was her plan. Then he moved up to her calf.

"Oh," she exclaimed. "You have to stop."

"Why?"

"Because I said so."

Wes threw up his hands. "I hear you."

Alex smiled and tried to regain her composure. If she was honest, she'd have to admit that it had been a long time since she had been touched like this.

David Jenkins. He had good hands and sweet kisses, but such a small dick. She shuddered inwardly, thinking that it had been two years since she had sex and it had been the most unsatisfying experience in her life.

Alex eased her foot out of Wes's hand. "Why don't we do what we came here to do?"

"And that was?" Wes quipped.

"Eat dinner in the moonlight because anything else you think may happen isn't about to."

"There you go, assuming the worst about me. I was just trying to help you feel better. When a woman's feet hurt it's a feeling one doesn't get over."

"You're right about that, and I guess this is where I pretend I'm grateful?" she said as she rose from the edge of the bed.

"No," he said as he closed the sliver of space between them and wrapped his arms around her. "This is where we kiss again." He covered her mouth with his and kissed her deeply. Alex nearly melted in his arms as their tongues danced together. Her body heated like a firecracker as his hands stroked her back. The kiss deepened and Alex moaned. It was a loud moan. Seemed to come from the bottom of her soul.

She knew if this kiss didn't stop, she was going to end up naked in her bed with this man. Alex brought her hand to his chest and pushed back from him. "Dinner is going to get cold."

"You're right," he said with a slight smile. Alex walked over to the balcony doors and opened them. She was disappointed when she was splashed in the face with raindrops.

"Damn it," she muttered, then turned around and bumped into the food cart and Wes. "It's raining."

"Then it's a good thing we decided to come inside." He took a step back from her and pushed the cart over to the small table near the window.

"Yeah, isn't it a good thing I'm full of amazing ideas," Alex said.

Wes lifted the lids that covered their meals and smiled at the steak on Alex's plate. "I see you weren't kidding about eating meat."

"Again, you have the wrong sister."

"How many sisters do you have?"

"Three."

"And you're the youngest?"

Alex dipped her fork in the butter sauce, then dug into her lobster tail. "You're cute, you know that. I'm the oldest."

"So, the other three must be toddlers."

"You can stop now," Alex said as she bit into her lobster. She frowned because it was way too salty. "You would expect seafood on a cruise ship to taste better."

"The lobster is sometimes hit or miss, but try this," Wes said as he dug into his crab cake and held out a forkful to her.

Alex took the meat into her mouth, and she had to it admit it was delicious. She moaned as the flavor exploded in her mouth.

"Damn," Wes intoned. "It's that good."

"Or maybe I'm just that hungry," she replied with a slight smile. "I wonder if I can get some of these."

"If I can take you to the pool, you can have mine."

"Didn't I tell you that I wasn't ready to be around you at the pool yet? You ruined a designer dress with your shenanigans."

"Yet here we are, sharing a meal. I tell you what, let's go to the midnight dance in the ballroom and then I will officially make my second first impression and we can take a swim in the morning."

Alex cut into her steak and took a bite-size piece into her mouth. "You're still trying to make me spend my day with you tomorrow. What's that all about?"

"Nothing other than you are a joy to be around. And I'd hate to have to do another cannonball to make you all wet again."

Oh, if only you knew how wet I am right now, she thought as she returned to her meal.

Alexandria was spectacular and Wes knew he wasn't going to leave her side on this trip. But there was something about her that made him wonder why she seemed to turn her heat on and off.

"Is the steak better than the lobster?" he asked after a beat of silence.

She shrugged. "I've had better."

He offered her another bite of his second crab cake. "I told you, you could have mine."

"I didn't want to be selfish," she said before she took the bite he'd offered her.

"Since I offered, it wouldn't be selfish." Wes was transfixed by her lips as they covered the fork. Her kisses were delightful and he wondered how those lips would feel all over his body.

Alex pulled back from him and smiled. "Thank you for sharing. I think I'm just going to skip to dessert," she said as she reached for her chocolate cake.

"Wait," he said, then slid the rest of his crab cake on her plate. "Just eat this and I'll take your lobster. It can't be that bad."

"Well, why don't you eat and let me know," she said with a grin.

Wes took a chunk of the lobster tail and when he popped it in his mouth, he realized she was right. That was some salty-ass tail. "And we neglected to bring drinks. That was a really bad idea."

"Dinner is a bust, let's just admit that now. I'm going to change and meet you in the ballroom later," Alexandria said with a sigh.

"Change? Out of that amazing dress? Why would you do that?"

She pointed to a drop of rémoulade sauce on her dress. "I have to get this stain out or Yolanda is going to lose her mind. So, do you want to meet later?"

He wanted to stand there and watch her take off that dress. He wanted to see if she wore a matching bra and panties set or if she was wearing panties at all. "Yes," he said as he rose to his feet. "You're not going to break my heart and stand me up, are you?"

"I'm a woman of my word. If I say I'm going to do something, I'll do it." She folded her arms beneath her breasts and shot him a questioning look.

"I like that," he said.

"So, I'll see you in a few hours, unless you're going to finish what's left of your dinner here while I try to get the stain out of my dress."

Wes was tempted to ask her if she planned to take the dress off first, though the look on her face told him he should leave. But Wesley Prescott didn't follow directions very well.

"Why don't you work on your stain and I'll eat my strawberry shortcake?"

She hitched her right brow at him. "You're not going to see me naked tonight, so enjoy your cake," she replied as she crossed over to the closet. Wes hoped she'd pull something out that would show off those killer legs. He was disappointed slightly when she grabbed a jumpsuit. A pants jumpsuit.

As she walked into the bathroom, Wes dug into his dessert. As sweet as the strawberries were, they had nothing on Alexandria's lips. Succulent and divine. He dropped his fork as he heard the shower start. Now, he couldn't walk into the bathroom and join her, but thinking about her standing underneath that shower spray and getting all soapy and clean made his dick harder than a brick.

"Let me get out of here," he muttered. "This isn't how things were supposed to go down tonight." Wes took one last bite of his dessert, then rose to his feet. As he headed for the door, he heard the shower shut off. He was tempted to see if Alexandria was going to walk out of the bathroom wrapped in a towel with water glistening on her shoulders and those legs. But he wasn't going to invade her privacy like that.

"Alexandria, I'm heading out," he said.

"See you soon," she replied.

Once Wes left her room he smiled and wondered what other secrets he'd discover about Alexandria tonight.

Alex felt like a fool when she stuck her head out of the bathroom to make sure Wes wasn't still in the room. Sure, they had kissed, and she was sure things would've been different had it not been raining outside. But she needed a minute alone to get her senses back. More specifically, she needed to get her hormones under control. Her short shower brought her back to reality. Had she really come that close to having a one-night stand with this man and the vacation had just started?

What if it had been bad? Then she'd have thirteen days of trying to avoid him. And if it had been good and he decided he wanted to move on to the next one? "Stop it," she muttered as she walked into the main room and took a look at herself in the mirror. Once again, Yolanda had chosen a great outfit. The white halter jumpsuit accented her body and fit amazingly. She was beginning to feel bad about underestimating her sister's taste over the years. As much as Yolanda and Alex fought, Alex had to admit that she was damn proud of her sister for living her dream. And now she was a wife and mother with a thriving business. Maybe Yolanda, Robin, and Nina had been right all along: Alex should've focused on living her life instead of trying to micromanage the family.

Now here she was, trying to figure out how to flirt with this man and not make a fool of herself. Yes, Alex knew she was attractive and because of working as her father's right hand, she'd played down dating and flirting. She wanted to be taken seriously as a businesswoman. She'd gotten that taken care of because she was known in Charleston as one of the toughest people to do business with. While Sheldon was known as the velvet glove, Alex was the steel fist.

There had been a few men who had the balls to ask her out. And she'd always said no, thinking they had only wanted to get her tipsy and figure out how to get what they wanted from her at a business meeting.

She never wanted to prove her father's old friend right. So, yes, she'd hardened herself and thrown everything into work. But she'd promised herself that this cruise wasn't going to be about who she was in Charleston. The only problem with that was, she didn't know how to separate the two.

Expelling a deep sigh, Alex decided she was going to do all the things she had accused Yolanda of doing and just have some fun without thinking of the consequences. It wasn't as if she was going to see this man again once the ship returned to Charleston.

Standing at the mirror, she decided to braid her damp hair into two goddess braids and pretend she was a heroine from one of her dad's favorite seventies movies. She would be Cleopatra Jones tonight.

CHAPTER SIX

Wes looked at his watch for the third time in fifteen minutes. It was twelve-thirty a.m. and Alexandria still hadn't walked into the ballroom. This didn't happen to him. Women didn't stand him up; that was why he had enemies.

Who the hell did she . . . There she was, in an ivory halter jumpsuit, with two braids in her hair that gave her face an angelic look. Okay, it was worth the wait. But it was not worth watching those dudes trying to hit on her before she could get through the door.

Wes crossed over to her and smiled. "Alexandria," he said as he took her hand in his while ignoring the man standing on the other side of her.

"Wes, I'm not normally late like this, but the hair took longer than I expected."

"I would've waited all night for you just to see you in

that amazing outfit," he said with a smile as they headed for the bar. Wes ignored the angry look he received from the man who had been vying for Alexandria's attention. He couldn't blame Thirsty McThirstyson for wanting to dance with Alexandria. That jumpsuit hugged her body like a second skin and highlighted her luxurious curves. After kissing this woman, Wes wondered what it would feel like to do more with her. If she was sweet all over.

Bring it down. Tonight is about the dance, he thought as she ordered a Jack and Coke.

"I'll have the same," Wes said, then turned to Alexandria. "You made quite the impression when you walked in here."

"That's what I do," she said, then took a sip of her drink.

"I have no doubt." Wes took her hand in his and gave it a kiss. "Shall we dance?"

"Depends on the song."

Wes rose to his feet and held out his hand to her. "That's not an answer, but if you can't dance to Prince, I think you're not interested," he said.

Alexandria took his hand and they headed for the dance floor. Prince's silky voice sang about being scandalous as they ground against each other. Her moves made him want to scoop her up in his arms and rush back to his stateroom. Her hips moved to the rhythm and he was hypnotized by them. He pulled her closer and brought his lips to her ear.

"You're amazing."

"Why, thank you," she said as she took a step back from him.

"Another drink and something to eat? I know you didn't enjoy your dinner."

Alexandria nodded. "Do they have anything other than bar food here?"

"I'm sure I can get you anything you want."

"Oh, you got it like that?" she asked with a smile.

"For you, yes, I do," Wes said, then stopped a waiter crossing the floor. He asked the younger man if he could get an entrée instead of the midnight snacks at the bar.

"I don't know, I mean . . ."

Wes placed his arm around the man's shoulders and spun him in Alexandria's direction. "You see that woman?"

"Yes. She's very pretty."

"I know. And I promised her some really good food. She didn't enjoy dinner and she just isn't the cheese stick type, you know."

"Oh I get it, and you want to feed the fineness before she gets hangry. I'm going to check and see what we have available. She's not vegan, is she?"

"No, but make sure whatever you have is fresh and not salty. That was her problem with dinner."

"Had the lobster, didn't she? Tonight was a bad night for lobster. I'll see if I can make it right for you guys. But I'm not going to be able to serve it to you here."

Wes nodded. "Can you deliver it to my room? I promise I'll make it worth your while." He reached into his pocket and handed the waiter a fifty-dollar bill.

"Yes, sir! And do you want a bottle of champagne, too?"

Wes shrugged. "If it's not too much to ask."

The waiter dashed off and Wes crossed over to Alexandria and smiled. "Don't take this the wrong way, but I have a surprise in my room for you."

She slapped her hand on her hip and glared at him. "Seriously?"

"You have a dirty little mind, you know that? I told you I was going to get you some decent food, right?"

"And it has to be eaten in your room?" She rolled her eyes. "Really original, Wes."

"Because it isn't original or the smartest thing I could do, you should really trust me on this or enjoy some cheese sticks." He nodded toward the finger food on the bar.

Alexandria turned up her nose at the fare. "Fine," she said. "Let's go."

Wes smiled and slipped his arm around her waist as they headed for the exit. She shot him a cold look, but he didn't let her go.

"If you try anything other than feeding me, we're going to have a problem," she said.

"I'm a complete gentleman," he said. "Until you ask me not to be."

She shrugged his hand away. "That's what's scary; you think someone would actually ask you to be a hoodlum."

"You sound like someone's overprotective auntie," he said.

"I'm on my way to being just that person. My sister had twins a few days ago."

"Wow, no wonder you ran off for the ocean."

She tilted her head to the side, then shook her head. "That's a horrible thing to say. I came on this cruise because . . ." She stopped talking abruptly, as if she was on the verge of revealing a secret she didn't want to share.

"The important thing is that you're here and you're with me."

She hitched her right brow at him. "I'm here for the food."

When they arrived at his stateroom the waiter was waiting outside with a cart and a smile. "Mr. P . . ."

"Call me Wes," he said as unlocked the door.

"Well, I have a special dinner and hopefully it will make up for the meal you two had earlier," he said as he pushed the cart inside.

"This must be something magical because my dinner was horrible," Alexandria said, then folded her arms across her chest. The waiter offered her a smile.

"I heard the lobster was a little salty, but one of the chefs and I have access to some really good stuff." He removed the silver top from the tray revealing two lobsters, grilled shrimp, and crisp green salads.

"Looks good," Wes said.

"So did the first meal," she snapped. "I need to taste this first."

Wes crossed over to the waiter and handed him two hundred dollars and cracked open one of the lobsters. With the silver seafood fork, he picked some of the meat from the tail. Then he held the fork out to her. "Take the first bite and let's see if it meets your approval."

Alexandria smiled and took the fork from his hand. When she took the meat into her mouth she moaned. Loud and deep. "This is so fresh," she said after swallowing. "It doesn't even need butter."

The waiter nodded. "Try the shrimp."

Wes had forgotten the man was still there as he watched Alexandria's lips close around that fork. "I'll take it from here. Thanks for everything," he said. The waiter shot him a thumbs-up sign and headed out of the cabin.

Alexandria had picked up a shrimp and licked the sauce from it. Wes was sure he needed a cold shower. "This is already turning out better than dinner," she said before biting into the shrimp. Those lips. How could she look so sexy enjoying something as simple as shellfish?

"I'm sorry," she said when their eyes locked. "Want one?" She speared a shrimp with her fork and held it out to him.

"Thank you," he said as he took the fork from her hand. The shrimp was good, but he needed to kiss her again. "Better than dinner, right?"

She nodded as she took another piece of shrimp. "Much better. Thank you for doing this."

"Want to sit down?" he asked as he pulled out a chair for her.

"Yes, where are my manners? But this food is so . . ."

Wes couldn't take another minute of not feeling her lips against his. Before she sat down he pulled her into his arms. "I've never been jealous of a crustacean in my life, until I saw how that shrimp made you smile."

She pressed her hand against his chest. "It was the fact that it wasn't overly salty."

Wes brushed his lips against hers. Alexandria wrapped her hand around his neck and brought his mouth closer to hers. Slow. Deep. Wet. Kissing her was an adventure that he was more than beginning to enjoy.

She pulled back and smiled at him. "Why don't we eat and then return to the dance floor?"

"If that's what the lady wants," he said, then let her go.

Alex was hot, heated from Wes's kisses and what he was doing to her body. She couldn't stay in this cabin alone with him. She was tempted to follow Yolanda's advice about a vacation fling. If she was going to do it, Wes would be worth it. But she could at least make him wait until tomorrow.

It's after midnight, it is technically tomorrow, she thought as she tried to focus on her dinner and not Wes's lips.

When she'd had her fill of lobster and shrimp, Alexandria rose from her seat and smiled. "Ready to go?"

"Sure," he said as Alex glanced at his half-eaten lobster tail.

"Wait, so you really just got this meal for me?"

Wes nodded. "So, if I haven't made a better first impression, I don't know what else I can do."

"I think you've redeemed yourself," she said with a wink. "But it's time to work off this food."

"Let's hit the dance floor," he said as he opened the door. They headed back to the ballroom. The place was packed. Instead of the live band, there was a DJ playing some old-school music and the dance floor was packed with people doing the electric slide.

"I love this song," Alex said as she joined the crowd and started grooving to the beat. Wes fell in line with her moves as he stood beside her. She glanced at his hips as they slid to the right. That man had some amazing moves. And how would those hips move against her body, between her thighs? The thought made her nearly trip. Wes reached out for her and kept her upright.

"Okay, twinkle toes," he said as he pulled her against his chest. "You all right?"

She released a nervous laugh. "I'm good. Just got a little distracted."

"Want to take a break?"

Just as she was about say something a Teddy Pendergrass classic started playing. Wes pulled her against his chest and they began to slow grind against each other as Teddy sang about closing the door. Wes brought his lips to her ear. "I like the way you move."

"You're not bad yourself," she said as she pulled back from him. The heat of his breath made her body tingle.

"Want to check out the moon? Hopefully it isn't raining anymore."

"Why do I get the feeling you just want to get me wet again?" she quipped.

"You have no idea how true that is," he said with a smile.

He was the one who didn't know the mission had been accomplished, Alex thought behind her smile. "Why not? We could both use a cooldown."

"Both of us?" he teased.

Alex rolled her eyes. "Did I stutter? Let's go." They headed out on the deck and there was no rain. But the sky was still full of clouds. Alex sighed because she still wanted to see the stars and the moon.

"Cool enough for you?" Wes asked as a breeze blew across them.

"Yes." Alex inhaled the salty air, then turned to Wes and smiled. "I just wish these clouds would go away."

"It's just the first night. You will get to see stars before you go home."

"You're going to see that I'm a woman who wants what she wants when she wants it."

"And what happens when you don't get what you want?"

She shrugged and flashed him a slick smile. "If I get bored, I move on."

"Then I see I have my work cut out for me," he quipped. "Got to keep you interested."

"Yes, you do."

Wes eased closer to Alex and wrapped his arm around her waist. "Another dance?"

"Only if it's out here," she said as she bumped her hip against his. "We don't need an audience."

Before Wes could respond Alex pressed her body against his and brushed her lips against his. She hadn't made a first move on a man since she was drunk at her first solo hospitality conference. Unfortunately, the man she'd made her move on that night had been Randall Birmingham. Alex usually pretended that night never happened. She'd even threatened him with a lawsuit if he ever said anything about that night or that almost kiss.

But kissing Wes was something she wanted to shout from the rooftops. His lips were soft, sweet, and delectable. This kiss was different—a sensual dance that made her knees quiver. It was as if Wes's lips were a sweet nectar she couldn't resist. Nor did she want to. He pulled Alex against his chest as their tongues danced against each other's.

Wes took a step back when they broke the kiss. "So, that's what it feels like."

"What do you mean?"

"Being kissed senseless. I've heard that I've done that before."

"Is that so? You need to prove it to me, then."

He stroked her cheek and smiled. "Thought you'd never ask." Wes scooped her up in his arms and carried her from the deck to his cabin. Alex surprised herself when she wrapped her legs around his waist. She wasn't going to overthink what was going on or what she and Wes were about to do.

She wanted this man and prayed it wasn't going to be a colossal disappointment. When his lips captured hers, Alex was hopeful she'd be pleased.

CHAPTER SEVEN

Wes felt as if he was on fire when Alexandria's lips brushed across his neck. Then she ground against him, making his erection tent his pants. Then she had the nerve to thrust her body against his and made him want to explode. What kind of lover would she be? He lay Alexandria on the bed and smiled.

"You are so beautiful," he intoned.

"And you're doing a lot of talking," she said as she tugged at the waistband of his pants. He grabbed her hand. "Slow down. We're going to do this all night. And there is something I need to do first."

"What's that?"

He reached up and untied the top of her jumpsuit and slid it down to her waist. Her skin was smoother than silk and reminded him of the finest French chocolate. Locking eyes with her, he grinned. "I have to know if you're sweet all over." Wes glanced down at her breasts. The definition of perfection. Perky, firm, mouthwatering. The best place to start his exploration. He ran his fingers down the valley of her breasts, eliciting a soft moan from Alexandria. Leaning in, he rained kisses down on her breasts. She arched her body into his lips as if his kisses were controlling her body. As if he needed to test his theory, Wes licked and nibbled at her right nipple. Alexandria's body moved at his touch, their passion in sync with each other. Her moans growing louder as his kisses went deeper. His tongue lashed her hard nipples while he tugged off her jumpsuit. Those thighs. Wes had never seen a body more exquisite than Alexandria's, at least not outside of a museum. This woman was a work of art.

"This is totally unfair," she said, her voice a husky growl. "I'm naked and exposed."

"I'm almost done with my fact-finding mission," he quipped. "So far, so sweet." Wes slipped his hand between her thighs. Alexandria gasped as his fingers danced across her inner thighs, finding their way to her valley of desire.

Her wetness drenched his fingers as he stroked her throbbing bud. "Yes," she gritted. Wes couldn't wait another minute to taste her nectar. Easing between her thighs, Wes licked and sucked her until she began to quake. Alexandria gripped the back of his neck and called out his name.

"Wes, Wes, Wes," she moaned before exploding in his mouth.

He now knew the answer to his question. Alexandria was sweet all over.

*   *   *

Alex closed her eyes and expelled a cleansing breath. When was the last time she'd been so satisfied and relaxed? It felt like never. That man had a magical tongue, and Alex had never come like that from a man's mouth. She closed her eyes and tried to determine whether she'd just had a wet dream or if she had really had multiple orgasms.

"Are you going to sleep on me, beautiful?" Wes whispered in her ear.

"Just five minutes," she said. "I didn't expect . . ."

Wes drew her into his arms and held her against his chest. "Relax, we're on vacation."

When he said *we*, Alex felt a twitch in her chest. It wasn't as if they were together or were going to spend the rest of their time together. Instead of making a big deal out of a minor issue, Alex nestled against Wes's chest and drifted off to sleep.

Five minutes turned into the whole night. Alex didn't wake up until sunlight hit her. Then reality slapped her in the face and across her naked body. Things felt different in the daylight. Had she made a mistake last night? Did she owe it to herself to go all the way with the man with the magic tongue?

Wes was still slumbering as Alex fought her desire. She gave him a slow once-over, noticing for the first time that he'd taken off his shirt and pants during the night. Boxer briefs, Alex was impressed. Her eyes fell on his crotch and her admiration grew like his morning wood.

You're still on vacation and there's no reason not to take a ride, she thought. *Just got to find a condom.* She tried to quietly ease out of Wes's arms, but he held her waist. "Are you trying to sneak out of here?" he asked.

"Actually, I was trying to figure out where you keep your condoms."

She felt him chuckle. "I guess I should've let you wander around so I could've seen all this poetry in motion." Wes stroked her bottom and Alex moaned.

"You have the touch, I see. I just wonder what the stroke is like."

Wes reached underneath his pillow and pulled out a condom. "Then I guess the time is now," he said as he kicked out of his underwear. Alex drank in his naked body. Sculpted. Toned. Everything about him was big. And the big-dick energy he exuded was well earned. "Are you disappointed?" he asked.

"Nope. Quite the opposite."

Wes tore the condom package open, then carefully rolled the prophylactic in place. Then Alex took control, pressing her hand against his chest and mounting him like a prized steed. She hadn't realized that watching a man sheath his erection could make her so wet. But when she drew Wes inside her, she was gushing. He whispered, "Sweet Jesus."

Alex gripped his shoulders and ground against him slow, then fast. He met her thrusts with the same power and intensity until he couldn't. But as he slowed down, Alex took even more control, bouncing against his dick until he exploded. Collapsing against his sweat-covered chest, Alex wondered what was supposed to happen now. Was it still a one-night stand if the sex happened in the middle of the morning? What time was it anyway?

"Um, I uh, need a shower," Alex said. These were new feelings for her: uncertainty, fear, and bitch-ass-ness. This wasn't who she was. Alexandria the Great, even if she hated hearing her sisters call her that, showed no fear.

Is this what having a few, okay, seven orgasms did to the brain?

"Want to save energy and water and do that together?" he asked.

Alex wrapped the sheet around her naked body. "I'd rather shower alone," she said as she rose from the bed. "And since my moisturizer is in my cabin, I should head back there."

Wes flipped over on his stomach and watched Alex pull on her jumpsuit. "So, this is it?"

"Excuse me?"

"I've been on the other side of this. You could at least fake a family crisis or something."

Alex tied her suit and rolled her eyes at Wes. "I don't lie about my family and . . . Look, last night and this morning were amazing, spectacular, and every other adjective that means phenomenal. But it was what it was. You don't owe me anything else."

"What if you owe me?"

Alex tilted her head to the side. "Now you're being ridiculous."

"That's you, pretty lady. I was going to order us breakfast and spa treatments. But if you want to slink out of here and ignore me for the rest of the cruise, go on and break my heart." Wes rolled over on his side and pretended to cry.

Normally, Alex would've called him out on his childish act, but she laughed. "Okay, okay. Listen, I hate to sound like a cliché, but what happened between us isn't something I do regularly."

"We're both adults and we did what we wanted. And," he said as he rose to his feet and slowly closed the space between them, "I'd like to do it again. As long as you agree that you want to have another spectacular night and morning."

"Hmm, just one?" she quipped. "What if I want more?"

"Then the lady gets what she wants."

Alex smiled, then slowly removed her jumpsuit. "Let's start with that shower."

Wes smiled and scooped Alex into his arms, then headed to the bathroom. Alex felt carefree and festive as he carried her. When had she ever felt this kind of bubbles in her stomach and a happy rhythm in her heart? How about never? All right, maybe Yolanda had been right about a vacation fling being fun. After the ship returned to Charleston she'd never see Wes again. Why not let her hair down and enjoy the ride?

"Please tell me you don't have to have the water set on hell," Wes said as he stepped in the shower and placed Alex underneath the showerhead.

"I don't take cold showers," she said as she reached back and turned on the water. The spray rushed out and blasted them in a cool burst before heating up.

"Shit, woman," Wes exclaimed. "That water is boiling."

"Stop being a crybaby, man!" she quipped. "it's not as if I didn't warn you." Alex turned the hot water down. "Now we are officially even."

"Even?"

"Your little splish-splash in the pool."

"And I thought I had redeemed myself."

Alex snorted as she wrapped her arms around his neck. "Well, I've been told I hold a grudge like a purse, so you're lucky all you got was hot water to the chest."

"That's cold," he replied as he dipped her underneath the spray, soaking her hair.

"You know this means war!"

"Bring it, babe," he said.

"You're going to regret that invitation," Alex replied.

"Before we start fighting," Wes began as he reached for the fragrant soap, "we should at least get clean." He wet the rose-shaped soap and rubbed it across Alex's breasts. She moaned in delight as his fingers circled her diamond-hard nipples. In a swift motion, he leaned in and replaced his fingers with his tongue and lips.

"Um, you don't play fair," she gritted.

He winked at her before tearing his mouth away. "Something we have in common. Now, let's clean between those amazing thighs." Wes slipped his hand between her thighs and made her purr when his fingers found their way inside her wet valley. "W-Wes," she gritted. "Right there!" His fingers drummed against her clit until she came. Alex grabbed his shoulder to steady herself as the waves of her orgasm subsided.

"Still want to go to war?"

"Your tongue is the peace treaty you needed to end the war."

Wes shut the water off and smiled at Alex. "Just wait until we get dry," he said.

"Maybe it's time for me to show you my peace agreement," she replied as they stepped out of the shower. She drank in the power of his ebony body as he wrapped a towel around his waist. It was the thighs that made her shiver. Thick thighs did save lives, and Wes could probably save the universe with his. Then there were that sculpted chest and those arms that looked as if they had been cut from the tree of life. And for the next two weeks this was all hers. All the pleasure, all the excitement, and none of the commitment.

Alex knew she and Wes could do any- and everything they wanted because she would never see him again. With that in mind, she didn't bother to wrap her body after she dried off. She felt Wes's eyes watching her as she moved to the bed.

"Take a picture next time," she joked.

"Don't get mad if I do."

Alex's mind raced as she thought about what would happen if a naked picture of her made it on the Internet. "Um, maybe a picture is a bad idea."

Wes hitched his right brow. "So, you're telling me that you've never taken a set of nude photos in your super-model career?"

"There you go with that model thing. I'm far from a model, okay?"

Wes gave her a slow once-over. "I can't tell. I'm sure I've seen you somewhere before, and not just in my dreams."

Alex crossed her legs and fanned her hand at him. "You know what, if you weren't super cute, I'd tell you how corny you are."

Wes walked over to her and stood in front of her. "Now, why would you want to hurt my feelings like that?"

Alex reached up and tugged off his towel. She ran her hands down his hips, then grabbed his erection. She stroked him slowly, making him moan with delight. Easing forward, she drew him into her mouth, sucking and licking him. Wes's knees buckled as she took him deeper down her throat. "Oh shit," he exclaimed, then pulled back from her magical mouth. "Wow."

"I wasn't done," she said.

"Yeah, I just wasn't going to make it," he said, then joined her on the bed. He captured her mouth in a fiery kiss that made her swoon. Wes pulled her on his lap as they kissed. She wrapped her legs around his waist, and for a split second she almost forgot they needed protection. "Um, you need to wrap it up for this ride," she said, lifting her hips a few inches above his erection.

"Yes, ma'am." Wes reached back and grabbed a condom from underneath the pillow. Alex took the gold package from his hand and slid the sheath into place. Then she mounted him and gave him a slow ride, taking him deeper inside her wetness with every stroke.

Their moans filled the air as they ground together. Wes gripped her hips and threw his head back as he reached his climax. Sweat covered their bodies as they collapsed on the bed. Alex expelled a satisfied breath as her thighs quaked. Wes stroked her back and kissed her neck. "Well, I can't think of a better way to start the day," he whispered.

"Maybe with some food," she replied.

"You definitely got my appetite worked up." Wes made no effort to let Alex go and she wasn't upset about it at all. Who was hungry anyway? Wes's arms were like heaven. She was a few seconds from drifting off to sleep when there was a knock at the door.

"Expecting company?" she asked.

"No. If we ignore them, maybe they will go away."

The knocking continued. Wes groaned and let Alex go. He grabbed his robe while she wrapped up in a sheet. She figured Wes had forgotten that he'd placed an order for breakfast. Then she heard a woman's voice.

"Wes, I owe you an apology," the singsongy voice

said. Alex didn't know what she was supposed to feel at that moment. She wanted to hop out of the bed and storm out. But she was naked.

"Liz, what the hell?"

"Are you going to invite me in, like the old days?"

"No. How did you find my cabin? You do realize this is the behavior that prompted the restraining order."

"You overreacted then and you're doing it again now," she said.

This was weird and Alex wasn't sure what her next step should be.

Wes needed Liz to go away. Like jump off the side of the ship, get in a lifeboat, and sail away. A smarter man would've ignored Liz the first time she mentioned marriage after he'd given her a back rub with coconut oil. But he'd allowed his erection to think for him that night. And hell was unleashed for the next six months.

Now she was ruining his vibe with Alexandria. "Leave," he said and attempted to close the door.

"I guess you have found your vacation booty call already. That's fast even for you."

"Go away and don't come back."

"Why are you like this?" She took a step forward and Wes held his arm out to stop her.

"You need to leave and I don't want to say it again."

"Girl, you better watch out. He likes to play with your emotions, then it's on to the next one," Liz yelled. If Alex hadn't heard Liz's squawking, his neighbors had. Wes didn't miss the cabin doors cracking open to get a glimpse of the drama.

The only thing Wes hated more than a well-done steak was unnecessary drama, which was all drama in his opinion. Now Liz had him looking like the ship's resident Lothario. "This is the last time I'm asking you to leave," he snapped. There was no need to play nice anymore. He imagined Alex was getting dressed and ready to leave. If Liz's plan had been to ruin his vacation, she'd succeeded.

"Ta-ta," Liz said, as if she has accomplished her mission. Wes slammed the door and headed back to the bed. Alex was perched on the edge of the bed with the sheet covering her nakedness, and that damned jumpsuit was right beside her. He was really starting to hate that damned suit.

"Alexandria, let . . ."

She held up her hand and shook her head. "If this is your thing, then this your thing. We didn't promise each other anything. I don't know what you did to the chick at the door, but that isn't my business. But I will happily move out of your way so you can . . ."

"Pause," he said. "I know what that sounded like, but . . ."

"Wes, we had a good time," she interjected. "You don't owe me anything else."

He crossed over to the bed and kneeled in front of her. "Then let's talk about what you owe me."

Alexandria hitched her right brow. "Excuse you?"

"I'm supposed to be given the chance to redeem myself and I feel like I haven't gotten the full opportunity I need."

"You know what, you have a damn nerve," she said, then broke out laughing. "I guess I could be benevolent and let you continue this redemption task of yours."

"I like you, Alexandria."

"Most people with good taste do. Now, if we don't get food, and soon, you're going to meet my hangry side."

Wes rose to his feet. "I get the feeling she's not really nice."

She shrugged. "That's what I hear. But do you really want to find out?"

"I don't," he said as he reached up and grabbed the phone from the nightstand.

CHAPTER EIGHT

Alex tried not to question her sanity. But why in the hell was she still in this man's cabin? She was making the same kind of bad decision she'd always gotten on Nina about. No, this wasn't the same. This was more like her acting like the old Yolanda, when she said she controlled her sexuality and did who and what she wanted with her body. And that was when the argument would start.

Now, she was doing everything she had always judged her younger sisters for doing. *Just go with it*, she heard Robin whisper in her ear. Now, she was losing her mind.

"Why are you so quiet?" Wes asked as the cabin attendant wheeled in their breakfast.

"I told you I was on the edge of hangry," she said, then thanked the attendant for the food. He smiled at her before heading out.

"Then you better eat fast. I don't want to meet the hangry side of you."

Alex shook her head as he filled her mug with coffee. "Then you're going to need to meal plan better and stop your former vacation babes from showing up at your door."

Wes took her coffee mug. "If you want to be rude like that, I'll keep the coffee for myself."

"You can't be that cruel," she said as she reached for the mug.

"Aww, now I know your kryptonite. Coffee."

Alex rolled her eyes as he released the mug. "Anyway." She took a slow sip of the coffee. It was good, but nothing really compared to the robust blend from the Richardson Bed and Breakfast. Sure, she was biased, but Clinton was trying to figure out a way to market the coffee and sell it online. Alex knew this was going to be a huge moneymaker and . . . *Stop it. How are you sitting here naked thinking about business? Work can wait*, she thought as she turned away from Wes's stare.

"What's going through that head of yours?" he asked as he cut into his eggs.

"Just thinking about home and work. Then feeling silly because I promised my sisters no work."

"Then I guess it's a good thing I'm here. One thing I know well is how to leave work in the office."

"Unfortunately, that is a skill I don't have."

"We'll work on that for the next two weeks. Whatever you do, since you claim you're not a supermodel, I'm sure you trained the people who work for you to do the right thing."

"And how do you figure I'm in charge?"

"Because I don't see you as the worker bee. You have that run-the-world energy."

Alex smiled. "It's almost as if you know me. I . . ."

Wes held up his hand. "If you tell me about your job, that means you're thinking about it and not me."

"Your ego knows no bounds, huh?"

He tilted his head to the side. "I know I'm more interesting than your job."

She tossed a napkin at him. "Whatever. What's on the agenda today, fun coordinator?"

Wes gave her a slow once-over. "If I had my choice, we'd get back in bed and . . ."

"Negative, ghost rider. We stop in the Bahamas today."

"Okay, this is one of my favorite stops. Pack your bathing suit. There is a spring that I know where we can have a quiet swim and a nice lunch."

"You come to the Bahamas that often?"

He nodded. "If I don't make you fall in love with this place today, I've lost my touch." Wes reached across the table and stroked the back of Alex's hand.

"I'm going to my room to get ready," she said as she stood up and dropped the sheet she had been using as clothing.

"You know, we got a few more hours before the ship docks and no matter what you pick to wear, you're going to look stunning."

"What are you suggesting?" she asked with a slight grin.

He nodded toward the bed. "It's comfortable over here," Wes said.

"Nope," she said, then crossed over to the bed and grabbed her jumpsuit. "See you in an hour."

Wes looked down at his smart watch and set the timer for an hour. "Tick tock," he quipped.

"Wow, something is wrong with you." Alex pulled on her jumpsuit and shook her head.

"Or maybe I just can't get enough of you? Especially since that suit looked better on the side of my bed. But you said an hour and time is wasting," he said.

"Then stop talking so I can go," she said as she headed for the door. Wes smiled as she left and Alex was excited about what was going to happen in the Bahamas.

Alex wasn't sure if she should be so giddy about this man. Did she not just witness some lady throw a fit about him while she was naked in his bed? What kind of insanity was happening here? Part of her wanted to lock herself in her cabin and just hold on to the memories she and Wes had made. She'd had the vacation fling Yolanda kept telling her she needed.

Who was she kidding? Alex knew she was going to pack her bag, change into another one of the outfits Yolanda had packed for her, and enjoy Wes.

His backstory didn't matter since she wasn't planning a future with him. Did his life in Brooklyn even matter to her? When this cruise was over Wes would go his way and she'd go back to Charleston. Maybe she knew everything she needed to know about him.

A cruise ship gigolo? she thought as she unlocked her cabin door. *It's a singles cruise; you had to know there would be someone like him here. Just enjoy the ride and stop overthinking everything.*

Alex walked inside. Heading to her closet, she grabbed the two-piece bathing suit she'd said she wasn't going to wear, the romper that clung to her breasts a little too tightly, and a pair of strappy sandals. Before packing her bag, she reconsidered the shoes. What if she and Wes were going to do a lot of walking? She needed sneakers. This felt like getting ready for a first date. The man had seen her naked and had blessed her with several orgasms. Why in the hell was she nervous?

"Get it together," she muttered as reached for her straw tote bag. After packing her things she called room service and ordered a bottle of wine. She figured a few glasses of chardonnay would calm her down. Even though she knew the call was going to cost her a fortune, Alex decided to call Robin. For a change she was the one in need of advice.

"Hello?" Robin said when she answered the phone.

"Robin, it's me."

"Alex? I know you better not be calling to check on the bed-and-breakfast."

"No, and you need to listen since I'm using the ship's phone."

"Is everything all right?" Robin asked, her voice filled with concern.

"I think so. I met someone and . . ."

"*You met someone!*" Alex had to move the phone from her ear because Robin was so loud.

"This is where you shut up and listen," Alex gritted.

"Yes, yes, because this I have to hear."

"You would hear a lot more if you'd stop talking," Alex said, then told Robin all about Wes, from the splash at the pool and the salty dinner to the night they'd spent together.

"Wait, you spent the night with him? Who are you and what have you done with my sister?"

"My first mistake was letting Yolanda get inside my head," Alex said with a sigh. "Now he wants to spend the day in the Bahamas and show me his favorite spots."

"Would you rather he ignored you? You're over-thinking the vacation booty. I bet you've googled him already."

"Honestly I don't even know his last name."

"Well, Alex, that doesn't seem very safe. What do you even know about this man?"

"I know just as much about him as he knows about me. We obviously enjoy having sex with each other. I don't know what I was thinking."

"The fact that you were thinking with something other than that big brain of yours actually makes me happy. Just enjoy the moment. And if anything goes wrong, call ship security."

"Here I thought you were going to be my voice of reason and you sound like Yolanda."

"Think about it like this, Alex, you're never going to see this man again. Why not have some fun?"

"You're right. That's what I said. I was going to do it anyway. It's just . . ." Alex sighed. "I haven't had fun in so long. I don't know what it's supposed to feel like."

"It's supposed to feel good. And from what you just told me I think you are feeling good. Keep it going and don't call me again unless it's an emergency."

"Thank you for all your support. I guess I'll head back to his cabin now."

"Please do, and don't get weird and google him because that's just too much."

"Robin, don't tell anyone that I called or what we talked about. I'll see you when I get back." Alex hung up the phone, grabbed her bag, and headed out the door. She was going to have fun with Wes and not worry about what happened at the end of the cruise.

Wes checked his watch for the third time since his alarm chimed. Alexandria's hour was up and here he was, waiting for her again. *She must be used to people waiting for her*, he thought. But if he was honest, he knew he'd wait as long as she took to get there. Wes was excited to see Alexandria in her bathing suit. Based on all her other outfits, he was sure it would be one sexy piece. Reaching for his swimming trunks, he wondered how this afternoon would go for them. Why was he so concerned? This was just a vacation hookup. If she changed her mind about hanging out with him, maybe he'd find someone else. But Wes was pretty sure there was no one who could compare to Alexandria. Now he was starting to feel crazy, like Liz.

Wes was about to consider last night a beautiful memory and remind himself that he was on a singles cruise when there was a knock. He crossed over to the door and opened it.

Alex stood on the other side with a smile on her face, dressed in a curve-hugging sundress. White looked good on her. But all he could think about was peeling it off her body. "Do you even have a watch?" he asked.

"I do, but I haven't put it on yet," she replied. "And a hello would've been nice."

"Hello, beautiful."

Alexandria reached into her bag and pulled out a bottle of malbec. "I was held up waiting for this. I figured I owed you a drink or two."

Wes took the bottle from her hand, then drew her into

his arms. "I don't know why I keep expecting you to disappear."

"Let's make a deal: no more timers. This is a vacation. I spend my entire life chained to a clock."

"Got it. Time is irrelevant as long as you're spending it with me," he said with a randy wink. She pinched him on the shoulder and then pushed out of his embrace.

"Let's get out of here," she said. "We can sit by the pool for a while before you get the wrong idea."

Wes had been thinking about taking her back to bed, but how in the hell did she know that? He took a quick look at his crotch and it was pretty obvious how she knew. Being around Alexandria was a natural aphrodisiac.

"All right, let's go," he said.

"You're not taking a change of clothes or anything?"

Wes shrugged. "I'm wearing everything I need."

"That doesn't include underwear?" She hitched her right brow at him.

"Who needs underwear?"

"What about swimming trunks?"

He shrugged again. "You'll see. Let's move." Wes opened the door and smiled at Alexandria as she crossed over to him. Damn, this woman was fine. Before heading to the pool Wes stopped by the snack table and grabbed some fruit for them to share. As he filled the plate with pineapples, he thought about how sweet Alexandria tasted, from her lips down to the heat between her thighs.

"What's wrong?" she asked when she noted his silence.

"Nothing, just thought about something that's even sweeter than these pineapples."

Alexandria rolled her eyes, then pointed to a tray of star fruit. "There it is right there."

Wes offered her a smirk before adding the succulent fruit to their plate. "I'll take your word for it."

She reached for a piece of the fruit, then rubbed it across his lips. "Now, lick your lips," she ordered. Though he did as he was told, the only thing Wes really wanted to lick was covered by a pretty sundress. "All right, let's go," he said after fighting through his lusty thoughts.

Alexandria smiled as they headed outside. The pool area was pretty crowded with everyone waiting for the ship to dock. But Wes found two seats for them.

"Hopefully I won't get splashed today," Alexandria quipped.

"Well, if you do, it won't be my fault this time."

"I'm still not sure if I've forgiven you completely. So, whatever you have planned for the Bahamas better be amazing."

"Don't worry, it will be."

She picked up a piece of fruit and held it out to Wes. "Want a bite?"

``How can I say no to an offer like that?" He leaned in and took the fruit from her fingers with his lips and tongue. He felt her shiver when his tongue brushed against the pad of her finger. "That was delicious. Let me try something else." Wes captured her lips and kissed her slow and deep. Alexandria melted against him, moaning as his tongue tangoed with hers. Normally he wasn't one for PDAs, but Alexandria's lips were so damn irresistible. Another three seconds and he was going to forget there were people around at all.

"Um," she said, not paying attention to the looks people were giving them. "Stick to trying the fruit."

"That's no fun."

"Neither is having an audience."

Wes looked around and caught a few stares, but he didn't care. Not even when he locked eyes with an angry Liz. "Maybe you're right. As soon as we get to the Bahamas, we're going to have a lot of privacy."

"And why isn't this magical place on the list of places to visit?" Alexandria asked.

"That's when a place loses its magic. The fewer people who know, the better."

"So, I'm the first you've taken there?"

Wes cleared his throat. "You want the truth or a nice flex?"

"I think I have my answer," she replied. "Maybe old girl was right about you?"

"You don't believe that we're the same?"

"The same?"

"Grown, single, and sexy. Living and enjoying life any way you see fit?"

Alexandria smiled. "Sounds about right when you're talking about me," she quipped.

"That's just wrong," he said, then picked up a piece of pineapple and held it out to her. "When you take your bite it doesn't mean you're going to get another kiss."

"Please! If I want one, I can get one."

She wasn't wrong, but Wes had to save face and pretend he would've turned her down. But the moment she leaned into him, they were kissing all over again. Wes pulled back and smiled. "What was that about not wanting an audience?"

"I'm enjoying life and doing what I want. Be happy that I want you."

"Excuse me, ma'am," he said, then offered her a slight bow. "Thank you for wanting me just as I want you."

She grinned at him and took another piece of star fruit. "Your pleasure."

Before he could reply the announcement came that the ship had reached Nassau. "Time for some magic," Wes said as they followed the crowd toward the exit.

Alexandria picked up her bag and Wes took her free hand in his. "Let's do this," she said.

CHAPTER NINE

If Alex was expecting to hit up the places on the list the cruise line had given the passengers as they exited the ship, Wes had other ideas. They walked downtown and had a quick lunch at a local restaurant that Alex would've called a hole in the wall, but the fried fish and conch salad were to die for. Alex loved fresh seafood and she hadn't tasted anything that good since . . . well the last time she'd kissed Wes. Which they had done after lunch, after walking three blocks, and when he announced they had reached their destination. She looked at the lush green area and gasped.

"This is beautiful," she said as she crossed over to a yellow elderflower bush. It smelled like vanilla and she wanted to have one of them at the bed-and-breakfast.

"When you stand beside it, there is a lot of competition," Wes replied.

"You're great for my ego," she said as she picked one of the blossoms and stuck it behind her ear.

"I speak the truth. So, ready for the magic?"

She nodded. They took a few steps into the fragrant bushes and Wes pointed to a spring that looked like a mirror. Three butterflies floated above the water and Alex was one step closer to believing in magic. "Wow, this place is magnificent," she exclaimed.

"Wait until you feel the water against your skin. But you're going to have to take your clothes off to get the entire experience."

"Why do I feel like you're just trying to get me naked?"

"That's always my endgame. But you have to experience this without anything coming between you and that water."

"All right. I'll try it." Alex stripped out of her dress. Even though she had on the bathing suit Yolanda had designed for her, she peeled it off.

She noticed how Wes was drinking in her image. It wasn't as if he hadn't seen her naked before. But there was something about the way he looked at her. She was intrigued by the magic of this place.

"You're acting like you've never seen me like this before," she quipped.

"The flower sets off an amazing body."

"So, when the cops come, I'm getting arrested for being naked out here and there you stand, fully dressed." There was a part of Alex that couldn't believe she was standing naked in a secluded yet public space. Hadn't she given Yolanda hell when she had streaked across Spelman's campus and nearly got expelled?

She was going to have to sanitize the story of this cruise when she talked to her younger sister. Hell, Robin, too. But right now she was going to live in the moment. And at the moment Wes was standing beside her naked. She looked down at their reflection in the water and smiled. "We're so going to jail."

Wes dove into the water. "Come on in," he beckoned. Alex jumped in and was surprised by the warmth of the water. Wes swam over to her and pulled her against his chest. "Just like being in a hot tub."

"I wasn't expecting warmth. But it does feel good." Alex kicked her legs forward like a mermaid.

"And you look good in it," he said as he ran his hands down her sides. "Feels good on you, too."

She spun around and faced him. Wes's smile warmed her heart. There was something about him and the sparkle in his eyes. She'd never felt more wanted or desired. Maybe there was some truth to what her sisters had said to her over the years about not living her life and having fun.

Though it felt good now, Alex knew when she returned to Charleston she had tons of work waiting for her. But right now she was going to allow this man to worship her, show her new things, and give her an unforgettable time on the friendly seas. She ran her hand down the center of Wes's chest. "So, what's next?"

"Anything you like." He brushed his lips across her forehead. She swam across the spring and toyed with the blossoms on the bushes surrounding the water. Wes followed her and encircled her waist with his arms.

"This place is what fairy tales are made of," Alex said. "Thanks for sharing, but I really think we should get dressed and head back."

"Why? We have plenty of time before the ship sails off. What's wrong?"

She shrugged. "I'm still waiting for the cops to show up."

"Trust me, we're safe here and things will be fine. I'll tell you a secret," he said bringing his lips to her ear. "I own this spot."

"What? Come on. Really?"

Wes nodded. "The third time I visited here, I knew I wanted it. And I was about to stop some development from happening here."

"What are you, some sort of environmentalist?" Alex asked, her anxiety about going to jail subsiding.

"A jack-of-all-trades, you know."

Alex shrugged and dipped underneath the water. She looked up at Wes, wondering who this man was when he wasn't on vacation. He clearly had means if he could just purchase a piece of land in the Bahamas because he liked it. She returned to the surface and pressed her body against his.

"Well, Wes, since we're here and it's so beautiful, why don't we . . ."

"Make love underwater?" he asked.

"Yeah, why not?"

"Just one problem," he said. "No protection."

She playfully slapped his chest. "I guess you weren't a Boy Scout."

"Well, looks like I have some atoning to do later."

Alex nodded, then brushed her lips against his. "I might agree to that if there will be conch salad involved."

"I believe I can handle that." He kissed her slow and deep as they relished the soothing spring water. Alex pushed back from him and shook her head.

"Don't start a fire you can't put out," she quipped, then climbed out of the spring. While she dried off underneath a mango tree, Alex wondered what other secret places

Wes could show her. But when he climbed out of the water, his ebony brown skin glistening in the sun, all Alex wanted to do was ride him like a race car.

"What's wrong?" he asked when he noticed her stare.

"Nothing," she replied breathlessly. "Do-do you need a towel?"

Wes shook his head. "The sun can take care of me." He pulled on his shorts but didn't bother putting on his shirt. What a tease.

"Thanks for sharing your space with me," she said.

"And just know you're one of the only people in the world who knows I own this place."

"What makes me so special?"

Wes smirked. "Everything," he replied as he wrapped his arms around Alex's shoulders.

"We'd better go before I decide we should stay here for the rest of our vacation."

"You'd get tired of mangos and conch salad in two days. Besides, we'd miss the beaches in the Cayman Islands."

"Can't be better than this," Alex said with a grin.

"You haven't done a lot of island traveling, huh?"

She shook her head. "I spend most of my time working. But we're not talking about that, remember."

"Oh, trust me, I only discuss work when I'm sitting in my big office."

Alex threw up her hands. "Excuse me, Mr. Big Office."

"I'm sure you have a corner office you spend too much time in."

She nodded and folded her arms across her chest. "Anyway, let's head back."

"But first, there is this amazing dessert we have to

get," Wes said as he glanced at his watch. "We got just enough time."

"What is this dessert that's so amazing?"

"It used to be my favorite until I tasted you," he said with a wink. "But it's a coconut tart."

"Sounds interesting." Alex inhaled deeply.

"You have to try it with ice cream. And any bit of cream that drips on you, I get to lick it off."

Alex laughed. "All right, but I'm not doing the same."

"That's because you've never had a taste of this ice cream before," he said before taking her hand in his.

They walked about half a mile in comfortable silence. Alex enjoyed being off the boat and seeing parts of the Bahamas that weren't tourist haunts. Clearly Wes spent a lot of time on Nassau. Part of her wondered how much work he actually got done when he wasn't on vacation.

Not important; he has a life off this ship that has nothing to do with you.

"Why are you so quiet?" Wes asked as they approached the restaurant.

"No reason, just thinking about how beautiful everything is here and . . . How much time do you spend here?"

"A lot. It's a great break from the city. I like to explore and see different things. But if I like something, I'll continue to come back and see it."

"Or buy your favorite part of it."

Wes nodded. "That too." He nodded toward the long line at the restaurant. "We'd better hurry and get in line."

"I hope it moves fast and we don't miss . . . Let me just go with the flow."

"I'm seeing that is something you don't normally do."

"Not unless I'm leading the flow." She smiled and followed him to the line, even if she was filled with anxiety. What if they got left here and she only had one set of clothes? She'd never hear the end of it if her sisters found out.

Thankfully, the line moved swiftly. Wes neglected to tell her that the restaurant only served one thing—the coconut tart. When they made it through the line and got their treat, there was still plenty of time to make it back to the ship.

Wes scored two seats at a table near the sidewalk. "You must be my good luck charm; this never happens."

Alex shrugged as she sat beside him. "Then I guess this is going to be your best trip ever."

"If these past few days are any indication, you're right."

Alex dug into her dessert and was surprised by the taste of the ice cream. It had a cinnamon flavor that meshed well with the tart. Being mindful of Wes's stare, Alex tried to take ladylike bites of her dessert, but it was so good, she lost herself in the taste.

"So, the lady does like it," he quipped.

Alex nodded as she took another bite. As a bit of cream dropped down on her chin, Wes leaned forward and licked it away.

"I wish I could bring this back to the ship tonight," he whispered.

"You are incorrigible," she said.

"Yeah, I am. You know the Caymans is an overnight port stop."

"All right."

"Not trying to be presumptuous, but I'd love for you to spend that time with me."

"I think we can arrange that," she replied with a smile. "I can only imagine what you know about the Cayman Islands."

"The first thing I know is that you're going to look amazing against the white sand on Smith Cove and Rum Point Beach."

"You're just an amazing tour guide," she quipped. "Is this your calling?"

"Only when I have a beautiful guest, and you fit the bill."

Normally, this would be the moment when she'd question how many women had gotten this type of treatment from him in the past. But she had to remind herself that it wasn't that serious. They were having fun on vacation. This wasn't going to be anything more.

"We should head back to the ship," she said. "I need a shower and a change of clothes."

"Is that an invitation? I'm pretty dirty, too," Wes said with a grin.

"That's very true, but we're showering in my cabin. That way we won't be interrupted again."

Wes groaned. "So sorry that happened."

"Guess that's what happens when you're irresistible to someone." Alex shrugged.

"Okay, remember that when we meet up on your next cruise and you're trying to act brand-new."

Alex laughed. "You know we probably won't see each other again. You have a real life in New Jersey, right?"

"You got jokes, Alexandria. You know it's New York. And when Fashion Week kicks off next year, I'm sure you'll be walking a runway pretending you don't even know me."

"You have such an imagination," she said as they walked toward the ship.

"I'm just going to have to find the magazine you were

featured in. Then you can stop acting as if you aren't a model."

"Please find it so I can prove you wrong," she said as they stood in line to board the ship. He wrapped his arm around her shoulders.

"I'm never wrong about pretty women." He gave her a kiss on the cheek.

"This time you couldn't be more wrong." She squeezed his hand and smiled broadly at him.

"That smile sold a million dollars' worth of products or broke a million hearts. One day I'll find out which one is the truth."

Alex was about to respond when Liz bumped into them. "Oh, excuse me," she said flatly. "I guess he took you out for conch salad."

"And coconut tart. It was delicious," Alex said. "You should try it next time, and watch where you walk."

Liz's mouth dropped open as if she was expecting a fight from Alex. She had no idea that Alex had perfected passive-aggressive swipes that stung. One of the ways she always won her arguments with Yolanda was to ignore her. Liz needed the same kind of treatment. Alex could almost see the angry steam fizzing out of her ears as she and Wes boarded the ship. She noticed Wes's grin. "What?" she asked.

"Remind me to stay on your good side."

"I didn't do anything that a mature adult wouldn't do."

"I see no one gets one over on Alexandria. I like that."

"Well, wait until we get out of these clothes—you can tell me everything you like."

"I–I, damn . . ."

CHAPTER TEN

A lex was sure she'd lost her mind as she unlocked her stateroom door, stripped off her clothes, and pulled Wes against her chest. "I'll get the shower started."

"You think I'm going to let you do that alone? Remember the shower we took in my room? Not taking a shower in hell this evening," he said as he pulled off his clothes.

"Fine, but I don't take cold showers," she said as she drank in his image.

"I can warm you up without a doubt," Wes replied with a wink. They dashed to the bathroom like two kids about to have a water balloon fight. When they stepped underneath the spray, Wes and Alex toyed with the temperature for a while. But Alex had finally gotten her way when she'd grabbed Wes's hand and slid it between her thighs.

"You know the water is fine," she cooed.

"Yes. It is," he said as his fingers danced across her thighs. "But you can turn it off. It's time for us to get dirty again."

"I like the way you think, Wes," she moaned as she gripped his shoulder. Wes lifted Alex in his arms and carried her to the bedroom. It didn't matter that they were soaking wet, or that she was going to have to call House-keeping to change her bed again; she needed to feel him deep inside her. How had she become that woman? It was Yolanda's fault and that was what she was going to stick with.

If there was anything sexier than a woman who knew what she wanted, Wes had never seen it. Well, not until Alexandria gripped his dick and licked him as if he had been dipped in the ice cream they'd shared in the Ba-hamas. Throwing back his head in delight, Wes called out her name. What in the hell was she doing to him? Making his body tingle with pleasures that he'd never felt in his life. She was like him, no inhibitions in the bedroom. She got joy from giving and receiving. And being on the re-ceiving end of her generosity was heavenly. Alexandria locked eyes with him as she gave his dick a long, slow lick. Wes was nearly undone.

"Oh, shit," he cried, then stepped back from her. She smiled and crossed her legs.

"I'm not sure what was sweeter, you or the coconut tart."

"I guess it's my turn to make that taste test," he said, then reached for her. Wes pushed her back on the bed and spread her thighs apart. He slid between her legs, lapping her wetness and sucking her clit until she screamed.

And yes, she was sweeter than any dessert he'd ever tasted, and he wanted to devour her until she melted in his mouth. Lick. Suck. Lick.

Explosion. Alexandria shivered and threw her hands above her head. "Yes," she moaned. "That was amazing."

"You beat the tart, for sure," he said with a wink.

"Well, thank you."

Wes wanted to bury himself inside her and stay there. But once again, he didn't have protection. "I want you so bad," he intoned.

"What's stopping you?"

"We need protection."

"I got you," she replied with a smile. Alexandria tapped his shoulder so that he would roll off her. When she rose to her feet, Wes was mesmerized by her naked body once again. She was totally a supermodel, despite her denials. Alexandria returned to the bed with three condom packages in her hand. "The Boy Scouts aren't the only ones who are always prepared." She handed him one of the gold packages, and Wes was ready to feel her pretty pussy gripping his erection. Ripping the package open, he sheathed himself, then joined her on the bed.

"Alexandria," he intoned. "You are so beautiful."

"Stop talking and get ready to work," she wantonly replied. Wes took his marching orders and went to work on giving her the pleasure she deserved. They ground against each other slowly, lips pressed together, moans becoming the soundtrack of their lovemaking. She matched him stroke for stroke, thrust for thrust. Wes almost felt as if he couldn't keep up with her pace, and that never had happened to him before. He loved every minute of it. "Wes," she screamed, indicating that she was about to come. This was the moment he liked the most. She was so wet, creamy, and her face was filled with bliss. Wes didn't fight back his climax, giving in to his own pleasure. Holding each other tightly, Wes and Alexandria drifted off to sleep.

Wes woke up with a start when he felt Alexandria shift in his arms. She was sitting up and easing toward the edge of the bed.

"You leaving me?" Wes asked.

Alexandria turned around and smiled at him. "I'm not leaving you, but I didn't realize we slept so long. It's a clear night out. I wanted to go and look at the stars."

"Oh yeah, you and those stars. You know they pale in comparison to you."

"There you go, gassing my head up again. I'm going to get dressed and head outside. You're more than welcome to come with me."

Wes winked at her, then licked his lips. "I think I'll take you up on that offer. But clothing should be optional."

"Whatever. I'm putting some clothes on because the ocean breeze isn't that warm at night."

"I know." He reached out and stroked her back. "So, after seeing the stars, is your vacation complete?"

"Um, yeah. I came here to relax, clear my mind, and try some new things. I just didn't expect to do all that stuff in three days."

"So, what you're saying is thank you," Wes joked.

"Excuse you?"

"I sparked all this when I splashed you at the pool."

"I need you to stop acting like that rude little stunt of yours was cute. And I'm still going to get you back. That's when my vacation will be complete." She grinned before rising to her feet. "Watch your back, Wes."

"It's much more enjoyable to watch your front."

Alexandria shook her head and then strolled into the bathroom. A couple of beats passed before she stuck her head out of the bathroom door. "Are you going to join me or not?"

"Here I come," he said.

Over the next few days, Wes and Alexandria spent their days and nights together. Hitting the different ports together and trying new things around the islands. Wes was starting to wonder how he was supposed to forget this woman when he returned to Brooklyn.

Alex didn't expect to feel some kind of way when the ship pulled into its last port. By this time the old Alex would have been ready to go back to work. But there was something about this vacation coming to an end that left her feeling a little different. It was Wes.

Now Alex wasn't crazy enough to think that sharing a vacation fling with this man meant there was something more between them. They'd had a great time. He'd given her many orgasms. And he was funny. But she knew that once she got off the ship and headed back to Charleston, Wes would just be a sweet memory.

She glanced at him as they walked across the white, sandy beaches in the Caymans. His body had become so familiar. But every time they were together, there seemed to be something new that he taught her about making love. Alex knew she'd never forget these lessons, but when was she actually going to put them to use when she got home?

There was so much she had to do. The bed-and-breakfast was going through a renovation. And as much as she trusted Clinton, she couldn't be sure he would follow her instructions on what she wanted the new wing to look like. And if her dad wanted to make changes, she wasn't there to approve them. Although Sheldon Richardson really didn't need her approval for anything. Still, Alex was used to being there when big decisions were being made, and now she was starting to feel as if she'd spent these last couple of weeks ignoring her responsibility.

"Why are you so quiet over there?" Wes asked.

"I was just thinking about everything that's waiting for me when I return to home. Work is going to be hell with . . ."

"No," he said as he placed his finger to her lips. "We are still on vacay. And that's not a business suit."

Alex twirled around, showing off her high-waisted bikini. "You're right, this isn't a business suit," she said with a smile. "And it's a good thing, too."

"It also means we're not talking about work or anything work-related or work-adjacent," Wes said.

"So, the boogie board thing," she began as she nodded toward the short boards he had underneath his arms. "It's not going down."

"What?"

"I feel bad that I had you carry them all the way out here, but um, I'm not doing it."

Wes dropped the boards. "You've got to be kidding me."

"I'm not," she said with finality.

"I can't believe you're punking out on me. Those boards aren't light and you said you'd try it."

"I don't recall those words leaving my mouth," Alex replied with a laugh. "I'd be happy to watch you, cheer you on and kiss you when you come out of the water. What more could you ask for?" Alex watched a huge wave crash on the shoreline and shivered. He really thought she was going to get on that little board and dive face forward into that water.

Nope.

"Wes, this looks sort of dangerous."

"Dangerous? That's your fear talking. Come on, I'll teach you everything you need to know."

She ran her hand across his shoulder. "I'm going to pass on that."

"Come on, this will be a great memory of your vacation."

Alex ran her hand across his smooth chest. Oh, she had memories. Memories that would give her something else to think about when she was knee deep into the renovations at the bed-and-breakfast. Why was she allowing work to creep into the last few days of her vacation?

Because that was who she was. The work came first and playing came last. She just needed to focus on getting out of this boogie board thing. "I'm good. We've made some amazing memories."

Wes wrapped his arms around her waist. "And we're about to make some more," he said as he lifted her off her feet. Alex, surprised by his move, wrapped her arms around his neck.

"Stop it." She grinned.

"Not until you agree to crashing these waves with me." Wes brushed his lips against hers. "Please."

"Um, no."

"I'm not too proud to beg," he replied, then slid his hand down her back.

She shivered at his touch despite the heat of the sun beating down on them. Alex wanted nothing more than to head back to the ship and spend the rest of the day in bed. Naked and wrapped in Wes's arms. She knew she needed to get as much of Wes as she could handle before she had to go back to the real world.

"Sorry, it's still a hard no for me," she replied.

"So, if I tell you no the next time I'm . . ."

"You won't, so don't even play like that."

Wes nodded. "That is a fact. But you can't leave me like this."

"Leave you like what?"

He dropped to his knees and stroked her feet. "Begging you to step out of your comfort zone."

Alex shook her head. "Fine, whatever. I'll try it, but you better make sure I don't drown."

Wes rose to his feet. "No harm will come to you, beautiful," he said.

Alex glanced at the ocean waves and inhaled deeply. What had she gotten herself into?

Wes knew Alexandria was going to enjoy riding the waves, but he had no idea she'd be as good as she was at it. Now, he knew she'd look good doing it, with those hips, that booty, and the way her suit clung to it making him want to hop on that board with her. He couldn't wait to dry her off and rub her body down.

But this woman wasn't making any effort to get out of the water. It had been two hours already. As he walked toward the shore, Alexandria rode another wave. As the water crashed against her body and she rose from the board, Wes was sure that was what a sea goddess should look like. "And she said she didn't want to do this," Wes said when she crossed over to him.

"It was a lot of fun," she said. "Thank you for talking me into stepping out of my comfort zone."

Wes drew her into his arms and kissed her on the cheek. "You looked amazing doing it, if I do say so myself."

"I'm sure I looked like an idiot when I fell off the board."

Wes laughed, thinking about her first try on the boogie board. She didn't look crazy, but he had been sure she'd want to quit trying. But he was starting to see that she had a lot of fight in her. And he liked that a whole bunch. "Ready for lunch?" Wes asked.

"Um, I was thinking that we should head to the room I got for us since this is an overnight stay."

"I didn't know you had secured a room for us, Alexandria."

"You're not the only one who can arrange surprises," she replied with a wink. "We can order room service and get a good night's rest in a king-size bed."

"All I'm hearing is music to my ears," he replied with a smile.

Alexandria returned his smile. "I knew you wouldn't mind." He reached for her hand, brought it to her lips, and kissed the back of it.

"Who would ever complain about spending time with you?"

"You'd be surprised. I'm sure there are a lot of people who have been enjoying these last two weeks without me."

"There's a name for those kinds of people. We're

going to call them stupid," he said. "This has been the most enjoyable vacation I've had this year."

"And how many vacations have you taken this year?"

"Four."

She hitched her brow at him. "When do you work?"

Wes shrugged. "When I feel like it."

Alexandria opened her mouth but didn't say anything. Wes took that as an opportunity to remind her that they weren't here to discuss work. "Tell me about this room again," he said.

"Why don't I just show you?" She grabbed his hand and they dashed across the sand.

The place where Alexandria had gotten a room for them was a quaint bed-and-breakfast. It actually reminded him of his project in South Carolina. He stopped in the lobby and looked around at the décor. Bright. The yellow walls were the star of the room. He wondered how this would look at the bed-and-breakfast in the States.

"Are you all right?"

"You got me thinking about work," he said with a laugh. "But that's done."

The desk clerk smiled at the couple before handing Alexandria the room key. "Secret getaway?"

"Something like that," Alexandria replied. "I have to say, this lobby is extraordinarily beautiful. I love the brightness."

The woman beamed. "It's a tribute to the owner. She was such a warm spirit, and when she passed away we wanted to make sure her memory and her spirit touches every guest, no matter how long they stay."

Wes and Alexandria exchanged a knowing look. "Well, it's working," Alexandria replied. "It's beautiful here."

She gave them directions to their room and told them to enjoy their stay. Wes felt as if she thought they were a real couple. And for some odd reason he wondered what being with Alexandria beyond the vacation would be like.

Where in the hell did that thought come from? He glanced over at Alexandria as she headed for their corner room. Alexandria stopped and looked at him. "Don't tell me you're tired."

"No, I was just thinking about how we're going to see each other after we get off this ship."

Alexandria tilted her head to the side. "We're not. You don't have to pretend you owe me anything beyond this vacation."

"I know that, but maybe I want more."

"Suppose I don't?" Alexandria asked. "My life on the mainland is different, and it certainly isn't four vacations a year."

"Are you saying that you're one of those all-work-and-no-play type of folks on dry land?"

Alexandria shrugged. "I have a lot of responsibilities. Maybe I won't wait so long for my next vacation."

"Of course, if I'm not there, you're not going to have half as much fun."

"So you say. Maybe next time I can finish my reading," she said as she unlocked the door to the room.

Wes drank in the king-size bed, the candles, and a basket of fruits and chocolate sauces. "You had this place set up right."

"Wait until you see the tub," she said. "I hope the pictures online match the real thing."

They headed into the bathroom and were happy to see a huge garden tub. "This is perfect," she exclaimed.

"Not yet," he said. "You still have clothes on."

She looked down at her bathing suit. "That's really quick and easy to fix." In a quick motion, Alexandria stepped out of her suit. "Your turn."

Wes pulled off his shorts and smiled. "Now that we're naked, what shall we do?"

She closed the space between them and wrapped her arms around his neck. "First, we have to fill the tub, and then we get down and dirty." Alexandria brushed her lips against his. "Let's get it going."

Wes turned on the water and looked up at Alexandria. "This water will not feel like a pot of soup."

CHAPTER ELEVEN

Alex was skeptical about how the water would feel when she stepped in. She knew about Wes and his ice-water showers, but she was pleasantly surprised when her foot touched the water. It was as warm as one of his kisses. "Nice," she said.

"I must have let it get too hot," he quipped, then joined her in the tub. Alex splashed some water on him.

"Just take the compliment."

"There are many things I want to take right now," he said. "I'm going to start with those lips." Wes leaned in and kissed her deep and slow. Alex melted against him as his tongue traveled the depths of her mouth. Wes pulled his mouth away and smiled. "Sit down and let me wash your back."

She nodded, then followed his directive. Wes reached for one of the heart-shaped bars of soap and dipped it in the water. He stroked Alex's back with the soap, lathering her shoulders, back, and hips. She moaned as his fingers danced against her skin. "You are so soft," he breathed against her ear.

Alex moaned and closed her eyes. "This feels amazing."

Wes sat down in the water, pulling Alex between his legs as he stretched out. "So," he said as he ran his hand down the center of her chest. "What needs cleaning next?"

"You have the soap, you control it all," Alex replied with a smile.

Wes grinned, then rubbed his hand across her flat belly. "I want the thighs first."

He ran his fingers up her inner thighs. Wes's soft touch made her shiver. "Ooh," she moaned as he slipped his finger inside her. The pad of his finger danced against her clit, making her so hot and wet. She wanted to pounce on his dick and ride him until the sun came up. But Alex released her control, allowing Wes to please her. And he was about to make her come with his fingers. She quivered and moaned.

"I need to taste you." Wes rose to his feet, then scooped a dripping Alex from the tub. Despite not drying off, he lay her on the bed and spread her thighs. Wes dove in and sucked the precious bud he'd been stroking. It was as if his tongue controlled her body. He licked and she pressed deeper into his kiss, wanting more, needing the most. Orgasmic waves washed over her body as he licked, sucked, and swirled his tongue around inside her.

"I need you inside me," she gritted. "Need. You."

Wes tore his mouth away from her and smiled. "Your wish is my command."

Alex reached underneath her pillow and retrieved a condom. He took the gold package from her hand and sheathed himself. Alex pressed her hand against Wes's chest, pushing him backward on the bed.

"I want to ride," she said, then climbed on top of him. Alex gripped his shoulders as she ground against him with a deliberate pace. Their moans filled the air as Alex moved fast, then slow. Wes matched her thrust for thrust, grabbing her hips so he could thrust deeper. "Oh yeah," Alex exclaimed as his dick danced in her G-spot. "Oh you feel so good. Yes, yes."

Wes tried to hold back his release, but seeing the look of bliss on Alex's face and feeling her heat made that impossible. He exploded with a guttural groan as she collapsed against his chest. Seconds later, they were both sleeping.

Alex woke up with a start. She didn't feel the waves, but Wes's arms around her reminded her that she was still on vacation. *Don't get used to this. There is a ton of work waiting for you when you return to Charleston.* There was that voice of reason she'd been able to ignore the entire cruise. Well, from the moment Wes splashed her at the pool anyway. She knew after he got off at his port, she'd never see him again. But they'd made good memories, and that would be nice to keep tucked away in the back of her mind. Alex knew the things she and Wes did while on this cruise she couldn't get away with in Charleston. And as much as she loved Yolanda's designs and how good she looked in them, she couldn't dress that way when she returned to the bed-and-breakfast.

"Why are you awake?" Wes asked, his voice deepened with sleep.

"I don't know," she fibbed. "I didn't mean to wake you."

"Since we're up now, whatever are we going to do?" He kissed her shoulder blade.

"How about some food?"

"I wouldn't mind eating again, but I'm sure what I want isn't on a menu in the world."

Alex smacked her lips. "You know what, you're incorrigible. I'm hungry, and as much as I like having parts of you in my mouth, that isn't going to fill my belly with what I need."

"All I got from that was you like tasting me as much as I love tasting you."

"Anyway, there is a restaurant close by that's open late." Alex rose from the bed and stretched her arms above her head. Wes watched her every move with a lustful gleam in his eyes. She laughed at him and shook her head. "What?"

"We're just going to go out in our wet swimsuits?"

"No, but we could since this restaurant is outside and on the beach. Check the closet, though."

Wes climbed out of the bed and crossed over to the closet. "What's this?" he asked when he saw the clothes hanging in the closet.

"Me being prepared. We can get dressed and go," she said as she walked up behind him. Alex wrapped her arms around his waist. "I think the black linen will look so sexy on you."

"Say no more. I'll wear the black."

Alex let him go and reached for a purple wrap dress. "I thought you were going for the pink strapless one," Wes said, nodded toward the dress. "Looks like something that will hug your curves as much as I do."

She sucked her teeth and grabbed the dress. "Since you took my suggestion, I'll take yours." Alex gave him a sly smile.

After they dressed the couple headed out to the restaurant Alex had found online. When they saw the number of people waiting outside and sitting on the patio, she was sure the Internet had been right.

"This looks fun," Wes said.

"I wonder where the ocean bar part of the restaurant is. I wanted to try it."

"Aren't you a mermaid now? What are you going to do when you're back in your landlocked life?"

"Who said I'm landlocked? Maybe I'm just going to have to start taking advantage of the ocean outside my door now."

"Ah, she's going to relax. Next thing you know, you'll be taking two vacations every five years."

Alex pinched him on the arm. "You don't get to do that. It's bad enough my sisters say crap like that all the time. But if you want, I can treat you just like I treat them."

"I'm going to pass on that. Because that doesn't sound like fun."

She hitched her right brow at him. "Trust me, it isn't."

After a bit of a wait Alex and Wes were seated at an outdoor table near the ocean bar she'd been excited to see. And it was everything she'd hoped it would be: the waves kissing your feet while the bartender poured some of the strongest cocktails Alex had ever tasted.

Wes wrapped his arm around Alex's waist as she drained her last drink. "Hold up there—you're about to be taken out to sea."

"Not with you anchoring me. Isn't this place amazing?"

He nodded. "Now, let's get some food in you."

"Works for me." She grinned. "I kinda don't want this to end, you know."

"Just book another cruise next month," he replied with a shrug.

"Oh, I wish I could just throw everything aside and live my life constantly on vacation."

"That sounds like a dig at me," Wes quipped.

She placed her hand on top of his. "No, that wasn't what I was trying to convey."

Wes brought her hand to his lips. "Whatever. Let's order our food."

"You know we're different people and I'm not trying to judge you," Alex said, not understanding the need to explain herself. Because she never did that.

"Since this is one of our last nights together, let's keep it beautiful," he said, then leaned in and kissed her cheek.

"I like the way that sounds," she replied. "Swimming after dinner?"

"Only if you're naked, little mermaid."

"I'm not going to be naked alone," Alex said.

"I'd never allow you to be naked alone," he said with a grin. Before Alex could reply, the waitress walked over to take their orders. Alex decided to go with fish run down and Wes shocked her when he ordered turtle stew. He grinned at her as she scowled at him. "What?"

"Turtle stew?"

"Never tried it? It's delicious."

"It could be someone's pet."

"It doesn't work like that, darling. Just like chicken farms," he said.

Alex held up her hands. "I don't think I want to hear any more."

"You're missing out."

Alex shook her head and frowned. "I'll take your word for it."

Once their food was dropped off Alex was happy with her meal and a tad bit curious about Wes's soup. "You know you want some," he said, then held out his spoon to her.

"How about no? I've tried a lot of new things with you, but this is where the line is drawn, buddy."

Wes slurped his soup and shrugged. After they finished their meal and Alex rebuffed the turtle soup offers, they headed back to the bed-and-breakfast. Holding Wes's hand made her smile, so Yolanda had been right. A vacation fling wasn't that bad after all.

"So, how would you rate your first cruise?" Wes asked.

"Five stars. And the company was amazing. Ten stars for you," she quipped.

"Don't forget about me when you return to your model life. Maybe we can get together for another cruise this year."

"I don't know about that. When I get home there's a lot of work I have to do."

"Alexandria, you should never let your life be consumed by nothing but work. I tried to live like that once and it almost killed me."

"So that's why you take four vacations a year?"

"Something like that. When I work I do work hard, and I play harder."

"Maybe I can be like you one day when I grow up."

Wes smiled and pulled her closer to him. "I'm glad we met."

"So am I. Even if you ruined my book and my outfit with your splashy introduction."

"And here I was thinking all was forgiven,"

"You redeemed yourself, and even if I forgave you, I didn't forget what you did." She bumped her hip against his.

"Well, thank you, my lady."

When they arrived at the bed-and-breakfast, the couple decided they didn't want to go skinny-dipping after all. Still full from dinner, they decided to call it a night.

The next morning Alex woke up early enough to watch the sun rise over the ocean. It was a beautiful sight, seeing the light sparkle on the waves and bathe the sand in warmth. She thought about how often she'd ignored the sunrises in Charleston as she rushed to work.

Alex silently promised herself that she would take more time to enjoy life and the beauty of home.

"How did you sneak out of bed so quietly?" Wes asked as he encircled her waist.

"I guess you sleep really hard." She leaned against his bare chest. "And I've been sneaking out of bed quietly my whole life."

"Details?" He stroked her arm and brushed a kiss against her temple.

"I used to wake up earlier than my little sister Nina. She'd climb in my bed in the middle of the night, and she was so cute when she was sleeping I didn't want to wake her up. So, I figured out how to ease out of bed without making a sound."

"You're close to your family, huh?"

"They might say too close. I'm the oldest, and maybe I

order them around. Not as if they listen. But Nina was my baby. Then she messed around and grew up."

Wes laughed as he swayed with her. "If my brother had ever gotten in my bed, I would've whooped his ass."

"That's kind of harsh," Alex said with a laugh. "I bet you're the youngest."

"Nope. It's just two of us, and I'm the sexiest and the oldest."

"Modest much?"

"I think you can attest to the fact that I don't have to be modest."

"Going to leave that alone," she laughed.

He spun her around and captured her lips in a soft kiss. "We'd better go have breakfast and head back to the ship," Alex said when they broke the kiss.

"Or we could say *forget the real world* and stay here for a month."

Alex pinched him on his shoulder. "You make it sound so simple and easy."

Wes shrugged. "It really is that easy, if you want it to be."

"Right now, I want coffee and another kiss."

He cupped her face and smiled. "I got the kiss."

As their lips met, Alex knew she would miss mornings like this the most when she returned to Charleston.

After breakfast Wes and Alex had a little time to take one last walk on the beach. "Where is your port?" she asked.

"Miami."

"But I thought you were from New York."

Wes nodded as he stopped to pick up a dried starfish. "I am, but I have a place in Miami because I'm a snow-bird."

"Nice. I would love to be around snow in the winter."

"Where's your port?"

"South Carolina. So, I get to float on a little longer without you."

Wes handed her the starfish. "You know when I get off this ship, things are going to get really boring."

"Or super exciting," she said with a smile. "You give yourself way too much credit for making my vacation great."

"Do I?"

"Yes. Someone has to keep that ego in check," she said with a wink.

"So, you're coming back to my cabin to kiss me good-bye?"

"Um, you could bring your bags to my cabin and we can have a long good-bye."

"Love that. And I'll bring us a special snack."

"Sounds great," Alex said as she kissed him on the cheek. They headed back to the ship holding hands. She knew reality was just over the horizon, but today she was going to stay in fantasyland with Wes.

Alex walked into her cabin and took a quick shower while Wes packed in his. After her shower she dressed in a white cotton dress, then fluffed the pillows on the bed. Even though Wes said he was bringing a special treat, Alex ordered some star fruit. After she placed her order there was a knock at the door. "That was fast," she muttered. She opened the door and Wes stood there with his bags and a waiter.

"Hello, beautiful. I'm moving in for the next four days," he said with a wink. "And I brought food." Wes stood aside and allowed the waiter to bring in the food. He followed him inside and set his bags in the corner.

"You certainly pack light," Alex said, noting the four bags he'd brought in.

"Yeah, always ready for the next adventure. Let's see what they picked for us. I just asked my dude in the kitchen to surprise us and make sure it wasn't salty."

Alex laughed. "Good job."

The waiter cleared his throat as he lifted the silver covers from the plates. There were scallops, shrimp, grilled pineapples, rice and tomatoes, and star fruit. "Is everything to your liking?" he asked.

"It looks delicious," Alex said, then reached for a shrimp. When she tasted it she moaned in delight. "And it is not too salty."

"Then we're really good," Wes said as he tipped the waiter. "Thank you."

The man smiled as he took the bills Wes handed him. "If you all need anything else, let me know."

"All right," Alex said, ready for the waiter to leave.

The man headed out the door and Wes pulled Alex into his arms. "I'm glad we're alone now," he said. "Now, I can do this." He captured her lips in a hot, sweet kiss. Alex moaned as his hands roamed her back.

"Um," she said when they broke the kiss. "I think that kiss was better than the shrimp."

"I need to do it again so you know for sure."

Alex pressed her hand against his chest. "Slow down, my guy. We got to try this food."

Wes relented and crossed over to the cart with Alex. She picked up a shrimp and brushed it across his lips. "It's good, right?"

Wes nodded as he took a bite. "But you taste so much better."

"How about we get to that later?" she replied with a wink. They fixed small plates of food, then hopped on the bed.

"After we eat what do you say we hit the pool for a while?" Wes suggested.

"Sounds good." She smiled at him, thinking she would get him back for the so-called cute way they'd met.

CHAPTER TWELVE

Wes smiled as Alexandria walked out of the bathroom in a blue-and-white-polka-dot bikini. "Beautiful," he said.

"Thank you. I figured this suit will help me get rid of the tan lines from the other suits."

"You could always sunbathe in the nude," he said with a wide smile.

Alexandria sucked her teeth and rolled her eyes. "Let's go."

Wes stood in front of her and stroked her cheek. "Alexandria, you know this has been the best vacation I've had in a long time. Thanks for sharing it with me."

Her smile made his heart tingle. She was a special kind of woman and he wasn't sure he wanted their interaction to end when they returned to their respective ports. He wanted to know her off the boat. Needed to know what made her tick and how she lived. Was she really the supermodel he thought she was? But what if this vacation was just her detaching from reality and she had a whole separate life on the shore? It wouldn't be the first time a vacation fling fizzled in the real world. *Just take it for what it is*, he thought as they headed out the door.

"We should get a couple of bottles of water," Alexandria said, breaking into his thoughts.

"Sure, and a daiquiri as well," he replied.

She shrugged. "Not a bad idea, but let's wait until we get to the pool."

They headed outside and Alexandria pointed to two lounge chairs. "That's a perfect spot."

Wes couldn't help but remember that was the seat where she'd been that first day they'd met. "Are you sure?"

"Yes, there's great sun over there."

"Now, don't have a flashback while we're there."

"Sweetie, that is all water under the bridge," she said, then planted a kiss on his cheek. "Come on." Alexandria grabbed his hand and Wes felt sparks. He wasn't a sparks type of guy. The last time he felt sparks had been with his ex-wife, and that fizzled. But Alexandria didn't seem anything like Jasmine, who could never relax, even on vacation. Wes gave her a slow once-over as she adjusted her chair. "What's up?"

"Nothing," he replied. "I just like what I see."

"A more sarcastic person would say *take a picture*, but I'm not that person today." She winked at him and leaned back in the chair. "Why don't you get comfortable?"

"I'd feel a lot better if you were sitting right here." Wes patted his thighs.

Before Alexandria could reply, Liz crossed over to them. "Well, well, isn't this special?"

"My goodness, I knew it was too good to be true." Wes groaned.

"What does that even mean?" she snapped.

"That you'd gotten a clue."

Wes looked past Liz when he heard Alexandria get up. She smiled, then sauntered over to the bar. "Liz, why don't you just go away?"

"This is what you do, come on cruises, sell some dreams, and then pretend she means nothing."

Wes dropped his head. "Liz, I never promised you a damn thing. I don't even understand why you thought there was something more than two adults enjoying sea and sand together."

"Because you made me feel so special, so . . ."

"We had good sex that was better for you than it was for me," Wes said.

"Surely you overestimate your prowess because it wasn't as great as you think."

Wes snorted. "Then what keeps you chasing me? My personality? Liz, let it go."

She glared at him. "One of these days someone is going to bring you to your fucking knees and I hope it hurts." Liz stormed away from him and headed over to her group of friends. Wes could tell by the cold stares that they were talking about him. He was going to chalk it up to bitterness and bad decisions when all of a sudden he was drenched with water. "What the . . ."

Alexandria's laughter filled his ears as he wiped his face. "That's how you feel?" he asked. She hung on the edge of the pool.

"You didn't see the set up?" She laughed. "Same spot where you met me, no towels or books."

One of the pool attendants walked over to the couple with fresh towels. "Everything all right?" the man asked, trying and failing to hide his laughter.

"Oh, everybody knew this was going down?"

"She didn't," Alexandria said as she nodded toward Liz and her friends. "Everything good over there?"

Wes shrugged. "I hope if I see you on another cruise you'll be happy to see me and not harboring delusions of a relationship."

"Never that," she said, then giggled. "The best thing about a vacation fling is that when the vacation is over, so is everything else."

Wes gave her a slow look because the last thing he really wanted was for things between him and Alexandria to be over. Wait. Was he turning into Liz? "So, if I asked you for your number, you wouldn't give it to me?"

Alexandria raised her right brow, then said, "Maybe. But I wouldn't be sitting by the phone waiting for you to call."

"I'd text first anyway," he replied with a grin.

"We still have a few days left on this ship before you give me the brush off. Let's worry about that when the boat stops in Miami."

Wes tilted his head and gazed at Alexandria. "Well, when you put it that way."

She held up her hand. "Wes, I'm a fully grown woman. I know how life works. You owe me nothing when we get off this ship. But right now I want my daiquiri."

"Yes, ma'am," he replied with a mock salute. "Strawberry or mango?"

"Mango for sure," she said as she dried off.

Wes shook his head. "Of course, you like it sweet," he said as he started for the bar.

She stretched out in the chair and placed her hands behind her head. There was something about her that drove him crazy. Maybe she *was* turning him into Liz. Or maybe Alexandria was special, a woman he needed to get to know a lot better. But he wasn't going to stalk her. So he wasn't Liz.

He ordered the drinks and watched Alexandria talking to the pool attendant. She was so personable and sweet to everyone. Was there something hidden underneath all that? He wanted to see her layers, wanted to know what made her happy, sad, and excited. *Where in the hell is all this coming from?* Wes took a deep breath and walked over to Alexandria. "Mango, my lady."

"Thank you," she said as she took the glass from his hand. "No hard feelings, right?"

"Not at all. You got me. I see you play the long game. I have to watch myself around you."

"I warned you, but you chose not to listen," Alexandria said. "My father always said, *hard heads make soft bottoms.* You're like a bag of cotton."

"I still have time to get you back; don't forget where I'm sleeping tonight."

"Then I'm going to have to keep you up all night," she said and gave him a quick peck on the cheek.

"Holding you to that," he said, then returned to his drink. Alexandria flipped over on her stomach, soaking up the sun, and Wes had to stop himself from kissing her shoulders. *Sexy* wasn't a big enough word to describe this woman.

"I told you to take a picture," she quipped.

"Maybe I should commission a painting," he said.

"What do you say we actually jump in the pool to-gether?"

Alexandria propped up on her elbow. "All right. Let's do it."

After a couple of hours of playing in the pool, includ-ing a game of Marco Polo with some of the other newly coupled people on the cruise, Alexandria and Wes headed back to her room to prepare for dinner. Tonight they'd dine at the captain's table, and Wes couldn't wait to see what Alexandria would wear. She'd been a fashion plate during the whole trip, even if he enjoyed seeing her naked more than any other way.

"Want to save water and shower together?" Alexandria asked, breaking into his thoughts.

"That depends on whether you actually want to eat dinner this evening."

"Good point," she said. "I won't be long."

Alexandria's shower wasn't long, but the steam that followed her out of the bathroom proved it was hot. Wes shook his head as he walked into the bathroom.

Alex smoothed shea butter over her body as she lis-tened to Wes humming in the shower. She had to admit she'd been having an amazing time with him. Part of her wondered how this was supposed to end. Did she tell him she wanted to keep in touch? How would that work? She wasn't going to visit him in New York in the winter. My God, the snow would kill a Southern belle like her. And she was not about to have him come to Charleston. Oh, her sisters would be out of control. Especially Yolanda, who always seemed to be in Charleston more than Char-lotte anyway.

Besides, she needed to focus on more important things—
the renovations at the bed-and-breakfast and her ideas
about upping their customer service based on the place
she and Wes visited in the Cayman Islands. The vacation
had been fun, but reality was right around the corner and
she needed to get her focus back. Alex crossed over to the
closet and pulled out a ruby red halter dress, the one dress
she'd said she wasn't going to wear. It was short, it was
bright, and nothing she'd even consider wearing in
Charleston. That was why she was going to put it on. Taking the dress off the hanger, she made a mental note to tell
Yolanda that she created clothes for women looking to
make a baby. That's probably how she and Chuck made
those twins, Alex surmised.

"Wow," Wes said, then let out a slow whistle. "That
dress is amazing."

"It'll be even better if you help me zip it up," she said.
Wes crossed over to her and zipped the dress.

"Red is definitely your color," he said, then leaned in
and kissed her on the back of her neck.

"You think so? Because I could've sworn you said
green was my color," she said. "You have to make up
your mind."

"You could swallow the rainbow and every color
would look amazing on you," he said. "I like taking the
colors off, myself."

"Don't you think you should get dressed?" she asked
as she took a step away from him.

Wes shrugged. "I guess, since I'm sure I won't get a
seat at the table in the towel."

"You wear it well, though," she said as she reached for
a pair of silver sandals.

A few moments later Alex and Wes were dressed and

ready to go to dinner. She thought he'd be the perfect replacement for the current James Bond actor, the way he filled out that tuxedo.

"Here's hoping the food isn't overly salty tonight," Alex said as they entered the dining room.

"If it is, you know I have connections to get you the satisfaction you deserve."

"You're too good to me," she replied as they reached the table. Wes pulled Alex's chair out for her and brushed a kiss on her cheek as she sat down.

Two other couples joined their table and they all fell into an easy conversation about the islands they'd visited, the local food, and the misery of the cruise coming to an end.

"This was one of the better singles cruises I've taken," a woman named Whitney said. "It's nice to meet people who are actually single." She squeezed the hand of the man sitting beside her, then leaned in to Alex. "I met a guy last year and he had a wife in Richmond. It was crazy because he was like, *come to Baltimore with me, let's see where this goes*. Honey, his wife was waiting for him. I was so embarrassed."

"It wasn't your fault that he lied," Alex said. "Why did you feel some kind of way?"

"Because his wife was my cousin," she said with a laugh.

Alex wanted to leave—she just wanted to pretend she wasn't thinking she'd run into something similar with Wes. Sure, it wouldn't be an unknown cousin, but suppose there was a wife, kids, or another Liz? She didn't need to hear horror stories because she was simply going to leave everything in the ocean. Alex turned to Wes and smiled. "I'm going to the bar," she said.

"I'll join you," he said as she stood up. She waited for him, then they headed for the bar.

"They have some stories," Alex said after they ordered their drinks.

"People sometimes come on these cruises with the wrong things on their mind. Marriage, meeting The One, pretending to be someone they're not."

"Which one are you?"

"I'm as real as they come," he said with a wink. "You mean to tell me you haven't figured that out yet?"

"That would require me taking you at your word." She shrugged, then broke out into laughter. "You seem like you're a good guy."

"*Seem like?* You know you've never met anyone like me," he said, then held up his glass. "Here's a toast to the best use of a cannonball ever."

"So, you finally admit you did it on purpose?"

"I didn't, to be honest, I was trying to avoid Liz."

"Guess you shouldn't have introduced her to the joy of Wes after dark."

"The joy, huh?"

Alex nodded. "Have to give credit where it's due. And you are a joy. I can't wait until dinner is over so I can get some dessert."

"Life is short; want to have dessert now?"

Alex pinched him on his shoulder. "No. We're going to be adults, have dinner, and then get naked."

"I can't wait," he said as they started for the table.

Dinner turned out to be delicious and uneventful. Alex listened to some of the couples making promises to stay in touch, and part of her wondered if she and Wes should make those promises as well. But since he didn't bring it up, she didn't either. Alex wasn't going to expect anything from him. They had a nice time together on the cruise. And it was soon to be over. She'd deal with it.

"Are you ready to head to the room now?" Wes asked.

"In a minute. I want to look at the stars."

"Ah, yes. You have been wanting to see a starry night over the ocean since we've been on this ship."

"I have. And tonight is the perfect night for that."

"Well, let's go," he said. They headed out to the deck, and the night was gorgeous, stars shining like diamonds against the velvet-black sky.

"I wish I could hang this on my wall," Alex said as she looked up at the sky. "So beautiful."

"Doesn't really hold a candle to you, though."

"You're really good for my ego."

Wes drew Alex into his arms. "You know, I think you're the most beautiful woman I've ever met. I mean that."

"You can stop laying it on so thick. You already have me."

"Then you know I'm telling the truth. What do you say we take a moonlight swim?"

She looked down at her gown. "You must mean later."

"Of course. There's no way I'd be responsible for ruining that dress, but I can't wait to help you take it off."

"Oh, really? You know it's only just one zipper. I don't think I need your help."

"Doesn't matter, you're gonna get it anyway."

Alex laughed as she leaned against his chest. "This has been a really amazing vacation. I guess I have to give credit where credit is due, you made this trip very special for me."

"I'm glad I was able to play a role in you having a

great vacation. You were definitely the highlight of the seas for me."

Alex wanted to say something, but she knew she couldn't get too caught up in emotions that would lead to nothing. "We better go change if we're going to spend some time out here."

CHAPTER THIRTEEN

Wes watched Alexandria's wide-eyed wonderment as they watched the stars. What was it about them that thrilled her so much? He didn't have time to figure it out tonight because the way she filled out that bathing suit had him watching her and not the stars.

"I should've brought my iPad," she said. "I'd love to have a print of this on my office wall."

Wes pulled his phone out of his pocket and handed it to Alexandria. "Take some shots," he said. "I'll text them to you."

"Was this just an excuse to get my number?" she quipped.

"Why would I need an excuse when you were going to give it to me anyway?"

Alexandria rolled her eyes, then lifted the phone upward. Wes watched as Alexandria twisted her body to get the shots of the sky. It didn't hurt that every time she moved, her suit rose, exposing her bottom.

"I should probably stop before I fill up your phone with my pictures," Alexandria said as she hopped off a lounge chair.

"You sure you got enough? Because you look amazing as a photographer."

"Whatever," she said as she walked over to him and sat in his lap. "Thank you for indulging me."

"No problem. I just hope you plan on thanking me really good and really hard later," he said.

She brushed her lips against his. "I'm going to thank you so good and so hard."

Wes captured her lips in a deep, hot kiss. Alexandria ground against him as their tongues danced against each other's. He pulled her closer to his chest and stopped himself from burying his hardness inside her.

She pulled back from him and smiled. "I guess you're ready for your *thank you*, huh?" she said as she reached down and stroked his dick.

"Absolutely," Wes replied, then lifted her in his arms as he rose to his feet. "You ready to thank me?"

Alexandria answered him with a long, slow lick to the side of his neck. He stumbled as he headed to her cabin. "Damn, woman," he moaned.

She winked at him. "I'm about to show you so much gratitude."

Neither of them paid attention to the stares from other people, particularly Liz and her crew. Once they made it to Alexandria's cabin Wes opened the door and pressed her against the wall. "So, that gratitude?" he said.

Alexandria wrapped her leg around his waist and brushed her lips across his. "Thank you," she breathed, then thrust her hips forward.

"Oh, damn," he moaned as his dick jumped in appreciation. "Do that again."

This time she ground against him, and his body throbbed. He captured her lips in a hot kiss, nibbling at her bottom lip as she thrust into him. He could feel her wetness through her suit. She was so hot and Wes wanted to melt with her without a thought about protection, but he couldn't be *that* irresponsible. Tearing his mouth away from hers, Wes rushed over to the bed and laid her against the sheets. "You're too much."

"I told you my gratitude runs deep," she said, then wrapped her arms around his neck. "And speaking of deep, I want you deep inside, now."

"Let me protect us," he intoned. Wes knew Alexandria was always prepared with condoms under her pillow. She didn't disappoint either. He grabbed a golden package and sheathed himself. Wes leaned back and opened his arms to her. "Ride me," he commanded. Alexandria mounted him and took his erection deep inside her valley. "Yes," he exclaimed as she rode him slow. Then fast. He thrust deeper into her, making her purr his name. Wes gripped her hips as she reared back and forth. There was something about Alexandria that just turned him on and made him harder and harder as she pumped up and down, up and down.

"So good. You feel so good," Alexandria cried out.

"Ah, ah," was all Wes could muster as he exploded inside her. Alexandria collapsed against his chest, reaching her own climax.

"Did I thank you thoroughly enough?" she asked.

"You did, but if you want to do it again, I'll be ready for more in ten minutes."

"Should I set an alarm?" she asked as she reached for the digital clock. Wes touched her elbow.

"Let nature wake us up," he said, then pulled her closer. A few seconds later they'd both drifted off to sleep.

The next few days on the cruise seemed to fly by. Alex and Wes spent most of their time in her cabin, wrapped up in each other. But the ship came to dock in Miami and Alex felt some kind of way. Was she missing this man before he even left? *Get over yourself*, she thought as she watched him gather his bags.

"You know, you could get off with me," Wes said.

"I've done that several times," she said as she crossed over to him. "As tempting as that sounds, I have to get home."

"Boo," he said, then kissed her on the cheek. "Don't be a stranger. We have each other's numbers. I plan to use yours, I hope you're going to do the same."

She smiled, thinking that telling him the truth would be harsh. Alex was old enough to know that long-distance entanglements didn't work. "We'll see."

"That doesn't sound very promising," Wes replied. "What's going on?"

"We're about to return to reality, and I'm not expecting phone calls and visits. I know I have a huge project coming up at work and my time is going to be limited."

"Are you saying this is good-bye?"

"Maybe it's for the best."

Wes chuckled. "Wow. So, is this where you confess that you have a husband and a couple of kids on dry land?"

"No. I'm not that kind of woman. But I have a lot of responsibilities with my family and my job. Besides, you're going to be in New York, living your life and taking more vacations. I don't think either of us should leave with expectations," she said.

"That's how you feel?"

"Those are just the facts, darling. I'm pretty sure you're going to forget all about me when you get back to the Bronx."

"Now you're just being petty. BK all day," he said.

"All right, whatever," she said with a nervous laugh. "We can try to keep in touch, but I won't hold it against you if life gets in your way."

"So, you're not going to call at all?" he asked as he hitched his right brow.

"I didn't say that, but . . ."

"*Don't hold it against you if you don't?*" He stroked her cheek, then pulled her close and kissed her softly. Alex moaned as his tongue brushed across her bottom lip. "If that's the last time I get to kiss you, I hope you enjoyed it as much as I did."

"Wes," she said.

"See you later, maybe," he said, then headed to the door.

Alex sat on the bed as it closed. She had done the right thing, hadn't she?

CHAPTER FOURTEEN

After the ship docked at the port in Miami, Wes waited for his driver and took his phone off airplane mode. The second his phone rang and he saw his brother's face on the screen, Wes wished he'd kept himself unreachable.

"Johnathan, what's going on?" Wes asked.

"Are you done with your vacation because we have some issues."

"I'm still in Miami."

"Good, then it shouldn't take you that long to get to South Carolina."

"What's going on?" Wes asked with a sigh.

"The Richardson project—the owner wants to make some significant changes."

Wes sighed. He wasn't ready to think about work. He was simply trying to understand why Alexandria's brush-off had gotten to him. He'd said something very similar to Liz. He wasn't Liz. But he didn't want to see the sexiest woman he'd ever met just become a memory. However, he had other things that obviously needed his attention. "What changes?"

"I spoke to the owner a couple of days ago and he said he wanted the building to look more like old Charleston or some shit."

"I thought this was a done deal? Why are they asking for changes now?"

"Because we haven't gotten construction started because someone was on another vacation."

"Don't start that bullshit. You were supposed to close the deal and get those folks to sign off on the designs. What happened?"

"I don't know, but I think you should go down to Charleston and meet with the Richardsons."

"Send me the files. I'll fly down there tomorrow."

"You must have had an amazing vacation if you're ready to hop into work like this."

"Get off my phone," Wes said, then ended the call. Working out this Richardson issue would give him a chance to think about something other than Alexandria. Maybe a trip to Charleston would be like a minivacation. But it was still South Carolina, and he remembered the horror stories he'd heard his grandparents tell about that place. That was why he'd hoped his brother would've taken care of this project. Of course, Johnathan played these games a lot. After every vacation Wes took there was always an issue when he returned. Why did he expect things to change because he was besotted with a woman he'd probably never see again?

* * *

Alex yawned as she waited for her luggage. As much as she hated being off vacation, she was happy to be at the Charleston Harbor. "Hey," Robin called out. "You look tanned and relaxed."

"I'm glad you picked me up. At least you're on time." Alex hugged her sister, then nodded toward her bags. "You want to help me with those?"

"No," she quipped, then grabbed two of the bags.

"I knew you loved me," Alex said when she reached for the other three bags.

"So, how was the cruise?" Robin asked as they walked to the car.

"It was amazing." She smiled broadly as Wes crossed her mind.

"Um, that doesn't look like the face of a woman who read books for two weeks."

"I did not read a single book," she said. "I have no regrets."

"Wait. What? Alexandria Richardson!"

"What I'm about to tell you does not leave this harbor or this car."

"I make no promises," Robin replied. "If this is a story about a business deal, I'm telling it."

"No business, all pleasure." Alex smiled again and Robin shook her head.

"Spill it."

Alex recounted the day at the pool, when Wes splashed her, and how he ended up at her dinner table.

"Hold up, who are you?"

"Do you want to hear the rest or not?"

"Of course, but first, on a scale of Idris Elba to

Michael B., how fine was he?" Robin wiggled her brows, then burst into laughter.

"You know the show *Leverage*?"

Robin nodded. "Aldis Hodge fine? Damn, Sis!"

"Robin, when I tell you this man made everything exciting. And he could kiss like a dream." Alex closed her eyes, her lips trembling at the thought of the kisses they shared and would never share again.

"Um, Alex," Robin said as she shot her sister a quick glance. "You're kind of scaring me."

"What?"

"That smiling thing you're doing, I'm not used to seeing that."

"You sound like Yolanda, and that is not a compliment."

"There, that's the Alex I'm used to. So, this good kisser—are you going to keep in contact with him?"

Alex shook her head. "What's the point? He's from New York, I have a lot of work to . . ."

"You are the worst. Grown folks can travel to see each other and . . ."

"Well, I'm not doing that, and I didn't want him to feel obligated to stick around. Real life eclipses anything that happened on the cruise ship."

"So, he feels the same?"

Alex cleared her throat and looked out of the window.

"Hello?" Robin said when she didn't get a response. "This is all your choice, isn't it?"

"Yes, it is. I'm not trying to get my feelings hurt over a vacation fling."

"Fling? You slept with him? Oh my God. Alex! I thought you'd just spent the night with him. Talking or doing whatever you do. Tell me more."

"Don't do that and don't say a word to your little sisters."

Robin laughed. "I don't know if I can hold this back. Please tell me it was good. Wait, your face says it all."

Smiling despite herself, Alex said, "We made great memories."

"That's good, but why are you stopping a good time?"

"Life gets in the way, and I'm not trying to have expectations that are going to fall through. Besides, we have these renovations at the bed-and-breakfast that I have to oversee with Daddy."

"Yeah, because he can't make his vision for the bed-and-breakfast happen without you," Robin quipped. "Come on, Alexandria. The world doesn't stop spinning because you aren't around to push it."

"Whatever. You know what I mean. Besides, this was my suggestion, so it's only right that I see it through."

"I'm pretty sure work has been done since you were on vacation because guess what, there are other capable people at the bed-and-breakfast."

"Never said that I was the only capable person, but I am the best."

"So modest. But serious question—are you going to call the man and let him know you made it back safely?"

Alex sighed and rolled her eyes at her sister. She knew calling Wes would be nothing more than a mistake. "Where is everybody?" Alex asked as Robin pulled into the parking lot of the bed-and-breakfast.

"Dad's golfing, Nina and Clinton are in Summerville."

"And Logan?"

"Sleeping," she said with a wink. "I don't deprive myself of a good time."

"That's your husband, you should always have a good

time," Alex said as images of Wes between her thighs danced in her head.

"Too bad you're throwing yours away."

Alex and Robin took her bags inside, then Alex plopped down on her bed. "I'm tired," she said.

"If you want me to leave, just say it." Robin laughed.

"'Bye, Robin," Alex said.

"I'll leave quicker if you tell me that you're going to call Mr. Vacation Booty," she said and took a slow step toward the door.

"I'm going to unpack and go to sleep. But you're still getting out."

"You're no fun," Robin said.

"Out."

Robin walked out of the room, and once Alex was alone, she pulled out her phone and looked at the pictures she'd texted from Wes's phone. Glancing at his number, she wondered if she should listen to Robin and call him.

And say what? You told that man that good-bye was forever. Alex stood up and started pacing. Why was she acting like this? Her vacation was over and so were mind-blowing orgasms and hot kisses. Calling him would only make being back home and back to work lonelier than she'd ever felt before.

That's the last time I'm going to listen to Yolanda Richardson-Morris.

Six a.m.—Wes knew it was six. He just didn't understand why his phone was ringing. Last night he'd hung out at two bars where he usually met all the beautiful people. But last night he had one person on his mind: Alexandria.

How had he allowed this to happen? Maybe it was just the fact that she'd turned him down. She was playing hard to get and that was his usual game. But she had been right; he'd probably never see her again because to hear her tell it, she didn't take vacations. He'd had three drinks last night and still couldn't get the sweet taste of Alexandria out of his mouth.

He'd gotten to his penthouse around one, but he hadn't fallen asleep quickly. Every time he closed his eyes he saw Alexandria's face. And when he did drift off to sleep his damn phone was ringing. "What?" he snapped.

"I hope you checked your e-mail," Johnathan said, forgoing a customary hello.

"Do you know what time it is, asswipe?"

"Yeah. Your flight to Charleston leaves in two hours," he said.

"Why did you book a flight and not tell me?"

"I sent you an e-mail," Johnathan said matter-of-factly.

"That. Does. Not. Count! What am I going to Charleston for?"

"Read your e-mail. I'm going to meet with a developer in Harlem. When I send you the meeting notes, how about reading them?"

Before Wes could tell his brother where he could stick those notes, Johnathan had ended the call. "Motherfucker," Wes muttered as he climbed out of bed. He took a quick shower, then checked his e-mail. Johnathan has sent the e-mail about his trip about the same time he was having his second drink at the bar.

And his brother wondered why he spent so much time on vacation. Wes packed an overnight bag and his tablet, then called his driver. He needed to get to the airport fast.

Wes figured he'd sleep on the plane and then make a reservation at the Richardson Bed and Breakfast so he could see what all the fuss was about.

When he got in the car he pulled up the bed-and-breakfast website. He started to click on the reservation tab, but he wanted to get some background on the company he was now going to have to deal with directly.

He clicked on the About Us tab and gasped. There she was. Alexandria. Not as a model but the co-owner of the Richardson Bed and Breakfast. "No freaking way," he muttered. "This can't be her, and I know that old man isn't her husband."

Wes released a sigh of relief when he read that Sheldon Richardson was her father. But what else would he find out about her—on her own turf?

This was going to be the most interesting business trip he had taken in a long while.

Alex stood in the kitchen of the bed-and-breakfast with a smile on her face. The blueberry muffins were almost done and her mouth was watering. The food on the ship had been good, but there was nothing as good as these muffins. Well, maybe the coffee.

"Glad to see you're back, Miss Alex," Roberta, the family's longtime cook, said.

"I'm glad to be back. I've been thinking about these muffins for weeks."

Roberta smiled. "Mr. Clinton told me, and I said I was going to make a special batch for you today."

"You are a true angel."

"And I baked enough for you to share," she said, then patted Alex on the shoulder.

"I understand, I'll definitely share," Alex said, then crossed over to the coffee machine and filled a carafe to take upstairs for the morning meeting. Alex was doing something she didn't normally do; she wasn't considering what all was on today's agenda, she was looking forward to lunch. When her phone buzzed she didn't know why she was hoping it was a text from Wes. *You told that man to leave you alone and there's no reason to think he isn't going to listen,* she thought as she looked at the calendar alert.

"Welcome back, Sis," Clinton said as she walked into the conference room. "I thought you would've taken the morning off."

Alex set the coffee and basket of muffins in the center of the table. "Now, you of all people should know better than that," she replied with a laugh.

"How was your vacation?"

Alex smiled widely, and Clinton was taken aback. He could count the number of times he'd seen her smile like that and it always caught him off guard.

"That good, huh?"

"It was much needed and I might have to do it again in a year. You and Nina should definitely take a cruise. Not the same one I took, but a nice couples trip."

Clinton nodded. "Nina said you went on a singles cruise. Any love connections?"

Alex rolled her eyes. "I'm leaving all that love stuff to my sisters. But I did have a good time and some amazing food. Let me show you something." Alex pulled up the pictures of the starry sky. "I want to see if we can integrate this design in some of the new rooms. Like maybe a ceiling scape or some photos on the walls."

"These pictures are nice," Clinton said. "Did you take them?"

"Yes. Seeing the stars and the ocean that night was so amazing. It's something I want to share with the guests."

Clinton nodded. "Must have been a special night."

"You have no idea," she said as the rest of the staff walked in.

Wes walked into the lobby of the Richardson Bed and Breakfast. It was clear to him that this place was special. His Uber driver couldn't stop talking about how historic the property was, and what it meant to the African American community in Charleston. Wes was impressed by what he heard. But more than anything else, he wanted to see the look on Alexandria's face. Maybe this was his chance to win her over and show her that fate was bringing them together again.

Wes crossed over to the front desk and waited for the clerk to end her call so he could check in. "Good afternoon, sir," she said. "I apologize for the delay. Do you have a reservation here with us today?"

"Yes, Prescott."

She smiled at him. "All right, I see you're here for a week, correct?"

"Yes. Do you know if Mr. Richardson is available?"

"I'll call his office and check for you, Mr. Prescott."

He nodded his thanks to her, then turned his focus to the lobby. It was warm with summer colors of sky blue, yellow, and green accenting the taupe walls. Whoever the interior designer was had done an excellent job capturing a seaside appeal and a homey feeling. Part of him was starting to understand all the questions and the need to preserve the history of the building.

"Mr. Prescott," the clerk said, breaking into his thoughts, "Mr. Richardson said he can meet with you in an hour. Does that work for you?"

"Yes, thank you very much," he said as she handed him the room key. Wes figured he'd put his things down in the room, then check out the property. Then he heard her laugh. Wes turned around and saw Alexandria walking with a man. He couldn't tell what their relationship was. But it was clear they were close. He ducked behind a potted plant and watched them leave the lobby together.

Maybe that was the reason she didn't want any contact; she had someone at home. Now he felt stupid. People are different on vacation than they are in real life, and whoever he met on the ship probably wasn't the same person he was going to run into at this bed-and-breakfast. He needed to get his work done quickly and get back to New York and begin to forget about Alexandria Richardson.

CHAPTER FIFTEEN

"Clinton, where are we going?" Alex asked as they crossed the parking lot.

"I'm just following orders," he said. "And your sisters are bossy, just like you. You taught them well."

"Now you're just being rude."

Clinton shrugged. "I told Nina we should play hooky one day while you were gone and she went off. *Just because Alex isn't here, it doesn't mean you can slack off. She's going to blame me.* I worked every day, just so you know."

"I expected nothing less," she replied with a smile.

"There's something different about you," he said as he nodded toward the picnic table where her three sisters were sitting. "Keep it up and be nice to my wife."

Alex looked at the smirks on her sisters' faces. "I make no promises."

Clinton gave her a quick kiss on the cheek, then crossed over to his wife, Nina, and gave her a passionate kiss before waving to his sisters-in-law. "See y'all later," he said, then headed back inside.

Alex eyed her sisters suspiciously, especially Yolanda. "Where are the babies?"

"With their father and aunties. Chuck's sisters came to visit and they decided I needed a break. So, Robin said you finally got some," Yolanda said with a grin.

"Robin!" Alex shrieked.

Robin kicked Yolanda underneath the table. "That is not what I said."

"You shouldn't have said anything," Alex said.

"But is it true?" Nina asked. "You, Alexandria the Great, got on a boat and had sex with a stranger?"

Yolanda nudged Nina. "Yes, she did. Look at her face; she's smiling. I didn't even know your lips could do that."

"Why are y'all interrupting my work day?"

Robin shook her head. "Well, most normal people would've taken the first day back from their vacation off. But since this is your first time, you didn't know the rules."

"Stop it. Dad said we have a meeting with the architect today about the designs for the remodel. I don't have time to play with y'all."

"Well," Robin said, "I have some news."

Nina smiled knowingly, while her sisters looked confused. "What is it?" Yolanda asked. "And it better not be you're leaving Logan again because . . ."

"Shut up and let her talk," Nina said.

"Logan and I are just fine and neither of us is going

anywhere," Robin said, then rolled her eyes. "But we are expanding our family."

"Aww," Yolanda exclaimed.

Robin smiled. "We're starting the process of adopting a baby boy."

"Wow," Alex said. "And both of you want this?"

Robin nodded. "It's a little weird how it all happened. Logan's partner in his practice also works at a women's clinic in North Charleston. One of the women he was treating also had a heart condition. Logan joined her health-care team and she was saying she couldn't take care of the baby with all her health issues. Logan tried to help her with finding the right social services programs."

"What about her family?" Alex asked.

Tears filled Robin's eyes. "They turned their back on her. Her father is a big preacher in Dallas. He put her on a plane to Charleston with ten thousand dollars and told her not to return."

"Oh my God, that is so horrible. How old is she?" Yolanda asked.

"She's only twenty-three. Could you imagine Daddy treating any of us like that?"

"No, thank God," Nina breathed. "How could any father do that?"

"That's horrible for her, but is this ethical?" Alex asked. "Logan is her doctor."

"Yes, it is ethical, and we're taking all the legal steps to do this right." Robin sighed. "I couldn't imagine that baby being left in the system. Spending time with Bradford and Nora made me realize that I still wanted to be a mom."

Alex thought about everything Robin had gone

through, and how much she wanted this adoption to work out for her and Logan. Robin had been devastated when a nurse claimed she had an affair with Logan and he'd fathered her son. Robin had gone as far as to file for divorce from her beloved husband. It had all turned out to be a lie. Thank God. But Alex hoped Robin wasn't in for another round of disappointment.

"Well, I'm happy for you," Nina said. "You and Logan are going to be amazing parents."

"And babies are not easy," Yolanda said. "I think Nora hates me. The minute I close my eyes, she starts crying. I can barely pump milk because they start crying. And it makes my heart ache because I don't know what's wrong with my babies."

Nina wrapped her arm around Yolanda's shoulders. "So, where's Chuck when all this is going on?"

Yolanda rolled her eyes. "Oh, he walks in the room and they turn into cute little cooing babies. He's so cute with them. But sometimes I feel like he's guarding the babies from me because I don't know what I'm doing." She dropped her head and cried. Alex and Robin crossed over to her and enveloped her in tight hugs.

"Oh, Yo-Yo," Alex said quietly. "You're a first-time mom with two babies. I know it's hard. But you have us, your husband, and Daddy. Reach out to us so we can help you."

Yolanda looked up at Alex and shook her head. "So you can tell my kids I couldn't handle it?"

"None of us would do that," Robin chimed in, then gave Alex the side-eye.

"I wouldn't do that," Alex said. "We love you as much as we love the babies."

Yolanda burst into tears. "Mommy was so perfect and I feel like I'm just making a mess and my babies are going to need therapy by the time they're two."

Alex wanted to laugh, but then she figured her sister was really suffering, so she just hugged her tighter.

"You should talk to someone," Robin said. "And no new mom is perfect. When you were a baby, Mom dropped you once."

"Robin," Alex exclaimed, then pinched Robin's arm. "She technically didn't drop you, you kind of rolled out of her arms like a little ball."

The four sisters laughed. "Was that supposed to make me feel better?" Yolanda asked.

"Did it?" Robin inquired.

Yolanda nodded. "Kind of."

"All right, what's going on out here?" Sheldon Richardson asked as he crossed over to his daughters. "Everything all right?"

"Daddy," Nina said as she hopped up and gave him a hug. "We thought Alex was still on vacation, but she said y'all have meetings today."

"We do. Mr. Prescott is here and I think it's time to go over his ideas."

"I thought we were happy with his blueprints?" Alex asked.

"You were happy with them. I have some concerns."

"Daddy, you know Alex thinks her word is law," Robin quipped.

Sheldon looked over at Yolanda's tearstained face. "What's wrong, my love?" he asked as he gave her a hug.

"I suck as a parent," she said.

"Aww, baby, so do I. There is no such thing as a perfect parent. It's amazing that you girls made it out of childhood. Make sure you're kind to yourself." He brushed a kiss across her forehead. "Are the babies okay?"

Yolanda nodded. "They're with their daddy—they're fine."

Sheldon hitched his right brow. "Then why is he on his way over here right now?"

"What?"

Sheldon laughed. "He said Bradford stops crying and Nora starts. Then Nora calms down, gets ready to go to sleep, and Bradford wakes her up."

Yolanda placed her hand on her chest. "Oh my goodness, he sucks, too," she said. "I'm going to go inside and wait for him."

"Good idea," Sheldon said. "Alex, we should get going since you decided to come to work today."

"We're all having dinner tonight, right?" Robin said as Alex and Sheldon started toward the B&B.

"Sure are. I'm so happy to have all my girls here. And I can't wait to hear all about your vacation, Alex."

Nina and Robin shared a knowing grin and ignored Alex's scowl.

Wes had questions for Clinton Jefferson, and they didn't have anything to do with the bed-and-breakfast. What was going on with him and Alexandria?

"We're going to meet in the conference room," Clinton said. "Can I get you a water or coffee while we wait for Sheldon and Alex?"

"Water is fine."

"Oh," Clinton said before ducking out of the room, "don't call her Alex unless she gives you the okay."

Wes hitched his brow. This goofy ass dude was what

she wanted? And they worked together? The way he called her Alex got under his skin. It was way too personal, and why would anyone shorten a beautiful name like Alexandria? When Clinton returned with Wes's water it took all Wes's composure not to snatch the plastic bottle from his hand. "Thank you."

"I understand you're staying here with us this week," Clinton said.

Wes knew this man didn't expect him to make small talk with him. "Yes. I wanted to get a feel for the property and understand the landscape."

Clinton smiled. "First time in Charleston? This bed-and-breakfast is historic. I remember when I applied for my job here, after trying to get Sheldon to sell."

Wes furrowed his brow. "Really?"

"Alex wasn't feeling me working here for a while." Clinton laughed. "But she's a wonderful boss."

Wes's anger at this man started to subside, then it flared again. This son of a bitch was using Alexandria to get ahead in the company. This was that sugary, underhanded cutthroat shit. At least you got stabbed in the chest in New York. "Um," he said. Wes was about to tell Clinton Jefferson that he was . . .

"Good afternoon," Sheldon boomed as he walked into the conference room. "Sorry I'm a few minutes late, but my daughters are here and I had to get my hugs."

"I totally understand," Wes said as he stood up to shake Sheldon's hand. "I'm Wesley Prescott, Mr. Richardson."

"Call me Sheldon. My right hand, Alex, will be here in a moment; she's grabbing the specs we've been going over." Sheldon nodded toward Clinton. "My marketing genius son-in-law is going to sit in with us."

"S-son-in-law," Wes stammered. So, she was married to this cornball doormat. "It's a real family business here, huh?"

Sheldon and Clinton nodded. "Yeah, that's part of the legacy of this place," Sheldon said.

"Dad, I . . . Wes?" Alexandria gasped. "What are you doing here?"

Sheldon looked from his daughter to Wes. "You two have met already?"

"Why is he here? I thought we were meeting with . . ."

"Wesley Prescott, that's me."

Alex nearly dropped her tablet. "I had no idea."

"Neither did I," he said. "And your husband was nice enough to show me around and entertain me until you and your father arrived."

She broke out laughing, as did Sheldon and Clinton. "This is my sister's husband. I thought we'd settled this already?"

"I'm sorry, but how do you two know each other?" Sheldon asked.

"We met on the cruise, but we didn't introduce ourselves properly," she said, then turned away from Wes with a bit of a blush on her cheeks. "Let's get started."

She took a seat at the table next to her father and across from Wes. She was beautiful even with her hair pulled back in a bun, nothing like the free and sexy styles she wore on the cruise. "Well," Sheldon said. "Since we're all friends here, let me say I don't like the design."

"But I do," Alex said. "However, I understand where Dad is coming from."

"I'm just a bit confused. What do you actually want?" Wes focused his question on Alex. He could've sworn he saw her squirm in her seat.

"I'm thinking something that has a nod toward history," Sheldon said. "What did you call it, Alex?"

"Mmm, what? I'm sorry. I think I left my notes in my office."

Wes nodded toward a folder she'd placed on the table when she sat down.

"Oh, I don't know how I missed that," she said. Sheldon and Clinton exchanged a strange look, then they started talking about the design for the new wing. Sheldon wanted a classic design, something that looked like old Charleston. Alex wanted a modern flair and a touch of history.

"I think I can come up with something that can incorporate both ideas. I just want to get a feel for the property and the city. Maybe you can show me around, Alexandria."

"Oh, sure," she said. "As a matter of fact, why don't we plan for something tomorrow?"

Wes nodded. "I'm sure you have access to my room; just give me a call."

Sheldon cleared his throat, "Sounds like we're done here. I look forward to seeing the designs by the end of the week." He and Clinton stood up and headed for the door. Alexandria started to stand, but then she sat down and speared Wes with a stare.

"Did you know who I was when we were on the ship?" Alex snapped.

"I didn't know who you were any more than you knew who I was. But look at this, we're seeing each other again."

"I'm going to my office. I hope you enjoy your stay," she said as she stood up and headed for the door. Wes quickly got out of his chair and crossed over to her, blocking her exit.

"Wait," he said. "I know this is jarring, but I can't get a hello kiss?"

"No. My husband wouldn't approve, since you're determined to find one for me," she quipped, then flounced out of the conference room. Even in her conservative gray slacks and ivory tunic, she had that sexy stroll. How was he going to get her to unleash the woman he'd met on vacation? He had a week to figure it out.

Alex felt as if she was going to pass out. Vacation Wes was *the* Wesley Prescott. World-renowned architect who just happened to be working on the bed-and-breakfast. How did a man who took four vacations a year get so much remarkable work done? How did she not know who he was? *Because you didn't do a Google search because your silly sisters told you to leave your electronics at home. Ugh.*

She plopped down in the chair behind her desk, then pulled up her Internet browser. Typing in Wesley's name, Alex read every article that populated about him. She noticed most of them didn't have a current picture, or there was no photo at all. Maybe he stayed out of the spotlight for a reason. Then she saw a line that said, "Wesley Prescott's wife."

"Son of a bitch," she hissed. "He's the one who's married."

"Alex, you all right?" Clinton asked from the doorway of her office.

"Yes, I'm fine. You need something?" she replied with a raised brow.

Clinton walked in and closed the door behind him. "What's really going on? You're in here cursing at the computer screen. And you actually got flustered in a meeting."

"You ever do something because you know it's a one-off-type situation and then it comes back to bite you hard?" Alex dropped her head for a moment.

"Who hasn't? None of us are perfect."

"Yeah, but only one of us is living this nightmare right now."

"So, you and the architect?" Clinton barely contained his grin.

Alex glared at him. "Don't do that. And don't you dare tell Nina."

He threw up his hands just as the door opened and Nina walked in. "What's up, people?" she asked, then kissed Clinton on the cheek.

"You know what, I'm going to go to my office so you two can talk," Clinton said, then gave his wife's shapely bottom a squeeze. "Come see me when you're done."

"No, just take her now," Alex said.

"What in the world is going on here? Alex, did you fire my husband again?"

Alex sucked her teeth as Nina sat across from her desk. Clinton grinned, then walked out the door. "Spill it, Sis," Nina said once they were alone.

"Clinton called you, didn't he? One day I'm going to go work for a company where everyone is a damned stranger."

"Yeah right. He said you were acting weird in your meeting and wanted me to check on you."

"I'm okay. It's just . . . I'm not telling you anything. I keep forgetting your mouth almighty."

"Then I'm going to sit here and ask you questions until you get tired of hearing my voice."

Alex knew Nina would do that because she'd been doing it her whole life. "Fine. My vacation fling is here. And not just a guest but the architect."

"Okay, two things—you really had a fling and you didn't know you were going to be working with him? How?"

"Of all the things we shared, our last names weren't one of them."

"Scandalous! You got on that ship and turned into Yolanda Richardson from Spelman."

Alex banged her hand on her desk. "Don't you ever say that again." Then she broke out into laugher. The sisters knew Yolanda had some wild times as an undergrad in Atlanta—including a naked stroll through the quad at the Atlanta University Center.

"Um, you're pretty close, sleeping with some random guy and not finding out who he is. Who are you?"

"A fool, obviously. I told Wes that we should just take the memories and not keep in touch. Then boom, he's here. And he had the nerve to accuse me of being married, when," Alex turned her computer screen around so Nina could see it, "he has a freaking wife."

"Click on the link," Nina said.

Alex did, and a picture of a beautiful woman filled the window. "Of course she's Beyoncé pretty. How do you take four vacations, meet all these different women, and have a wife at home? Trash!"

"Slow down and read the words. That is his *ex*-wife, who lives in London."

Alex's heart slowed to a normal pace. He wasn't the asshole she was propping him up to be in her mind. But he was still here when she wasn't supposed to ever see him again. "Okay, but he thought Clinton was my husband, so he's clearly an idiot."

"Oh, certainly." Nina rolled her eyes. "Stop looking for excuses not to talk to this man and find out why fate brought y'all together."

"Get out of my office, and you better . . ."

"Don't threaten me because I'm telling Robin. I can do it before dinner or at dinner in front of Daddy."

"You better not say a word about this to Daddy!"

"Okay." Nina rose to her feet. "I'm going to see *our* husband." Her laughter grated on Alex's nerves as her sister left.

Fate was for romance novels and fairytales; this was neither. This was just a lapse in judgment she was now paying for.

This is the last time I will ever listen to Yolanda.

CHAPTER SIXTEEN

Wes sat in his room, enjoying the lush carpet under his feet, but what he wanted was Alexandria. And he was sure the feeling was mutual. The sparks between them in the conference room were damn near explosive. But first he needed to get his thoughts together for the design of the new wing of the bed-and-breakfast. Business first.

Wes slipped into a pair of flip-flops and pulled on a tank top. It was time to explore the property and some of the surrounding buildings. He figured tomorrow he'd go to downtown Charleston and look around for historic inspiration. Wes knew he needed to temper his misgivings about the South as well. He thought of the dark Southern history his father and uncles decried. It wasn't that long ago. And Charleston was the very city where a white supremacist killed Black worshippers in the house of the Lord. He wasn't afraid as much as he was angry.

Heading outside, Wes took in the beauty of the landscape, the swaying palm trees and the golden sand. Pulling out his cell phone, he started snapping pictures. Then he thought about Alexandria on the ship, holding his camera and taking shots of the night's sky. And what happened next left an indelible mark on his brain.

"Hey!" a tall man with angry green eyes yelled at Wes. "What are you doing?"

Wes remembered he was holding up his phone, and the man was walking out of the hotel with two babies and a woman. He really did look suspect. Lowering his phone, Wes said, "My apologies. I'm Wesley Prescott and I'm working with the Richardsons on the new wing."

"So, that includes taking pictures of my wife and kids?" the man growled.

"I didn't take any pictures of your family, my guy."

"Chuck," the woman said. "It's okay. Daddy said he'd be around the property."

Chuck nodded at Wes. "My bad. I'm just a little overprotective of my family."

"Understandable. So, you're Alexandria's sister?" he said to the woman.

"Yes and don't hold me responsible for whatever she did. I'm Yolanda, by the way. And that's my dear husband, Chuck. I'm sorry, Charles. And our babies."

"Nice, so the whole family works here?"

"Hell no. And again, I apologize for whatever my sister did."

"Your sister is actually a wonderful person. If you see her before I do, tell her to call me; I have a question."

Yolanda's face was a mixture of shock and intrigue,

but she promised she'd pass the message along. Wes returned to taking photos, then he crossed over to the shoreline. This was a beautiful property and he wondered how a Black man built such a legacy in South Carolina. Wes knew whatever he created had to reflect strength, grace, and power. Grace and power—that was a great way to describe Alexandria. Or could he call her Alex now? Wes's phone rang, and he smiled when he saw stars and Alexandria's name.

"Alexandria," he said. "Good to hear from you."

"What can I do for you?"

"That is a loaded question, but I'm out here by the shoreline and I wanted to see you."

"I'm a little busy right now and I don't have time to . . ."

"It's about the new wing. I know we have other things to discuss, but I can wait."

"Wes, let me be clear as glass: We have nothing other than the new wing to discuss," she said.

Wes could tell she was trying to be tough and he'd let her do it over the phone. When they saw each other things would be different. "Can you meet me out here in the next half hour?" he asked, his voice calm and cool.

"Yes," she replied in the same tone.

"All right, see you then." Wes ended the call, then smiled. Part of him hoped she changed into one of the many sundresses she wore on the ship. But he mostly wanted to peel off any outfit she wore and make slow love to her once again.

Alex looked at her phone and shook her head. What had she agreed to and why was she pretending that Google-searching Wes was work? When Robin and Nina burst in her office she wished she had gone outside to meet him as soon as their call ended.

"Is Nina right?" Robin asked.

"Get out."

Robin smiled at her little sister. "Alex, you know what this means, right?"

Alex folded her arms across her chest and glared at her sisters. "It means Nina can't keep her damn mouth shut."

"You didn't just meet me," Nina quipped. "Yolanda said she ran into him when she and Chuck were leaving. Said he's quite the looker. You're sure you want to turn your back on all that?"

"I want to finish my work and . . ."

"Meet him outside?" Nina said. "Does Daddy know about you two?"

Alex leaped from her seat and glared at her sisters. "Why are you bringing Daddy into this? The last thing he needs to know is that I made a fool of myself with this man. How am I going to sit in a meeting with him knowing . . ."

"Hold up, what else happened on that ship?" Robin asked.

"Don't worry about it," she said. "But what if this was some kind of setup, some scheme that I fell for because I needed some hot sex?"

Sheldon cleared his throat as he walked in Alex's office. "What have I walked in on?"

Alex wished the floor would open up and swallow her. "Nothing," she said. "Um, I was about to meet Wesley outside to talk about his plans."

"Dinner is at six and I'm inviting someone special. Just wanted to give you a heads-up. Didn't expect all of you to be here."

"Maybe we're looking for jobs," Robin said.

Nina grunted. "Speak for yourself. Daddy, who's coming to dinner?"

"A friend of mine I want y'all to meet. And no hot-sex talk at dinner tonight," he said as he turned to leave.

Alex didn't join in her sisters' laughter. "Get out of my office and don't come back without an appointment," she said once their father was gone.

Robin and Nina waved to Alex and headed out the door.

Now, Alex had to get herself ready to be alone with Wes in the shadow of her family. By the time Alex headed outside she had told herself a ton of lies about not hugging him, not kissing him, and not getting lost in his eyes.

"Alexandria," he said when he spotted her coming his way.

She waved at him, drinking in his image in a white shirt and well-worn jeans. "Mr. Prescott."

"This is what we're doing?" He grinned at her and reached for her hand. Alex took his hand and smiled.

"We are here to discuss business. I just thought I should address you properly."

"Alex," he said as he pulled her against his chest. "I can do my job and you too."

"But I don't work like that. It's always messy when that happens and lines are crossed. Are you sure you didn't know who I was on the ship?"

"If I knew who you were, you knew who I was. This isn't the life I thought you lived in Milan."

"Oh, come off that supermodel crap," she said with a slight smile.

"Trust me, I had no intentions of coming to South Carolina until I saw your face on the website."

"So, you saw me and thought it was a good idea to come here and do what exactly?" Did her lip just quiver? Why was her body so turned on and needy? *Do better*, she thought as she turned away from him.

"I came for two things," he said. "The design for the new wing and to make you mine."

Alex laughed and dropped his hand. "Well, I–I'm not a property for you to possess. And nothing has changed since we got off the ship."

"You said you'd never see me again, yet here we are. I don't mean to sound corny, but someone is trying to tell us something."

Alex rolled her eyes. "Wes, you and I aren't the people we were on that cruise. I can't spend my life on vacation. My family needs me here, and I enjoy my work."

"I get that, but you have to have a life outside of work. I watched my father work himself to death and I refused to let that happen to me. I work hard and play even harder."

"So that's your motto, or is that why your marriage didn't last?" Alex groaned inwardly. He wasn't supposed to know she'd spent the better part of the afternoon researching his life.

Wes laughed. "One of many reasons. But we're not talking about the past. I want to talk about a future with you in it."

"We had some good times on a singles cruise. That isn't the foundation for a future. What do we even know about each other?"

"This is where we start. I'm Wesley Prescott; nice to

meet you, Alexandria Richardson. I grew up in Brooklyn. Has Charleston always been your home?"

She laughed and started to tell him that he was being ridiculous, but she decided to play along. "Yes, born and raised here. I love this city and my family's bed-and-breakfast."

"You always wanted to work here? No other dreams?"

That question gave her pause. Before Alex heard that old man telling her father that he didn't have a son to pass his legacy on to, she did have other dreams for her future. And she hadn't thought about them in years. "Um, I wanted to study botany," she said quietly. "My father always gave my mother beautiful flowers. I–I wanted to find out why they lived, why they died." She closed her eyes and inhaled sharply. "But someone had to go into the family business. You know what? This isn't why I came out here. I thought you wanted to talk about the new wing."

Wes fixed his mouth as if he was going to say something, but he inched closer to Alex's face and brushed his lips across hers. He kissed her slow and deep. Alex melted against him, forgetting everything she'd said she wasn't going to do.

Wes savored the sweetness of her mouth, reveled in the heat of her body as the soft ocean breeze blew across them. How in the hell did this woman get under his skin the way she had? He'd been struggling with his desire to kiss her since she walked into that conference room. Now he wanted more. He wanted to get her out of that suit and feast on her delectable body. But he also wanted her to know he wasn't just about having sex with her. Wes just needed his dick to understand that as well. Breaking the kiss, he looked into her eyes and smiled. "I'm sorry, but if I didn't kiss you, I was going to lose my mind."

"So, you decided to take mine? Wes, I can't do this. We have to work together, and I don't mix business and pleasure. You paint a pretty picture, but you keep leaving out reality."

"What am I leaving out?"

"Oh, the eight hundred miles between us, for starters."

"You know, there's this thing called an airplane . . ."

"Stop!"

"I'm not going to stop because that's not who I am, Alexandria. I want you."

"The Rolling Stones said it best, 'You Can't Always Get What You Want.' And as much as I want to believe fate or something brought us to this point, I know it will fizzle and I'm not trying to deal with that hurt." She pushed out of his embrace. "I have to go."

He watched her practically run away from him, but he wasn't upset. She'd given him an opening and he was going to walk right through it to get what he wanted. Alexandria Richardson was going to be his, no matter what.

CHAPTER SEVENTEEN

Alex slammed into her room and flung herself across her bed. Why was he like that? Why did this man who was such a brilliant architect and world traveler believe she was enough for whatever life he had in mind?

Alex had to face some serious facts: She wanted what her sisters had. If she was going to be with a man, he needed to be there. Not a flight away, but someone she could reach out and touch. Like she saw growing up with her parents. Like she witnessed with her sisters. There was no way in hell she was going to make it to this big age for a long-distance relationship. Fuck that. She'd been fine before she met Wesley Prescott and she'd be even better when he went back to his beloved Brooklyn.

Alex closed her eyes and groaned. Why was she allowing this man to affect her? He would be gone soon enough and she'd get back to normal.

Do you really want that? Wes whispered in her ear. Alex sat up and spun her body around, as if she expected to see him in the room. What she did see were the red numbers on her digital clock, telling her that she was about to be late for dinner. "Shit," she muttered as she hopped off the bed and headed to the bathroom for a quick shower. After drying off she decided to wear one of the sundresses Yolanda made for her. It was quick to put on and she loved the pink halter dress.

After slipping into a pair of tan ballerina flats, Alex headed out the door. When she walked into the lobby, she spotted Wes at the front desk talking to Lillian, the evening desk clerk. She was hoping he wouldn't notice her, but Lillian did.

"Miss Alex, you look amazing," she called out. Wes speared her with a smoldering look. Her knees quaked. But she found the voice to thank Lillian.

"I'm late for dinner. Have a good night." Alex practically ran into the dining room, silently praying Wes wasn't her father's special guest.

"Well, well, look who made it," Yolanda said when she noticed her sister marching toward her chair. "And I love the dress."

"You should. I have to say, you're a great designer," Alex said, then sat down.

"That's it? Just a compliment?" Yolanda asked. Charles shook his head at his wife.

"Just say *thank you*," he said. "You do look nice."

"I wonder why you're all dressed up," Nina quipped. "You look like you could pose on the cover of *Architectural Digest* or something."

Clinton coughed and Logan looked at his sisters-in-law. "Why are y'all being weird?" Logan asked. Robin smiled but didn't say a word to Logan.

Alex expelled a sigh. "Where's Daddy?" she asked.

"He said he was running late," Robin said. "You didn't invite your friend to join us?"

Alex narrowed her eyes at Robin, her usual ally when the sisters got together. "I don't have a friend to invite to dinner and y'all can stop this bullshit because it's not funny." She stood up and grabbed a bottle of merlot from the center of the table.

"Have you talked to him at least?" Yolanda asked. "I don't want him to think I didn't pass along his message."

"You saw him?" Nina asked.

Yolanda nodded and mouthed, *He is fine.*

Alex groaned as she uncorked the wine. "Mr. Prescott is a business associate. Leave it alone."

Nina and Yolanda exchanged conspiratorial glances. "So, what you're saying is . . ."

"I'm saying shut the hell up," Alex snapped.

"What's going on in here?" Sheldon asked from the doorway. "We don't argue at the dinner table."

Everyone looked at Sheldon and the comely woman standing by his side. She was petite, with a curly gray Afro and creamy brown skin that didn't have a wrinkle. She was dressed in a St. John's Bay navy blue pantsuit. And was she holding Sheldon's hand? *The hell?* Alex thought as she smiled. "Sorry, Daddy. Your kids are being rude."

Sheldon cleared his throat. "Anyway," he said, then turned to the woman. "They do have manners; sometimes they just forget."

"My sister and brothers are the same way, but it's all

love." Her voice was soft, as if she were a singer or something. And she was still holding his hand.

"So, Daddy," Alex said. "Are you going to make the introductions?"

"Real smooth," Yolanda whispered.

"Have a seat," Sheldon said to Alex. She fought the urge to roll her eyes. Sheldon and the woman sat at the two chairs at the head of the table. "Everyone, I want you to meet my lady friend, Lillian Crosland."

"Hi," she said with a little wave. Robin smiled at her, Nina opened her mouth as if she was about to ask a question, and Yolanda and Alex just looked at each other in disbelief.

"How did you two meet?" Nina asked.

"Golfing," Sheldon said.

Logan coughed and looked at Robin. "Told you."

"Shut up," she muttered.

"Oh," Nina said, ignoring her sister and brother-in-law. "You play as well?"

"Nina," Sheldon said, "this isn't a press conference. But yes, Lillian is a great golfer."

"Well," Lillian said. "I could learn a lot from you, Shel. Your swing is legendary."

Shel? Alex thought as she sipped her wine. *I was not expecting this.*

Sheldon introduced his daughters and sons-in-law to Lillian, then the kitchen staff brought dinner in. Shrimp and grits, collard greens, and garden salad.

They ate in a tense silence for a few moments, then Sheldon started talking about the new wing of the bed-and-breakfast. "I'm really impressed with Wesley Prescott's ideas. But . . ."

"You're not the only one," Yolanda quipped, eliciting a swift kick underneath the table from Alex. "Ouch."

"Sorry, my foot slipped," Alex said through a scowl.

Sheldon shot his daughters a stern, cut-it-out look. Then he smiled at Lillian. "They really get along better than this. Alex, I'm curious, though. How do you know Wesley?"

Can the floor just open up right now? she thought as she reached for her glass of wine. Sip, think, answer. "We were on the same cruise."

"Did you two talk about the new wing?" Sheldon asked.

Nina giggled and Yolanda smiled. "Yeah, Sis, did you turn it into a working vacation?" Yolanda asked.

"No, we didn't, Daddy. We weren't aware of who each other was because it was a vacation."

Sheldon nodded. "You know, you should take more time off. You work entirely too much."

"Like father, like daughter," Lillian chimed in.

"Ms. Lillian, are you and my father a couple?" Robin asked. "And if so, how serious is it?"

Everyone stared at Robin, who shrugged in return. "Listen, you all were wondering the same thing," she said.

"Well," Lillian began, "I'm very serious about your father. He's a very special man who has brought a lot of joy into my life."

"Lil, you already know I feel the same about you. And tonight I wanted to show you and my family what you mean to me," Sheldon said, then reached into his pants pocket and pulled out a red velvet box.

The Richardson sisters gasped as he opened the box,

revealing an emerald-cut diamond ring set in a platinum band.

"What the hell?" Alex exclaimed.

"Alexandria," Sheldon snapped.

"Daddy, how long have you known this woman? This is all so sudden," Alex said.

"We've known each other for over ten years," Sheldon revealed. "But ten years or ten days doesn't mean you can ruin this moment."

Alex folded her arms across her chest. While she wanted her father to be happy, she wished his happiness came from some other place. How could he want to marry someone else? Her mother was supposed to be the love of his life. What if this Lillian Crosland was just some old gold digger? She didn't even look at her sisters, who seemed as if they were watching some romantic movie as Sheldon slipped the ring on Lillian's finger.

"You've given this old heart a jolt I never thought I'd feel again," Sheldon said. "I'd be honored if you'd be my wife."

"Oh, Sheldon, yes. A million times, yes," she exclaimed.

Alex downed the last of her wine as everyone else clapped. What in the hell had just happened here?

Wes munched on the bed-and-breakfast's signature chocolate chip cookies as he sketched his idea for the new wing. Long, wide columns, wrought-iron gates that would match the railing on the balcony of the second-floor rooms. Rose accents? No. He ripped the page from his sketchbook. He needed to work the angles. And angles were nothing but curves. Alexandria had curves for days. As he drew the gate, he noticed that he had drawn Alexandria's frame in the design. *Her father is going to love this*, he thought as he ripped up this rendering as well. Wes stood up and paced the floor. He needed to get her alone again, needed her lips against his and those legs wrapped around his waist.

He wasn't getting any work done tonight. He needed to find Alexandria. But how? It wasn't as if she was a guest in the bed-and-breakfast. *Just call her*, he thought as he looked at his phone. *And say what?* Wes picked up his phone and started to dial her number, but there was a knock at the door.

Crossing over to the door, he looked out of the peep-hole and was surprised to see Alex standing there. "Wow, I was just thinking about you," he said when he opened it.

"I know this is improper, but I needed to see you."

He hitched his right brow. "And I thought I was going to have to talk you into realizing you needed to see me."

Alexandria smirked. "Are you going to invite me in or not?"

He stepped aside. "Please, come in."

She walked in, closed the door, and wrapped her arms around his neck. Without saying a word she kissed him hard. Wes was taken so off guard that he pushed back from her. "What's happening here?" he asked. "Not that I'm complaining because I've been wanting to kiss you all day."

"Then just go with it," she said in a low voice as she stroked the back of his neck. Wes was about to do just that, but he noticed something different about her. A tension he'd never seen before.

"Talk to me," he said as he led her over to the bed.

They sat down, and Wes wrapped his arm around her shoulders.

"I really didn't come here to talk. Maybe this is a mistake."

"No, but whatever you're going through we can't fix it through sex."

Alexandria rolled her eyes. "You know what?" she said with a groan. "You're absolutely right. I should be happy for them. It was unrealistic to think that my father was going to be alone for the rest of his life." She stood up and started pacing back and forth.

Wes furrowed his brows. "What happened?" he asked.

She stopped walking and looked at him. "My father just got engaged to some woman he's been seeing for years. How could he keep this from me?"

Wes was confused. He could tell the Richardson family was close, so he didn't understand why Alexandria was so upset about her father's happiness. "Maybe he knew this would upset you?" Wes said. "But why does it upset you so much?"

She blinked twice and shook her head. "This is going to sound crazy," Alexandria began. "I always thought it was my job to carry on the Richardson legacy. Since my mother died it was me and my dad as a tag team. We took care of my sisters, he taught me the business, and I just figured it was me and him against the world. Now . . ." Her voice trailed off.

Wes stood up and crossed over to her. "Your father has a life, and maybe this is a sign that you need to get one, too."

"I'm going to go," she said.

"Wait," he said as he pulled her into his arms. "Alexandria, you have to stop being so hard on yourself. You don't have to fix everything, or be the rock everyone depends on. You can have a life, and you should."

She rolled her eyes. "And this is where you sell yourself as the life I need? I'm good. I'm sorry I came here." Alexandria pushed out of his arms and rushed out of the room.

CHAPTER EIGHTEEN

Alex walked into the family wing of the bed-and-breakfast and wasn't surprised to find her sisters sitting at the dining room table. "Aww, look who came back," Yolanda said when she saw Alex.

"Where have you been, or do we need to ask?" Nina quipped.

"I'm not in the mood for this shit," Alex snapped, then took a seat at the table next to Robin.

"You didn't seem very welcoming to Lillian," Robin said quietly. "Do you know her?"

"No, and I'm just a bit concerned about this. Why would Daddy keep her a secret?"

Yolanda cleared her throat. "Because he knows his daughters. I was thinking about all Daddy's golf trips and stuff. He was developing this secret relationship to spare our feelings."

Alex raised her eyebrow at Yolanda. "Spare our feelings?"

Yolanda nodded. "Alex, you and Robin low-key showed your asses at dinner. You sat there shooting ice daggers at the woman, Robin acted all in a court of law, I'm going to ask rude questions. So, I don't blame Daddy."

"Oh please," Robin said. "I asked a simple question I thought Nina would've asked."

"Hold up," Nina said. "Why would I ruin that moment for Dad? You can see how much they care about each other. They have nicknames for each other."

Robin and Alex shared a look of confusion. "I know you two aren't sitting here happy for this relationship," Robin said. "We don't know this woman. And if she hurts Daddy . . ."

"She's going to be in for a world of hurt," Alex finished. "I don't understand why Daddy would keep this from us. Hell, me specifically."

"Okay, here's the real issue," Nina said. "You're pissed because Daddy didn't tell you he was seeing this woman."

Alex didn't want to say it out loud, but she was pissed that Sheldon had found another woman. He was supposed to love Nora and no one else, ever. Childish, yes. But her parents' marriage had been the fairy tale she'd believed she would never have. She wanted a love that never died, and seeing her father with another woman—asking her to be his wife—hurt.

"What's your excuse, Robin?" Yolanda asked.

"What do you mean?" Robin replied.

"Just what I said. You're acting like this one," Yolanda said as she nodded toward Alex. "If Daddy is happy, we should be happy for him. Think about all he sacrificed for us."

"I know what Daddy did and continues to do for us," Robin said. "We're also old enough to have concerns."

Sheldon walked into the room and grinned at his daughters. "I figured you all were here when I saw my sons-in-law at the pool."

Nina stood up and hugged Sheldon. "You need to talk to your oldest kids. They're tripping."

"I'm going to talk to all of you, because I know tonight was a little jarring," he said. "But I need you all to understand a few things. I'll always love your mother. Nora brought me so much joy and happiness, and she gave me the four of you. But I'm a man, and I want y'all to know I've dated other people over the years."

"What?" Robin asked.

Sheldon laughed. "Those relationships were casual, didn't go anywhere, and I didn't want to bring someone into your lives and then have her disappear."

"But you've been seeing this woman for years," Alex said.

"Yes. However, my daughters have needed me. And I didn't know I was going to fall in love with Lillian or that she'd fall for me."

"Oh, how could she not?" Yolanda quipped. "You're Richard-Roundtree-from-*Shaft* fine."

Sheldon laughed. "I can always count on you to make me laugh, Yo-Yo. Lillian and I were friends for many years before we . . ."

"No need for the details," Nina said. "She is a nice woman, isn't she?"

"I wouldn't be with her if she wasn't. I want you all to get to know her, make your own judgments once you

know her. But I'm not going to tolerate any disrespect."
He looked pointedly at Alex.

"What?" she asked.

"I know you feel some kind of way, Alex."

She sighed. "Daddy, why didn't you tell me?"

Sheldon shook his head. "Alex, darling, I don't expect
you to tell me what happened between you and Prescott
on your vacation, so why do you think I'd discuss my
love life with you?"

Alex's mouth dropped open and her sisters laughed.
"Anyway," Sheldon continued. "Lillian wants to have
breakfast with you all tomorrow."

"What if I have a meeting?" Alex said.

"I'll handle it. And you don't have a meeting," Sheldon said with a wink. "I'm asking you all to give her a
chance. A genuine chance."

"We will," Nina said. "And I'll keep these two in
check." She pointed her fingers at Alex and Robin.

"If she makes you happy, Daddy, I'm all for it,"
Yolanda said. "You've always cheered for our happiness
and now it's *all* of our turn to do the same."

"All right. See you in the morning." Sheldon kissed
each of his daughters on the cheek, then headed out of the
dining room.

Alex drank in what Yolanda said about Sheldon always supporting them. She needed to stop feeling slighted
and do the same for her dad. But was she denying her
own happiness because she was afraid to get hurt?

The next morning Alex woke up feeling stupid. Not
only had she made a fool of herself with Wes last night,
now she had to swallow her pride and get to know the
woman who she felt was taking her place in her father's
life. Was she going to work at the bed-and-breakfast once

they got married? She'd never be Nora Richardson, that's for sure.

Just be honest with yourself—you don't want to like her because you don't want to see him with another woman, and that's not really fair. Alex sighed as she climbed out of bed. After a quick shower she dressed in a sleeveless gray dress and a pair of red heels. Instead of her standard bun, she let her natural coils flow in an Afro. Glancing at her watch, she realized that she was way too early for breakfast. She picked up her cell phone and sent Wes a text.

Are you up? We need to talk about last night.

His reply came quickly. **You know where to find me. And I agree, we do need to talk.**

She sighed and headed for the main building. As she walked through the lobby, Alex hoped she could make it to Wes's room without any of the staff spotting her. It was just after six thirty, and the front desk wouldn't be manned until seven. The housekeepers wouldn't be on the guest floors until ten, so she had time to visit and make it to breakfast with that woman. Sighing, she headed to the elevator and closed her eyes as she waited for the door to open. The ding seemed louder than Alex had ever heard it before, or maybe it was her imagination. *Or maybe you're just losing your damned mind*, she thought as she stepped on the elevator. As the car rose to Wes's floor, Alex willed her heart to stop beating overtime. She was just going to walk in, apologize, and be on her way.

But why was she so nervous?

Wes had never felt anxious waiting for anyone, whether it was a CEO of a multimillion-dollar company or a capital investor. Alexandria Richardson made him anxious. He didn't know what she was going to say when she walked into his room. *Just listen to what she has to say,* he thought as he pulled on his tank top.

He crossed over to the door and looked out the peephole to see if he could spot Alexandria coming his way. He spotted her walking up the hallway. She still reminded him of a model. Wes wanted to open the door and pull her inside. He wanted to kiss her until they were breathless. But she said they were going to talk.

She knocked on the door and Wes took a deep breath before opening it. "Good morning," he said.

"Hi," she said. "May I come in?"

He stepped aside and Alex seemed to rush inside. Wes touched her shoulder. "Are you all right?"

"I just wouldn't want the staff to see me in a guest's room," she said. "It's not proper."

"Okay," he said as he crossed over to the desk in the corner of the room. "You said you wanted to talk and I'm here to listen."

"Last night I was wrong to come here and try to get you involved in my emotional drama. I have to stand by what I said about us not setting up unrealistic expectations."

"So, what would've happened if I had taken you up on your offer last night?"

"I would've been out of your bed before the sun came up and I probably would've called in sick to avoid dealing with you today."

"Wow, you act like this is something you've done before," he said with a laugh.

Alexandria rolled her eyes. "I haven't, but I know how to work my way out of difficult situations."

"Is that how you see me? A difficult situation?" Wes drank in her delicate features as she stared at him with her lips slightly parted. Inching closer to her, Wes pulled Alexandria against his chest. "You look amazing this morning. Like a well-balanced breakfast."

"Stop it," she whispered.

"What if I just want to kiss you?" He brought his lips inches from hers.

"Wes," she breathed. "I want to kiss you too."

He captured her mouth in a hungry kiss. Alexandria pulled him closer as the kiss deepened. His tongue danced with hers, exploring the sweetness of her mouth, making her moan with delight. Wes knew he should've let her go. But the softness of her lips and the heat of her body felt too good. Alexandria made the decision to end the kiss. "I–I have to go," she said.

"Alex," he said. "Will you stop running from me?"

"That's not what I'm doing. It's just that . . . Wes, this isn't going to work out the way you think it will and . . ."

"You can read minds now? Why are you so afraid to step out of your comfort zone?"

"I'm not afraid. I'm realistic," she snapped. "I know I'm not putting myself in a place where I'm going to end up hurt."

"So, you're going to let fear keep you from being happy? All right, if that's what you want, I'm going to stop trying to convince you otherwise." He stepped back from her. "Have a wonderful day, Alexandria."

She paused for a second, and Wes hoped he'd gotten through to her. When she walked out the door without saying a word, he knew he hadn't.

CHAPTER NINETEEN

Alex didn't know why she felt as if Wes had dismissed her when she had been the one who came to do that. He wasn't supposed to talk her into believing they had a future, but maybe that's what she wanted him to do. She wasn't trying to compare herself to her father, but if he could find love, why was she running from it?

Oh, stop it, she thought as she stabbed the elevator button. *You were right when you said it wasn't going to go any further than the cruise ship.* Just before the elevator doors opened, Wes walked out of his room and over to Alex.

"I lied," he said. "I'm not done convincing you otherwise." In a swift motion, he drew her into his arms and kissed her slow and deep. Alex didn't try to resist or pretend that his kisses didn't make her feel like magic. She wasn't going to act as if she didn't want him when she absolutely did.

"Wes," she moaned when they broke the kiss. "This is crazy."

"No, you acting like you don't want to see where this goes is crazy. Alexandria, I crave you. And I'm not talking about just sleeping with you. I want to know all about you. I want to be a part of your world and make you my everything."

She shook her head. "Why me?"

"Because you're Alexandria Richardson," he said. "Who in his right mind can resist your brains and beauty? I mean, why not you?"

"But you don't even know me."

"Then let's fix that. Let me get to know every part of you."

She opened her mouth to respond just as her phone went off, indicating she had a text message. "I have to check this," she said as she pulled her phone out of her pocket. It was Robin, asking where she was. "I have to go. We're having breakfast with my dad's fiancée."

"Are you all right with that?"

She shrugged. "I told my dad I was going to make an effort, so that's what I'm doing."

"Interesting," he said.

"Can we put a pin in this and come back to it later? Like over dinner?"

"Only if dinner is off the property." Wes smiled and she couldn't say no. Alex didn't like that at all.

"I'll text you later and we can go have a low country boil."

"A what?"

She smiled this time. "You're going to love it."

"And if I don't?"

Alex stroked her chin. "Um, you're not human and I'll have to find some way to make it up to you."

"Then I'll see you at dinner," he replied with a wink.

Alex couldn't explain what took over her mind, but she looked up at Wes and said, "How about a kiss for luck?"

"Absolutely," he said, then brushed a tender kiss across her lips. Alex gripped the back of his neck, cajoling him for something deeper. And that's just what she got, hot tongue. Wet and a lip nibble.

She pulled back and smiled at him. "Thanks."

"I can kiss you again to double your luck."

Her phone buzzed again. "I have to go. See you tonight." Alex pressed the elevator button and smiled at Wes. Just what in the hell was she doing?

When she made it to the lobby Robin was standing by the front desk watching the front door, as if she was waiting for her sisters.

Alex crossed over to her. "Am I late?"

Robin turned around. "Where did you come from? Have you been up in your office this whole time?"

"Yeah. I was working off some nervous energy with work," Alex lied.

"Well, Nina and Yolanda are in the dining room waiting for their stepmom."

"Don't call her that," Alex deadpanned. "We are all too old to be looking for a mother figure."

"I don't like this," Robin admitted. "I want Dad to be happy, but why does he have to marry this woman? She can be his special friend and call it a day."

Alex wanted to agree with her sister, but were they being selfish because they saw the magic of the Sheldon and Nora love story? "I know how you feel and I understand, but Daddy sacrificed a lot for us. He didn't date while we were growing up. He did so much to protect us."

"I know that, but part of me wants to know why it has to stop."

"Because we're grown."

Robin hitched her brow at Alex. "Really?"

Alex nodded. "Maybe we need to take a page from Yolanda and Nina's book for a change."

"Who are you? Did you know Dad was seeing this woman or something?"

"No, but Robin—" Alex stopped short when she saw Lillian walking into the lobby. "We better go to the dining room."

Robin followed Alex's eyes and saw Lillian crossing over to them. "Good morning, ladies," she said. "I hope I'm not too early."

"No," Robin said, "you are just on time."

"Great. I'm so glad you ladies agreed to have breakfast with me. I know last night was a lot to process."

Robin and Alex exchanged a look before Robin said, "Well, Nina and Yolanda are waiting for us."

"Okay," Lillian said. "Let's go."

Alex looked at Lillian and couldn't help but compare her to Nora Richardson. There weren't any physical similarities. Lillian was shorter than Nora. She had a short Afro that highlighted her face. She kind of reminded Alex of Pam Grier. No wonder her father liked this woman. When they walked into the dining room Nina and Yolanda stood up to greet them.

"Good morning," Nina said. "I was beginning to think we'd been stood up."

"I know, right," Yolanda said. "These two are never late."

"They were kind enough to greet me in the lobby," Lillian said, then took a seat. Alex and Robin sat down and glared at their younger sisters.

"We're having shrimp and grits, if that's all right," Nina said.

"And a veggie omelet for you, Robin," Yolanda chimed in.

"Can I get one of those, too?" Lillian asked. "I try to have at least one plant-based meal every day."

"Are you getting Daddy on board with that?" Robin asked.

Lillian laughed. "Heavens no. But I want to strive for better health."

"Yet you feed my daddy bacon," Alex muttered. Nina kicked her under the table. Alex glared at her.

Stop it, Nina mouthed.

"So, how did you and Daddy meet?" Alex asked. "And when did you meet?"

Lillian poured herself a cup of coffee and smiled at Alex. "We met ten years ago on a golf trip," she said. "I couldn't get over his swing. So, I asked him if he could teach me. We found out that we were both from Charleston. And when he said he was Sheldon Richardson, I was floored that he'd even paid me any attention."

Robin rolled her eyes. "Miss Lillian, I don't mean to be rude, but this is new for us. Dad has never introduced us to a woman and you came in as his fiancée. Do you really love our father or what he has to offer?"

The other sisters gasped at Robin's question. Alex was trying to build up to asking that very question. But since Robin dove in, she was all ears.

"I love Sheldon for the man he is and I don't need anything from him but his love," she said with a smile. "Have you ever heard of Miss Ebony's Hair Cream?"

Nina nodded. "I swear by that stuff. When I went natural it was a godsend."

Lillian clasped her hands together. "I love to hear that. I'm the creator of Miss Ebony's Hair Cream. Just like your dad, I have a successful business. But even if I didn't, I wouldn't be marrying anyone I didn't love. I love your father so much."

"Did he tell you about us?" Nina asked. "I mean, when y'all met, we were grown."

Lillian took a sip of her coffee. Then she looked at the sisters. "Your father didn't know how you all would accept our relationship and he was concerned about how you all felt. But I wondered why he didn't want to tell his daughters about us. I was considering leaving him, wondering if I was fighting a ghost. He told me about Nora and wondered if Alexandria and Robin would accept me."

"Well, Dad knows his kids," Yolanda said. Nina laughed and reached for a mug to fill her coffee with.

"I know Dad isn't looking for permission from us to marry you or anything like that," Alex began. "Robin and I always wondered if Dad would date and find love again. I know he sacrificed a lot. All of us want the best for our father."

Lillian nodded. "I understand and I'd never do anything to hurt Shel. I love him, but I know if you ladies don't believe that, we won't be walking down the aisle."

"Do you have kids?" Nina asked.

Lillian cleared her throat. "I had a son, but he died when he was five." Tears welled up in her eyes. "My first marriage ended after my son died, and I focused on work for years. Then I met Shel."

Alex wanted to hug the woman. So much pain and regret. Could that be what drew her father to Lillian? Did it really matter? They were together. And she seemed nice.

As the waiters brought over the food, the sisters stopped asking questions and dug into the food. Robin gave Lillian her omelet and opted for a fruit plate instead.

"So, are you guys having a big wedding?" Nina asked.

"I don't think so. It's more about the marriage than a big party."

Alex was impressed because she wasn't ready for another Richardson wedding. *No, you're happy being alone and lonely.* Alex looked at Yolanda because she could've sworn her sister said that. However, Yolanda was eating and not saying a word.

"So, what does your family think about you and our Dad?" Nina asked.

"I have a very small family. It's me and my two sisters. But they are excited."

"Are your sisters as annoying as mine?" Yolanda joked.

"Remember that when you need a baby sitter," Robin replied.

"You're going to need one, too, Rob. And since I'm the most qualified, you have no choice but to choose me," Yolanda said, then stuck out her tongue.

"You're pregnant?" Lillian asked Robin.

"No, my husband and I are adopting," she replied tersely.

"Oh, I'm . . ."

"But I have twins," Yolanda said excitedly. "They're a month old." She pulled out her phone and started showing everyone pictures of the babies. "Bradford and Nora—these babies have changed my whole world."

"Their outfits are so cute," Lillian said. Yolanda beamed. "I designed them," she said. "Chuck says I should do a line of baby clothes."

"You should," Robin said. "They look like little dolls. Speaking of the little ones, where are they?"

"It's Daddy day. Chuck told me to get out of the house and go buy some fabric."

"Wow," Nina said. "He really wanted to be alone with the kids if he's turning you loose in a fabric shop."

Yolanda hitched her right brow. "And I was going to ask you to come with me."

Nina threw up her hands, "I have to talk to a college basketball coach and I just don't want to go."

"Whatever." Yolanda turned to Alex. "What about you?"

"Sure," she replied.

"Wait? For real?"

"I'll even drive."

Yolanda shook her head. "I'll drive. I do want to get home before midnight."

Alex shook her head. "Miss Lillian, my sisters have a problem with riding in a car that goes the speed limit."

"Well, I have a hard time with the speed limit on the open road in my Camaro," Lillian said. "It's a classic."

"My husband has a '64 Mustang. Maybe we can race one day," Nina said.

Lillian laughed. "My racing days are over."

"So are hers," Alex said.

Nina rolled her eyes. "Anyway," she said, "does Daddy know you're playing hooky today?"

"Not yet. I'm sure he wants to meet with Wes alone to discuss the new wing."

"Wes?" Yolanda questioned. "Isn't that a little casual?"

Alex wanted to toss a grape at her sister, but she ignored her.

Lillian cleared her throat. "Well, I want to thank you all for a lovely breakfast. I hope we can all be friends. I love your father very much and I know you four are so important to him. When we met he couldn't stop talking about his *little women*. I was a little intimidated," she admitted.

"Why?" Robin asked. Yolanda shook her head.

"I know how protective daughters can be about their fathers. I was very close to my father. And there was no way that I would allow anyone to disrespect him or try to do anything to make him feel uncomfortable. It got me in trouble as a kid, but I know what it's like to have a superhero father."

"We *are* super protective of Daddy, but we also want him to be happy," Nina said. "As long as you make him happy and love him, we're going to be friends forever. But don't hurt our dad. That would be a huge mistake."

Damn, Alex thought. *That shook me.*

Lillian smiled and nodded. "Duly noted, Ms. Nina. Sheldon told me to watch out for you."

"He's right, you know," Nina said, then smiled sweetly.

After telling Lillian good-bye, Alex headed up to her office to tell her dad that she was going to spend some time with Yolanda. She was surprised to see Sheldon and Wes laughing in the hallway. "G–good morning, Dad, Mr. Prescott."

Wes nodded at her and smiled. "Please, call me Wes. You look very nice this morning."

Alex turned away from him. He knew he'd seen her already. *And you know you've moaned his name many times.* Alex exhaled, hearing Yolanda's voice again.

"Dad, I'm going to take the day off and spend it with Yolanda. I figured you and *Wes* could talk about the new wing design."

Sheldon looked from Wes to Alex and nodded. "You and Yolanda are spending the day together. Now, I hope y'all are going to act right today."

"I haven't had a chance to spend much time with her since the stalking incident and the birth of the kids. I think we have about four hours to get along," she said, then kissed her father on the cheek. "But if you need me, I can let her go to the fabric store alone."

"No, I'm glad you're spending time with your sister. We can talk about my decision tomorrow."

She gave Wes a brief glance and saw that he hadn't taken his eyes off her. "Have a good meeting," Alex said, then headed for the elevator.

Wes tried not to get caught staring at Alexandria. After all, Sheldon Richardson was her father. But when the older man placed his hand on his shoulder, Wes knew he'd been caught.

"Wesley Prescott, what is going on between you and my daughter?"

"I'm sorry?"

Sheldon laughed. "I'm not blind and I'm not too old to understand what those looks between the two of you mean."

"Sir, you know your daughter is a beautiful and intelligent woman."

Sheldon nodded. "And she's hardheaded, my right hand here at the B&B, and a little scared to live her own life."

Wes laughed. This man certainly knew his child. "I don't expect you to tell me how I can help her see that there's more to life than work."

"Nope, you have to figure that out yourself. All I ask is that you don't do anything to hurt her. If Alex finally decides to give in to what you two have going on, I don't want her to regret it."

"I understand completely."

"And that's all I'm going to say about what my adult daughter is doing with her life. Let's go in the conference room and look at your designs."

Wes spent the next three hours with Sheldon, revamping the sketches for the new wing and learning the history of the bed-and-breakfast. During segregation, many customers, especially the white visitors, thought Sheldon Richardson was a white man and the real Sheldon just worked there. In 1971 Sheldon and his wife, Nora, decided to stop hiding behind that lie and built a loyal following because they had a beautiful property with amazing service. Nora had laid much of the groundwork for the business.

Wes knew the new wing had to celebrate Nora before Sheldon even made the suggestion.

"I know I wouldn't be here without everything Nora did to make our family and business work," Sheldon said.

"She sounds like a special woman."

Sheldon nodded. "She was one of a kind. I was so

lucky to have her in my life. Nora was the love of my life and such a blessing."

"It's rare to find a love like that," Wes said.

"You've been married?"

"Yes. We weren't matched perfectly for marriage, but we were able to work together," he said.

"That's a good thing."

"And it doesn't hurt that she's in London," Wes joked.

"As long as you two weren't fighting and had to put all that space between you two."

"No, she just has a different way of living than I do, so we wouldn't fight, we just let it go."

"Smart. The worst thing a man can do to a woman is waste her love. I'm glad to know you're not that kind of person," Sheldon said.

"I'm going to go over your notes and have some more designs for you to go over tomorrow."

"I think you and Alex should go over the designs tomorrow before I make my final decision," he said with a wink.

"No problem. I'd love to meet with her," Wes said with a smile. "I'll make sure to bring some muffins."

"And coffee. Clearly you know my daughter pretty well. Muffins are her weakness."

"That's good to know," he said as he rose to his feet. "Mr. Richardson, this has been a great session and I appreciate the history of your business here and I'm going to make sure we capture the history in the new wing."

"I have total faith in you," Sheldon said.

CHAPTER TWENTY

A lex knew Yolanda was going to spend a lot of time in the fabric store, but they had been in Mount Pleasant for two and a half hours. If this was what it took to be a designer, Alex was glad it wasn't her calling, but Yolanda seemed to glow in it. Alex loved how she turned yards of fabric into beautiful clothes.

"So," Yolanda said as she started to the counter with her haul. "Why are you here?"

"What do you mean? I can't spend time with my sister?"

Yolanda pursed her lips at Alex. "I know we've gotten a little closer since everything, but I think you're here avoiding your lover boy."

"And there she is, my smart-mouthed sister. Wes is . . . You know what? You blamed Nina for Chuck and I'm going to blame Wes on you."

Yolanda placed her fabric on the counter and turned to Yolanda. "Excuse me?"

Alex frowned. "Who told me to have a vacation fling?"

"And when did you start listening to me? But no wonder you're looking so relaxed and you were nice to Dad's fiancée. You had the dust knocked off that box." Yolanda thrust her hip against Alex's. "Was it good, or are you avoiding him because . . ."

Alex was mortified as she noticed the clerk listening to them intently. She covered Yolanda's mouth with her hand. "I'm not doing this with you!"

"Um, eighty-five seventy-two," the clerk said. Alex dropped her hand so Yolanda could pay.

"Why are you hiding from the man?" Yolanda asked as the clerk wrapped and bagged the fabric.

"I'm not hiding from anything or anyone." Alex said. "You know you could've died, and I'm happy that you're not dead."

"Okay, you are the worst. Just be honest with me— you do like this guy, right?"

Alex sighed, then nodded. "I think I do."

"You think you do, yet here we are. Is Alexandria the Great afraid this might … be something real?"

"What's real about two people who only have sex in common?" Alex said. "I mean, every time I see him, I just want to strip naked and pretend we're still in the Caymans."

Yolanda's jaw dropped. "I don't know what to say. How have you been sitting in meetings with him and Daddy without falling on your face?"

"If I tell you a secret, will you keep it?" Alex asked.

"I'll try," Yolanda said with a wink as they headed for the car.

"I don't know why I try to talk to any of y'all," Alex bemoaned.

"Oh come on, this is richly delicious. You have been in our business our whole lives and now you have some business."

Alex sucked her teeth. "Forget it."

"No, no, tell me. I won't say anything to Nina. She's the one who can't keep her mouth shut."

"And had she not opened her mouth about your situation, you'd be dead, and I wouldn't have Bradford and Nora. But still, don't tell Nina what I'm about to tell you."

"All right, go on with what you have to say."

"I went to his room this morning," Alex said.

"Before you came to breakfast? That means you got some good old morning wood! All right, now."

"See, this is why I can't with you. We didn't have sex this morning. But we're having dinner tonight, and I'm not sure I can keep pretending I don't want him."

"Then stop pretending and get that man."

Alex sighed. "It's not that easy. Wes and I are too different for this to be more than just sex. And I'm too old for that, and . . ."

"Are you trying to fall in love and get married or do you just want a good time? There's nothing wrong with having a good time."

Alex sucked her teeth. "Listen, I had a plan for my life. I thought I would've been married and running this place by now. Yet here I am. Watching you all live your best lives while I'm still trying to prove that I can carry on the Richardson legacy."

Yolanda sighed. "You are the last person who needs to prove anything. Alex, you have given up your life for that place."

"And I don't regret it. I love this industry, this bed-and-breakfast as well as this city. Wes doesn't even like the South."

"Okay, but he's here now. And I'm willing to bet it isn't because he wanted to sit in the office with Daddy."

"He hangs out in Miami, so . . ."

Yolanda popped Alex on the arm. "Just stop it. As much as I love Charleston, I wouldn't leave Miami to come here and work."

"But I told him when we came to port in Miami that this wouldn't work. That man takes four vacations a year."

Yolanda placed her hand on her chest. "Throw that man away for working and enjoying life. Goodness, you could learn from him."

"Shut up and drive," Alex said.

Before heading back to the bed-and-breakfast Yolanda stopped at the farmer's market and picked up some green tomatoes, sweet corn, and plums. "I would invite you to dinner, but you better make sure you meet Wes for dinner and then serve him dessert. Ooh, what are you going to wear?"

"I don't know."

"Thank God I'm here."

"I don't need you to dress me," Alex said.

"Are you saying you didn't wear my designs on the cruise? Because I know you did and that's one of the reasons he couldn't keep his eyes off you. And those DSLs you got."

"What does the Internet have to do with anything?" Alex asked.

"DSLs aren't about the Internet. It's about what that mouth does. Dic . . ."

"Okay, I get it and you're the worst!"

"Whatever you say." Yolanda laughed. "Thanks for coming with me today, even if it was just to avoid your new boo. Alex, you really should give that man a chance. Look at Dad. He's opened himself up to love again. You should try it at least once."

Yeah, but what if it doesn't work out? Alex thought as Yolanda hit the highway.

Once they got back to the bed-and-breakfast Alex was still mulling over what Yolanda had said about their father. Sheldon had loved their mother with his entire being, but he was willing to give it another chance. She needed to know why and how. Alex helped Yolanda unload her bags, then headed to find Sheldon. When she arrived at the office she caught him as he was walking out of the office.

"Daddy," she said. "Where are you going?"

"I thought you had taken the day off," he said.

"I did, but I wanted to talk to you," she said. "Do you have a second?"

"For you, of course. Follow me downstairs. Lillian and I are getting together for dinner."

"She's a really nice lady," Alex said honestly.

"Lillian said she really enjoyed breakfast with you all this morning. I'm glad you girls are giving her a chance."

Alex sighed. "Can I ask you a serious question?"

"Sure thing. What's going on?"

"How did you know you could move on and love again?"

Sheldon stopped walking and placed his hands on Alex's shoulders. "It was a number of things that prepared me. Lillian reminded me that there was more to life than just work. After I lost your mother I never wanted to feel that pain again. I never wanted to pour my heart into another woman I could lose." He dropped his hands from her shoulders and sighed. "So, I started focusing on making a legacy for my daughters, and I think I made a mistake."

"A mistake? Daddy, you built something amazing here. The B&B is the number . . ."

"No, my mistake was with you."

Alex furrowed her brows. "What?"

"Somehow, I made it seem as if work was the most important thing, that you couldn't have a life outside work, and everything except family came in a distant second."

"You didn't do that."

Sheldon motioned for her to follow him downstairs. "I did, and I'm sorry. I had a few discreet relationships when you all were younger, but I never wanted y'all to think I was trying to replace Nora. And I couldn't if I tried because Nora is irreplaceable. All you saw was me working all the time, and you internalized that."

Alex opened her mouth to tell him he was wrong, but he wasn't. "Alexandria," Sheldon said. "You don't have to prove yourself to anyone and you never had to."

"You still haven't answered the question," Alex said.

"When you feel something you've never felt before, then you know. Maybe you have that feeling now?"

"Um, what do you mean?"

Sheldon laughed as they headed to his car. "Wesley Prescott."

"Oh, Daddy, please he's just . . ."

"A nice man who seems to care about you a lot."

"But we're so different, how can it work?"

"Why don't you get to know him and see how much you actually have in common?"

Alex took a deep breath. If she was honest, she'd admit that was what she was afraid of. What was going to happen when all the excuses were gone? "That's easier said than done. He lives in New York and . . ."

"There are planes, trains, and . . . well, in your case stick to planes and trains. It would take you forty days to drive to New York."

"Et tu, Daddy?" she quipped.

"Sweetheart, you drive like a fifteen-year-old with a permit in a stolen car with a police officer in the next lane."

Alex scoffed, "Whatever, Daddy. But I'd never drive to New York. Nor would I ride the subway. Can you imagine?"

"Actually, I can. Lillian and I went to New York a week and a half ago. We had a good time traveling on the subway and not waiting for taxicabs on crowded streets. She had business there and we were getting around just fine."

"So, you and Lillian are traveling together a lot?"

Sheldon nodded. "We have earned the right to take some time away and get a life. Your life doesn't have to revolve around the bed-and-breakfast."

"But . . ."

"Alex, we have a staff in place who can do the work. We have to focus on life and living. Me again and you for the first time. He's here because he wants you, not because he has to be. Just think about that."

Alex nodded, then gave her father a tight hug. "Thank you, Daddy. I really needed that."

"I know," he said, then kissed her on the forehead. "Give him a call."

"We're having dinner tonight," she said quietly.

"Good, and be honest about your feelings."

"I'll try."

"Do more than that. I know you don't need someone to make you happy, I know you're going to live your life your way, but there is nothing wrong with loving the right person. Maybe it's Wesley, maybe not. But you owe it to yourself to see if it feels right." Sheldon opened the door to his car. "And do me a favor, tell your sisters to leave you alone and let you navigate this thing on your own."

"Do you really think they're going to listen?"

"No, but you never did either. Enjoy your dinner."

"You too," she said, then looked at her watch. She needed to get ready.

When Alex walked over to the family wing she wasn't the least bit surprised to see her sisters sitting in the living room.

"Why are y'all here?" she asked. Yolanda spoke up first.

"Because I'm cooking dinner."

"Don't you and Charles have a huge, state-of-the-art kitchen in your house?" Alex rolled her eyes and shook her head.

"Okay, Alex," Nina said. "We're here to make sure you go on your date."

"I'm going," she said. "Jeez, you all are so annoying."

"Hi, pot," Robin quipped. "Where were you?"

"Hopefully riding some . . ."

"Yolanda!" everyone else exclaimed.

Yolanda shrugged. "Whatever. So, what are you wearing since he's already seen you in this outfit?"

Alex glared at her sister. Yolanda threw up her hands. "I didn't tell them where you were before breakfast."

"Say another word and I'm going to . . ." Alex sighed. She couldn't even joke about murdering Yolanda anymore after the stalking, when a powerful man hired a hit man to kill her.

"I brought you a gift and this is how you treat me?" Yolanda scoffed. "I'd take them back, but Bradford really wants his auntie to look nice tonight."

"When are you going back to Charlotte?" Alex groaned.

"It's Charleston month, so you're stuck with me. My store manager is more than capable of keeping things going."

Nina rolled her eyes. "I still don't like your number one customer."

"Well, think of it like this: He's getting me so much attention that I can actually launch my line."

"I can't be mad at that, but I heard he's getting traded. A trusted league source told me. So, good-bye tacky suit guy."

Yolanda rolled her eyes. "Are you ever going to let it go?"

"Um, no," Nina said with a smile.

"This is nice and all," Alex said. "But I need to shower and get dressed."

"Where are y'all going, and please don't say the dining room," Robin said.

"We're going to James Island. He's never had a low country boil."

"You're dating a serious Yankee," Robin teased. "So, y'all are going to the Crab House?"

Alex nodded. Yolanda clasped her hands together. "I have the perfect outfit." She leaped to her feet and ran into the sitting room. As much as Alex wanted to pretend she wasn't excited about the outfit, she was very curious. And she prayed it was another one of Yo-Yo's amazing jumpsuits.

"You have to wear this and I'm not taking no for an answer!"

"Let me see it," Alex said.

Yolanda held up the pink-and-white-polka-dot-halter jumpsuit. It was divine. "I want one!" Nina exclaimed.

Alex smiled at Yolanda. "I love it."

"Thought about you and Pam Grier when I made it. And since I'm sick of you in gray and black, I figured pink would be a nice change."

Alex reached for the jumpsuit and noticed the sides above the hips were cut out. "Yolanda, I don't know about this."

"Try it on first! You can pull this off."

Alex thought about some of the outfits Wes had already seen her in and the number of times he'd seen her naked. But could she wear this in *her city*? What if she ran into someone she knew? She looked at the suit again.

"If you see someone you know, who cares?"

Alex turned around to make sure that was Yolanda talking and not her thoughts. It was her sister's mouth this time. "Okay, I'm going to take a shower and try it on." She headed for her room, ignoring her sisters' chatter.

After a quick shower Alex dried off and stood in front of the mirror and held the jumpsuit against her body. The material was soft against her skin. "You can do this," she whispered, then stepped into the suit. She had to give it to Yolanda—that woman was an amazing designer. The cuts on the hips showed just a sliver of skin. She loved the way the suit framed her body. Now she needed shoes. She remembered a pair of silver sandals she'd purchased on a whim. They'd be perfect. As she slipped on the shoes, there was a knock at the door.

"Alex, you better have on that jumpsuit," Yolanda said as she knocked.

"Hold on," Alex snapped as she put on her shoes. She crossed over to the door and opened it. She thought it was just going to be Yolanda, but it was the whole crew.

Yolanda let out a low whistle when she saw Alex. "Damn, this suit looks even better than I thought it would."

"I can't pull that off," Nina admitted. "But damn, Alex. Who knew you had all that sexy going on?"

"Oh, hush," Alex snapped. "I need to get going, so can y'all go cook your dinner?"

"Before you go," Robin began, "we need to give you the Richardson dating speech."

Alex groaned. "Y'all make me sick."

"Oh, this has been a long time coming," Nina said. "Make sure he has you home at a decent time."

Alex rolled her eyes, knowing she'd said the same thing to Nina many times.

"And don't embarrass Daddy out there," Yolanda said.

"Get out. All of you. I'm going to be late," Alex snapped.

"Don't keep him waiting; he might think you changed your mind." Robin ushered her sisters to the door. Then she turned to Alex. "Please sit on that man's face tonight and don't come home until you do."

"Oh shit," Yolanda said as she and Nina left the room.

CHAPTER TWENTY-ONE

Wes entered the lobby about five minutes before he and Alexandria were scheduled to meet. He wondered what her home was like. Would she feel comfortable enough to invite him over after dinner? He wondered what her favorite places in Charleston looked like. But more than anything else, he wanted another look at the beauty of her naked body.

Turning toward the front doors leading into the lobby, he saw her walking in. And by God, she was so pretty in pink.

"Well, hello, gorgeous," Wes said as he crossed over to her. He was about to hug her when she placed her hand on his chest to stop him.

"Hi, Wes. Let's head outside. My car is parked out front." She nodded toward the desk clerk, who was watching their every move.

"No problem," he said, then they headed out the door. Once they were away from prying eyes, Wes drew her into his arms and hugged her tightly. "You feel as good as you look," he intoned.

"I can't do this in the lobby of my place of business," she said. "I don't want our employees to get the wrong idea about how we deal with our guests."

"I understand, but technically I'm not a guest. I'm working with the bed-and-breakfast," he said, then brushed his lips against hers. Alexandria moaned.

"Well, that is true, but the optics," she replied. "And . . ."

Wes cut her off with a hot kiss. She melted against his chest and Wes was about to say to hell with boiled low country or whatever she'd said. But Alexandria broke the kiss and smiled at him.

"If we don't leave now, I'm sure we won't make it to dinner."

"Is that supposed to be a bad thing? Because I know exactly what I could eat."

Alex pressed the Unlock button on her key fob. "Let's go. And you can eat your first choice later."

"You said it out loud, so no take backs," he quipped.

"Not you out here, trying to regulate my right to withdraw consent?" She shook her head, then laughed.

"That's not what I meant. One thing you should always know about me: I'll never stand in the way of anything you ever want or need."

"I know that," she said. "I have to be honest about something."

"What's that?" he asked as he opened the driver's side door for her. Alexandria locked eyes with him.

"I had to take a real hard look at myself and figure out why I didn't want to tell you that I like you."

"So, you like me?"

"You know, you could just listen," she said as she slid behind the wheel. Wes closed her door, then crossed over to the passenger's side.

"I'm listening," he said as he hopped in the car.

"I've been focusing on what I think are our differences instead of looking at what we have in common. And to know what those things are, I have to get to know you beyond the bedroom."

Wes took her right hand in his and gave it a kiss. "Alexandria, I really want to get to know you."

"You can start by calling me Alex. Although I do like it when you say it with your lips real close to my ear," she said.

"Noted. Why do you prefer Alex over Alexandria?"

She smiled as she started for the highway. "My mother started calling me Alex, and then so did my sisters and other people close to the family. Alexandria was the student, then the professional. When people know me, they meet Alex. And it didn't help that my younger sisters started calling me Alexandria the Great because they didn't like following the rules."

"Interesting. But you were Alexandria on vacation?"

She shook her head. "I thought I was a woman who'd never see you again."

"Yet here we are, about to boil the low country," Wes said with a laugh.

"First, it's a low country boil, and second, if you don't know, just be quiet," she quipped.

"Yes, ma'am," he said with a mock salute.

"Why did you become an architect?" Alex asked.

"My dad talked me out of drawing comic books, but I

still wanted to figure out what I could do with my passion to draw."

"Comic books?"

He nodded. "My dad was a practical guy, so you can imagine how that conversation went."

"Especially during those days when you didn't see or hear about Black comic book artists and writers."

"True, but Black architects from Brooklyn were even rarer. Still, that was our compromise."

"Do you regret it?"

"Not really. I used to tell myself that I'd do my own line, create characters who looked like me and my friends, but time got away from me and I created a successful firm."

"So, things worked out for you?" she asked with a shrug.

"Yes, because I'm sure the Richardson Bed and Breakfast wouldn't have hired a comic book artist to design the new wing."

Alex laughed. "You got that right. But it sounds like you gave up your dreams and . . ."

"What about your dreams, beautiful? I came to grips with not being able to do the exact thing I wanted, but have you?"

"What do you mean? I wanted to go into business with my father. The bed-and-breakfast was always like a member of the family. When people came here they were always so happy, and I loved that."

"We both know vacations make people happy," he said with a wink.

"Yes, they do. I guess that's why you take so many."

"You just can't let that go, huh?"

Alex pulled into the parking lot of the restaurant. "It's just different for me," she said as she shifted her car into Park. "I feel like I have to work, even if my dad says I've earned a lot of time off. I don't know what life is like without meetings and some sort of crisis."

"You remind me of my brother, and I hate thinking about him when I'm having a good time. But he works way too hard for no reason."

"You have a brother?"

"It's just the two of us."

"I wanted a brother, but after Yolanda came, my father said he and my mother were a daughter factory. Mommy said her girls were going to run the world someday." Wes noticed Alex's eyes had filled with tears. He stroked her cheek, suddenly understanding why she was so focused on work. She was still trying to please other people. "Have you ever thought about what you want?"

Alex gasped. "I–I haven't thought much about it, but it's not as if I'm going to start some new artistic endeavor or try to reclaim some childhood fantasy. I don't know what my next steps will be."

"Here's an idea: take another vacation."

Alex laughed and shook her head. "I don't think I want to become a regular on the singles cruise circuit."

"Oh, you won't. Your next vacation will be our first one together."

"Look at you, making plans for my life," she jibed. "I think I want to go to Alaska."

Wes stroked his chin as they waited for a table. "Spoken like a woman who doesn't see much snow. You know you can't wear a bikini in Alaska."

She smiled at him. "I'm sure the cabins are heated."

"Well, it's not the same as a beach."

"Look around, Brooklyn, I can see the beach anytime I want."

"It's nice here, but it isn't Hawaii or the Canary Islands."

"Well, who knew you were going to design the new wing and plan my next vacation? Is there anything you can't do?"

Before he could reply the host crossed over to them. "Good evening. Do you have a reservation?"

"The standing Richardson reservation," Alex said. The host gave her a slow once-over.

"Alexandria?" he asked. "My goodness, you look amazing, and so different."

"Thanks," she said flippantly as the man led them to their table. Wes couldn't hide his smile as he and Alex took their seats. "What?" she asked, noting his smile.

"I see you have many layers. Do you just come here for business meetings?"

"And a nice low country boil. Why?"

Wes took her hand in his, "So, I'm the first date you brought here? I feel so special."

"Whatever," she said as he brought her hand to his lips.

"Come on, this is a momentous occasion. We need champagne."

"Not here we don't, because I don't want anything getting in the way of you tasting the best meal ever."

"We'll see if it lives up to your hype," he said, then released her hand.

"It's not hype, it is life changing," she replied with a smile.

Their waitress walked over to the table with a pitcher of iced tea and two glasses. "Miss Alex, you look great. Pink is your color."

Did Alex blush? Wes wondered as she breathed a thank-you to the waitress.

"What can I get for you two?" she asked.

"We're going to do the low country boil," Alex said. "Is Cynda working today?"

"No, she's off."

Alex nodded. "We'll have to try the red rice next time."

"Oh, so I get a second date?" Wes said.

"Maybe. Just don't get ahead of yourself right away, buddy."

The waitress smiled, then headed back to put in their order.

Wes leaned across the table. "Would I be getting ahead of myself if I kissed you?"

"You're actually behind schedule," she replied as she stroked his cheek. Wes captured her lips in a tender kiss. He wanted to skip dinner when her tongue flicked across his bottom lip. He just wanted to devour Alex. On the table, in the car, in his room—everywhere. She eased back from him and smiled.

"We better stop before we cause a scandal in here," Alex said.

"If you want to take this food to go, I have an amazing room for us to eat in."

Alex shook her head. "It's so much better hot."

Why did she have to say that? "Don't I know it." He winked at her and Alex blushed. He liked that she was vulnerable with him. Wes knew she didn't show this side of herself to many people. That made him feel special. He stroked her hand. "Tell me something no one knows about you."

"What?"

"Come on, I can see all these people here know Alexandria, but I want to know Alex."

She smiled and folded her arms across her chest. "Okay. You know how I focus on work a lot, but I relieve my stress through ballroom dancing. I'm actually pretty good at it. The studio I go to wanted me to enter a statewide contest."

"So, when is the contest? I want to see those moves."

Alex dropped her head. "I'm not doing it."

"Why not?"

She expelled a sigh. "Because that's not who I am. I just dance for me."

"Oh, okay, so tell me you're afraid without telling me you're afraid."

She sucked her teeth. "Listen, I'm not trying to embarrass myself on a statewide level."

"Your words, you're pretty good at it."

"I am."

"Then you need to compete."

"It's in two weeks, I'm pretty sure you're going to be gone by then."

"I'm the boss. I can stay as long as I want. You should enter the contest."

She stroked her chin as if she was considering it. "My sisters are going to have a field day with this. All right, I'll do it."

Moments later the waitress returned to the table with a metal tray covered in newspaper, holding corn, new potatoes, shrimp, sausage, and onions. "This looks interesting," he said.

"Dig in," she said with a smile.

Wes took his first bite of the mix and moaned in delight as the flavor exploded in his mouth.

"This is everything you said it was. Damn!"

"Told you so," she said as she picked up an ear of corn.

They ate dinner in a comfortable silence, commenting on the taste of the food and how Wes wasn't used to presweetened tea.

"Wait, so if I order iced tea in Brooklyn, there's no sugar?" Alex asked. "Oh, that is horrible."

"When are you coming to Brooklyn?" Wes took another sip of his tea, deciding that it wasn't as sweet as Alex's lips.

"Maybe someone will invite me one day."

"Oh, that's an open invitation. Whenever you're ready, Brooklyn is willing."

Alex laughed. "You love New York, huh?"

Wes reached for his half-empty glass. "It's a great place. So much history, and New York is the center of the world. If you can't find what you're looking for in New York, you can't find it anywhere."

"You're going too far, and if you're interested in history, you're in the right place."

"I'm more interested in the beautiful woman sitting across from me. You want to go have some dessert?"

"I couldn't eat another bite," she said.

Wes smirked, then leaned into her. "But I won't bite unless you ask me to."

Alex waved for the waitress. "Check, please."

CHAPTER TWENTY-TWO

Alex was a stickler for the speed limit. But not tonight. Not when her pussy throbbed with the anticipation of Wes's tongue going in and out of her slit. She'd been doing eighty-five on the interstate before she slowed down.

"That's some fancy driving," Wes said as he stroked her thigh. "Remember that time we were in the lagoon?"

"Um-huh," she replied as she took the exit for the bed-and-breakfast. "That was one of the highlights of my trip. Everything was so beautiful."

"Especially you."

Three miles—she just needed to make it three miles to the bed-and-breakfast. She took a deep breath and fought the urge to close her eyes. The last thing she needed was to wreck the car because she wanted to be sucked like a church peppermint.

"Stop it," she moaned as she turned down the road leading to the bed-and-breakfast.

"I haven't done anything yet," he said. "But you remember that day and all the fun we had?"

"If I'm honest, that's something I can't stop thinking about."

"Then it's time to give you a lot more to think about," he said in a low voice.

Alex pulled her car around the back of the family wing of the bed-and-breakfast. She was happy to see none of her sisters' cars were there. "Wait, you've been on the property this whole time?" Wes exclaimed. "And I was trying to figure out how to get your address."

"And that doesn't sound like a stalker at all," Alex quipped.

"I wasn't going to show up, but the flowers were." He leaned over and kissed her cheek.

"You know, flower deliveries aren't a good thing around here these days."

"What woman hates getting flowers?"

Alex shrugged as she opened the car door. "The woman whose sister got death threats wrapped in roses."

Wes furrowed his brows. "What?"

As she and Wes walked to the building, Alex told him about the chaos before Yolanda had the babies. That while she'd been running her boutique in Richmond, she'd witnessed a murder outside her shop. About the man who'd done the shooting, who had some powerful connections in the city and put a hit out on Yolanda.

"Wow," Wes said. "That had to be scary."

"That's putting it mildly. Thank God for Charles."

"I thought that dude was going to take my head off

when I was out on the property taking pictures. Now I get it."

"Charles—or Chuck, as my sister calls him—is protective of his wife and kids. You practically have to do an eye scan to get in their house." Alex laughed as she unlocked the door. She led him to the sitting room. "Would you like something to drink?"

Wes walked up behind her and enveloped her in his arms. "You know what I want."

She faced him and took a deep breath. "Yes," she said as she wrapped her arms around his neck. Their lips met in a hot kiss. Alex melted against his body as his hands roamed her back. She moaned as his tongue caressed hers. Wes stepped back.

"Did I tell you how amazing you look in pink?" He reached up and untied the halter part of the jumpsuit. Alex was glad she hadn't been wearing a bra when his fingers danced across her diamond-hard nipples. Then he kissed her on the neck as he slipped down her jumpsuit to her feet. "Exquisite," he said as he drank in her naked body. He spun Alex around as if they were on the dance floor.

"You have me at a disadvantage," she said. "Why am I the only one naked?"

Wes scooped her up in his arms. "Because I'm about to worship this body." He leaned her against the sofa, then spread her legs apart. He licked her inner thighs and inched up to her throbbing pussy. Alex arched into his mouth and he sucked her clit as if she was the sweetest piece of hard candy. Her legs trembled as he made circles inside her with his tongue. "Oh my God," she exclaimed as she neared her climax. "Don't. Stop!"

And he didn't. Lick. Suck. Lick. Then she exploded, covering his face in her sweetness. "Um, so good," he said. "So good." Wes stroked her thighs and Alex shivered.

"I can't move."

"That's why I can carry you. Point me to your bedroom," he growled, then picked her up. Alex pointed him in the direction of her room. Once inside, he laid her on the bed, then stripped off his clothes. Alex took in a deep breath as she drank in his brown skin, his washboard abs, and his hard dick. She eased to the edge of the bed and wrapped her arms around his waist. "I've missed this," she said, the licked the tip of his dick. Wes shivered in delight as she took him in her mouth. So wet and so hot. Wes cried out her name as she sucked and licked his shaft like it was a special treat. When she grabbed his ass and took him deeper into her mouth, Wes's knees went weak. "Damn, damn, damn," he exclaimed as he pulled back and joined her in the bed.

"Um," she said. "I'm glad you liked it."

"*Like* doesn't even begin to cover it. That mouth is spectacular," he said as he wrapped her legs around his waist.

"Protection," she whispered.

Wes nodded as she reached into her nightstand drawer for a condom. He took the gold package from her hand, ripped it open, and slid the condom in place. Alex smiled as she pushed him back on the bed and gripped his shoulders. Straddling his body, she drew him into her wetness and moaned as she rode. Wes thrust deeper into her, turning her moans into screams of passion. Alex ground against him, getting hotter and wetter as his dick caressed her clit. "Yes, yes, ride me, baby," he exclaimed. Alex bucked harder, Wes went deeper, and she exploded. Seconds later, Wes reached his climax and they collapsed against each other.

"Whew," Wes expelled. "You all right?"

"I'm great," she said as she ran her finger down the center of his chest. "You know, you can spend the night if you want to."

"I couldn't imagine leaving you tonight."

Alex closed her eyes and rested against his chest.

Wes couldn't sleep with Alex in his arms. He just didn't want to miss a moment with her. He watched her breathe, smiled at the way her lips curved up at the edges, and inhaled her luscious scent. He ran his fingers through her wavy hair. He loved her hair, so soft and free. Much like he wished she would be. She stirred in his arms and her eyes fluttered open. "Why are you still awake?" she asked.

"Just making sure I'm not dreaming," he said, then kissed her forehead.

Alex snuggled closer to him. "Totally not a dream. But what time is it?"

"I know it's after midnight."

She sat up in bed and smiled. "Since my sisters are not here, we can raid the kitchen for cookies. Our chocolate chip cookies are legendary."

"Really?"

Alex nodded. "These cookies have been featured on the Food Network as one of the best things a certain chef ever ate. They're kind of a big deal. Let's get dressed and go."

"What happens if we get caught?"

"You are with the boss, so I think we're going to be fine."

Wes rose from the bed and picked up his pants from the floor as Alex grabbed a T-shirt dress from her dresser drawer. He watched her pull the dress over her curves and decided he wanted more of her than those magical cookies.

"All right, let's go," she said as she stepped into a pair of slippers. As they headed for the kitchen, Alex told him how she and Robin used to sneak into the kitchen, grab cookies, and talk about their future.

"What were those talks like?" he asked as they walked down the hall.

"Robin wanted a family, three or four kids. She always wanted to be a lawyer," Alex said as she opened the door to the kitchen.

"What were your dreams?" he asked.

Alex shrugged. "To take over the bed-and-breakfast. I always said I wanted to modernize the place. Until I started working here, I thought my father was stuck in the past. But you have to preserve history or you'll be erased from it."

Wes folded his arms across his chest. "You're telling me that you didn't have any other dreams when you were out here stealing cookies?"

Alex laughed. "Yes. Someone had to stay in Charleston and help the family. There's nothing wrong with the hospitality industry."

"I'm sure there isn't, but you had to want something."

"Okay," she said as she picked up a package of freshly baked cookies. "If I'm honest, I did want to be Lola Falana."

"Is that why you dance?"

Alex opened the bag of cookies and handed one to Wes. "Maybe. But I'm not Ms. Falana. Even when I tried to be Debbie Allen, I failed miserably. I don't think I paid enough in sweat."

"How do your sisters not know that you wanted to be a dancer?"

"Because I never told them." Alex bit into her cookie and closed her eyes. "So good."

"Tell me more about how you hid this dancing ambition from your sisters." He took a bite of the cookie and smiled. It was rich and delicious. He wondered what would happen if he ran the cookie across her hard nipples.

"It was something I never wanted to talk about. You know, it wasn't practical, and I had to carry on the Richardson legacy."

"That's a lot to carry."

Alex took another bite of her cookie and rolled her eyes. "I remember one night, Nina and Yolanda set off fire alarms when they tried to bake a batch of cookies. Those nuts forgot to remove the waxed paper before putting the dough in the oven."

"That's funny," he said.

"Maybe I should tell them," Alex whispered.

"What's that?"

"You know, one thing about this family is that we show up for the big things. If I'm going to make a fool of myself for the state to see, I'm going to need a cheering squad."

"I'm ready to cheer you on," he said after finishing his

cookie. "And I can start right now." Wes started clapping and Alex shook her head.

"Stop it," she said. "But thanks for joining the band-wagon."

"I'm the leader. Come here." He opened his arms to her. Alex thought he was going to hug her, but he spun her around and they started dancing cheek to cheek.

"Maybe you ought to be my partner. Can you do the paso doble?"

"No, but I'm a master of all the forbidden dances." He thrust his hips forward. Alex dipped low, then shimmied to her feet. Then she wrapped her left leg around his waist and leaned back and pointed her arm to the sky.

"This is so sexy," he said as they unfurled their bodies. "Next time we try this with no clothes on."

Alex laughed. "You're always thinking about me with no clothes on, huh?"

"Honestly, I'm just always thinking about you, Alex. You're the most intriguing woman I've ever met."

"I was just kidding. Wes, you don't . . ."

He placed his index finger to her lips. "Stop. Just hear me out. When we said good-bye on the ship I was deter-mined to find you because there was a spark between us that I didn't even feel with my ex-wife. And you wanted nothing to do with me."

She licked the pad of his finger and Wes moved it. "Full honesty," she began. "Part of me wanted to get off in Miami with you, but the practical part of me needed to prepare myself for the reality of life."

"The reality of life? What does that mean?"

She dropped her head and sighed. "You know, I'm not

like my sisters. They are the women fairy tales happen for. I'm not that person. I've never pretended to be her."

"You know, you always sell yourself short. You deserve happiness. It's not something that's just limited to your sisters."

"Usually it is," Alex said quietly. "I know I didn't have to, but I wanted to make sure Yolanda and Nina were always happy and had what they wanted. They thought I was being a jerk and trying to run their lives, but that wasn't the case."

"Your sisters are all grown and you don't have to look after their happiness anymore while ignoring yours."

"Wes, you're cute, but I know the other shoe is always going to drop on me."

"Sometimes the other shoe is just putting one foot in front of the other. But you can't live a life in the shadows, thinking you don't deserve the fundamental happiness people are born into."

"That's easy for you to say when you haven't been through . . . My parents had a fairy-tale romance and they didn't get forever. So, I hid behind everything else so I wouldn't get my heart broken. No one was ever going to mean that much to me." Tears spilled down her cheeks. "Now, you have me questioning everything at this big age." She wiped her eyes.

Wes pulled her into his arms and hugged her tightly. "Just know that I'm here with you every step of the way."

"Until your next vacation," she quipped.

"You're going with me, lady. I'm thinking we should head back to that bed-and-breakfast on the island."

She smiled. "That place was magical."

"So was the company."

"Let's go back to my room. You're going to have to get out of here before breakfast because I know at least one of my sisters will be here first thing in the morning."

"And you're hiding me because . . ."

"They've been waiting their whole lives for something like this to happen. You will thank me later."

"I'll take your word for it."

CHAPTER TWENTY-THREE

She felt a hand stroke her back. Warm and tender. Alex rolled over on her side and realized she wasn't dreaming. She was in her bed, in Wes's arms, and . . . Was her clock right? It was five after eight. He should've been gone two hours ago. They'd agreed on that, then they'd made love until four a.m.

And now . . . there it was. A loud knock on the door. "Alex," Yolanda called out. It *would be* her.

"Damn it," she muttered. Wes yawned and looked as if he was going to say something. Alex placed her hand over his mouth and shook her head.

"Alex, I know you're in there," Yolanda continued. "Open the door."

"She's not going to go away," Alex whispered as she rose from the bed and grabbed her robe.

"What if you just lay here quietly?" Wes whispered.

"You don't know my sister," Alex said.

"Is that man in there?" Yolanda called out.

"Go to the bathroom and I'll handle her," Alex told him. Wes laughed but headed for the bathroom. Alex waited until he'd closed the door before she crossed over to the bedroom door and opened it a sliver.

"What do you want?"

"To be invited in. Unless you have something to hide." Yolanda grinned.

Alex narrowed her eyes at her sister. "Where are the babies?"

"My kids are in the kitchen with Auntie Robin, wondering why there's no breakfast. Where is he?"

"Probably having breakfast," Alex said as she tried to block Yolanda from coming inside. "Give me a minute and I'll be in to kiss my niece and nephew."

"I don't know if that's a good idea. Who knows what you did with that mouth last night, or even this morning."

"Go away," Alex said, then attempted to close her door. Yolanda pushed her way in and scanned the room.

Yolanda spotted Wes's slacks and crossed over to them. "Well, well," she said as she picked the pants up. "You sent him to his room without these? Scandalous."

"Get out!"

"Why can't I meet him?" Yolanda pouted.

"Because he's naked, all right. Get out and we'll meet you and Robin in the dining room for coffee."

Yolanda looked at her watch. "Ten minutes or I'll be back."

"Yo-Yo, get out," Alex snapped.

"Ten minutes," she sang. "And not a second more." Yolanda closed the door behind her, and Alex made sure the door was locked before she called Wes's name.

He walked out of the bathroom laughing uncontrollably. "I have never in my life . . ."

"Stop it," Alex said, throwing up her hand. "We'd better get dressed and head out there."

"Why are you making it seem like we're about to face a firing squad?"

She tossed him his pants. "You'll see, darling."

Nine minutes and forty-five seconds later, Alex and Wes made their debut in the family dining room together. Robin gasped when she saw Wes. Alex thought she heard a *damn* float from one of her sister's lips.

"Good morning," she said.

"Well, well," Robin said as she stood up and handed Wes a steaming mug of coffee. "It is nice to have a face to go with the name."

"And what name is that?" he teased. "I only answer to *King of the World*."

Yolanda chuckled as she rocked the twins in her arms. "Handsome and a sense of humor. Okay, Sis."

Alex wanted the floor to open up and swallow her. "I know both of you have lovely homes in the city, yet here you are," Alex said. She glanced at Wes. "This is not the King of the World, but Wesley Prescott."

Wes nodded at the Richardson sisters while sipping his coffee. "Nice to meet you all as well," he said after finishing his sip. "This coffee is delicious."

"I made it," Robin said. "By the way, I'm Robin—the nicest of all the sisters."

Yolanda burst into laughter. "The lies you tell in front of babies. Wes, I'm Yolanda, and the reason you fell in love with my sister is because . . ."

"Okay, that's enough, you all can leave now, Wes and I have business to discuss," Alex interjected.

"When did you start conducting business meetings in the family wing?" Yolanda asked.

"And without a business suit and a fruit tray?" Robin added.

Alex gritted her teeth. "Good-bye."

Before her sisters could get themselves together to leave, Nina rushed into the dining room. "She hasn't kicked y'all out yet?" She looked up at Alex and Wes. "Oh my goodness, does Daddy know you had a boy in your room?"

It was official: Alex was going to lock out all of her sisters.

Wes hadn't laughed so hard in years. The Richardson sisters were funny as hell. But he could see Alex wasn't as amused as he was. Especially when Nina asked probing questions. The more Nina talked, it clicked where he knew her from. "Sweetheart-gate, that was you, right?"

"Damn it, Wes, I was starting to like you," Yolanda said. "Now we're going to hear the Cody Cameron saga again."

"First of all," Nina began, "everyone knows the story, but sadly, no one ever held him accountable, and he is the same jackass now he was then. I don't care if a certain Judas at this table has been supplying him with clothes."

"Do you think Cody was wrong?" Robin asked Wes.

"Absolutely," Wes said. Alex placed her hand on his thigh and stroked him. "Maybe I'm old-fashioned, but when I call a woman *sweetheart* it means something."

"Mostly condescending," Nina snapped.

Wes smiled and faced Alex. "Not if he's the right guy and leans in really close then says, *good morning, sweetheart*." He brought his hand to Alex's cheek and stroked it. She swooned under his touch.

"Well, damn," Nina and Yolanda breathed.

Alex turned to her sisters. "Don't you all have some-place to be? As in a place not here?"

Wes was surprised that the women got up and left without much pushback. Alex kissed her sleeping niece and nephew as she told her sisters good-bye. When she closed the door and locked the dead bolt, she faced Wes. "So, sweetheart has never made me wet before, but here we are," she said.

He crossed over to her and dropped to his knees. "Like I said, I want *sweetheart* to mean something when I say it to you." He lifted her dress and was happy she hadn't put on panties when she pulled on this cotton dress. His fingers danced up and down her thighs before spreading her legs apart and slipping his finger inside her wetness and stroked her throbbing clit. Alex moaned as his tongue replaced his finger. He sucked her until she was shivering with delight. Wes wanted to make sure she came. He wanted to taste it, he wanted to drown in her sweetness until she was weak.

"Wes," she moaned as she gripped his shoulders. Her juices covered his face like a Halloween mask. She kept coming and he kept sucking and licking. Pleasing her until Alex screamed at the top of her lungs, "My God, my God."

Wes kept her from falling when he stood up and held her melting body against his chest.

"You good, sweetheart?" Wes asked, then licked his lips.

"If you're going to keep doing that, you can call me sweetheart, sweetie pie, sweetness, hell—sweet potato pie," she replied breathlessly.

"Don't you have work today?"

"Um, just a meeting with some architect dude. I'm

sure I can push it back," she said as she pulled off the dress.

"Definitely think that meeting is pushed back or maybe even canceled." He captured her lips in a hot kiss.

Alex placed her hand on his chest. "We'd better take this to my room. I don't trust my sisters not to come back."

It was midafternoon before Wes and Alex got out of bed. He didn't want to move after making love to her all morning, he wanted more, but he wasn't just in Charleston to woo Alex. He had to create the new wing that would live up to the historical legacy of the bed-and-breakfast. While Alex showered, Wes called his ex-wife, Jasmine.

"Wesley," she said. "What's going on?"

"Saying hello is just too hard for you, huh?"

"You always have an issue when you call me. So, hello. What's going on?"

"I'm still working on the Richardson project. You said your family vacationed here, right?"

"Yes. They said it was a beautiful property. Have you seen it?"

"I'm here now. It is a lovely place and so is the family that runs it. They're one step away from royalty."

"Must be a princess in Charleston you find yourself interested in if you're in a part of the South that isn't Miami."

"Don't make me regret this call, Jazz. I want to design something that honors the history of this place without turning it into a museum."

"Whoa, you taking this really seriously. You sound like the man I thought I'd married. She must be really pretty."

"Jasmine, we were really young when we jumped into that marriage thing. Imagine if we'd taken more time to get to know each other."

"We'd still be divorced, but I'd have less stock options. We were in each other's lives for a season. And just like summer, it ended."

"I don't think I'll ever meet another woman like you as long as I live."

"Are you laughing right now?"

"Yes, I am, but I mean it. You're something special, always remember that."

"I'll let the world know I have your seal of approval."

"All right, Jasmine, good-bye. Hey, send me some pictures. I want to see the magic."

"Let me see what I got. We'll talk soon."

Wes ended the call and smiled. He didn't notice Alex's cold glare from the bathroom.

Alex was pissed. Had she just heard this man on the phone lamenting about never finding another woman like his ex? What was she? Chopped liver? Why did he think it was okay to sit in her bed and talk to his ex? She slammed out of the bathroom and rushed over to him. She promised herself not to be taken in by his brown eyes or his smooth skin. She was going to tell this nude-seeking son of bitch to get the hell out of her room and her life. *Damn it,* she thought. *He still has to design the new wing, and Dad has invested too much in this to allow sex and lies to ruin it. But still, this motherfucker has to go.*

"Hey," Wes said when he noticed Alex walking over to him. "Did you leave any hot water for me?"

"There's plenty in your room and that's where you should go," she said coldly.

Wes stood up and Alex turned away from him, trying to ignore the body that brought her so much pleasure and so many orgasms. "Did I miss something? What's wrong, Alex?"

"I missed something and I'm correcting it. We have business together and no business doing any of this." Alex pointed to the bathroom. "I'm going to get dressed and you need to be gone when I come out." She stormed into the bathroom and slammed the door. Alex plopped down on the toilet and cried silently. How could she be so foolish?

CHAPTER TWENTY-FOUR

Wes didn't understand what had happened while Alex was in the shower, but he needed answers. Crossing over to the bathroom door, he tapped on it. "Alex, you want to tell me what's going on here?"

"Please leave," she said. "I don't owe you anything and I don't want to make this ugly by calling security."

"What is this, Alex? Did I do something wrong?"

She snatched the door open and glared at him. A million things ran through his mind; maybe something happened to her father or one of her sisters. "Alex, talk to me, please."

She walked over to the bedroom door and opened it. Then she speared him with an icy look. Wes didn't want to fight and clearly she didn't want to talk, so he shrugged and walked out the door. Wes was confused and he didn't know what his next steps needed to be. His phone vibrated and he pulled it from his pocket to find that Jasmine had sent the picture he'd asked for. There was his ex-wife as a little girl, standing in front of the B&B with her grandparents. The happiness on their faces seemed to leap through the phone. Despite his drama with Alex, Wes had found inspiration for his design. He crossed the parking lot and headed for the main building. As he walked through the lobby, he ran into Robin, who was in tears.

"Hey," he said as he touched her elbow. "Are you all right?"

"No, I'm not. Is Alex around?"

"She was in her room when . . . Robin, I know you don't know me like that, but has something happened? Alex was . . ."

She shook her head and fought back a sob. "I'm sorry. I need my sister, I can't do this." Robin ran out of the lobby, and Wes was certain Alex's one-eighty had something to do with what was happening with her sister.

Alex had finally stopped crying. Now she was berating herself for acting like an idiot. Love had never been in her life equation. So what if her sisters were having good luck in love. Everything was not for everybody. *It's not as if you were in love with him anyway. It was just sex and he's not even over his ex. Asking for nudes like a fucking teenager.* Alex slammed her hand against her mattress and then stood up. He had made love to her, met her family, and called his ex while sitting on her damn bed. Just as she was about to rip the comforter and sheets off her bed, there was a loud knock at the door.

"Go away," she screamed, thinking it was Wes.

"Alex, let me in," Robin said. Alex crossed over to the door and opened it. When she saw her sister's tearstained face, she was worried.

"Robin, what's wrong?" Alex ushered her sister into the room.

She flung herself into Alex's arms. "The adoption, everything fell through. I'm never going to be a mother."

"Oh, Robin, I'm so sorry. Maybe . . . maybe this wasn't the right time or baby for you and Logan," Alex said as she stroked her sister's back. "Do you want to talk about what happened?"

Robin took a deep breath and a step back from Alex. She started pacing the floor. "Well, her family came around, and when we were going to sign the papers her dad and lawyer came in. I guess you can be a preacher and still need to find Jesus."

Alex knew what she wanted to say wouldn't bring comfort to her sister, but she was glad this mother wasn't abandoned anymore. But it hurt that Robin wouldn't have the son she'd been preparing for.

"Robin, there's nothing I can say that will make you feel better," Alex said.

Robin wiped her eyes. "But at least you get it. Logan was just so nonchalant. I wanted to punch him. And he had the nerve to say that he was happy that her family was accepting her and the baby."

Alex chewed on her bottom lip. "Well . . ."

Robin took a deep breath. "Just because I know she needs her family and I'm happy for her, it doesn't mean that my feelings don't matter. I'm hurt. But I sat there, smiling, asking her if this was what she wanted, saying prayers with her hypocrite-ass father. Then I watched them walk out of the room and I felt hopeless."

"I'm sorry, Robin. But you can't let this come between you and Logan after all you've been through."

Robin dropped her head. "I know. But what do I do with these feelings?"

"When I'm feeling like crap I have a secret way to work it out."

Robin raised her right brow. "You have edibles?"

Alex laughed. "Um, no. But I have a standing invitation at the Alice Davis Dance Studio. It helps me forget for a little while."

"Ballroom dancing? And all this time I thought you didn't listen to anyone."

"Anyway. Do you want to go?"

"Yes. Hopefully this will calm me down before I talk to Logan. I think I might owe him an apology."

"Do I even want to know?"

"I called him a heartless asshole before I left."

Alex shook her head before grabbing her dance bag. "I'll drive," she said.

"Why are you available to do this in the middle of the day? I thought you and Daddy had a meeting with your boyfriend."

Alex cleared her throat. "First of all, I don't have a boyfriend, and Dad is the one making the decision about the new wing. There's no need for me to be there."

Robin gave her sister serious side-eye. "Don't act like you have to babysit me when . . ."

"What if I need my hand held, too?" Alex blurted out. "What if I put myself out there and got my feelings stomped on?"

It was Robin's turn to hug her sister. "What happened?"

Alex expelled a sigh. "I let myself fall for a man who clearly hasn't gotten over his past, but that's over now."

"Alex, I'm sorry. How do you know that's true? Because what I saw this morning was . . ."

"All a fucking act. That man sat on my bed, telling his ex-wife to send him nudes."

"What?" Robin shrieked. "The same bed where y'all made love?"

Alex nodded. "Do you know what a fool I feel like right now?"

"It's not your fault. I can't believe he would do that to you."

Alex shut her eyes, trying not to think about all the things he'd said to her. His words, his touch, and his kisses made her believe she had a chance to love someone. To open her soul to a man who wanted her the same way. Someone who didn't see her as a means to an end. A way to get an audience with Sheldon Richardson. While her sisters acted as if Alex was so tough and strong, she wasn't. She was fragile, though she would never admit it.

"Do you want to go to the dance studio with me?" Alex asked. "I know it's not going to heal all our problems, but it's something."

"Why not? We can work some things out on the dance floor. And if that doesn't work, we can kick Wes's ass for being a dick."

"That's not a bad idea. But don't tell Yolanda. She might put Chuck on that man."

"You say that as if it is a bad thing."

Wes walked into the conference room with his sketches for the new wing of the bed-and-breakfast. He'd hoped

Alex would've been in there so she could tell him why she'd been so upset earlier. While he didn't know what had happened with Robin, he knew the Richardson sisters were close and looked out for one another in ways he and Johnathan didn't. The Richardson family dynamic was a marvel to him. Though everyone was different, they still got along, unlike his father and his only sister.

Clinton walked into the conference room. "Sorry to keep you waiting," he said.

"No problem," Wes replied as he stood up to shake his hand.

"So, my wife says you're a unicorn."

"What?"

"Somehow you've made Alex happy. Don't know what you're doing, but keep doing it," Clinton said.

"Where is Alex?"

"I was expecting her earlier, but I haven't heard from her today."

Wes stroked his chin. "I don't know if I'm out of line or not, but is something going on with the sisters? Alex and I were together earlier and she got really upset, then I saw Robin in the lobby in tears."

Clinton cleared his throat, then pulled out his cell phone. "I know Nina is on assignment in Columbia right now, but if something is happening with her sisters, she would've said something." As he scrolled through his phone, Clinton shook his head. "I don't see a text from her."

Wes shrugged, his confusion growing. Before he could ask another question, Sheldon walked in. "Afternoon, gentlemen." He looked around the room and furrowed his brows. "Where's Alex?"

Clinton shrugged. "I haven't heard from her today."

Sheldon shook his head. "That's fine." He turned to Wes. "If anyone deserves to play hooky, it's my Alexandria. What do you have for us?"

Though Wes was wondering where Alex was, he showed Clinton and Sheldon the new sketches and told them how he'd gotten the idea for the designs.

"I was married to a Southern girl once. She lives in London now, but she remembers the vacations she spent with her grandparents here. She sent me some pictures today, and the joy was palpable."

"What was her name?" Sheldon asked.

"Jasmine Brown. Her grandparents were William and Lorraine Smith."

Sheldon clasped his hands together. "I remember the Smiths. They were such a joy. Nora used to send Christmas cards to our guests, and the Smiths were one of the few guests to send a card every year."

"Jasmine said spending time here made them feel like royalty."

"That was our plan when we opened the bed-and-breakfast," Sheldon said.

"And that's what this new wing should be about, royalty," Wes said as he pulled out the sketches and laid them on the table. Sheldon's eyes lit up as he looked at the renderings.

"This is just perfect," he said, then passed the sketches to Clinton. "It's like you captured the history of the city in the details of the beach. But the archway, that is something that reminds me of my Nora."

"I wanted to ask you for a favor," Wes said. "I wanted to do a rendering of you and your family welcoming guests to the property."

"That's a great idea. Let me get some pictures together of me and the girls."

"Perfect. I'm sure Alex will want some input on this," Wes said. "Is she coming?"

"I don't think so. She said she was helping Robin with some stress or something." Sheldon shook his head. "At least they're sticking together."

Wes was feeling a little better about Alex's attitude earlier. If it was about her sister, he just needed to check on her later. "Well, unless you have any questions for me, I'm going to head out," Wes said as he rose to his feet and shook hands with Sheldon and Clinton.

"Head out, or are you going to find Alex?" Sheldon asked with a smile.

"Well—" Wes said, then smiled.

"When you see her tell her I forgive her for missing the meeting today."

"I'll tell her," he said as he left the room.

Robin watched in awe as Alex and her instructor, Alan, glided across the floor like professional dancers. Alex was pouring her anger and soul into every move. She'd caught Alan off guard with a couple of her twists and kicks.

"Miss Alex, we need a break," Alan said breathlessly. Robin clapped.

"You guys were amazing. Who knew seeing my sister dance was the salve I needed?" Robin asked as Alan and Alex crossed over to her.

"Why are you so mad today?" Alan asked Alex as he handed her a bottle of water.

"No reason," she replied, then opened the water. She downed it in two gulps.

"We're having boy problems," Robin said.

"Speak for yourself," Alex snapped. "My problems are over."

Robin looked at Alan and shook her head. He patted Robin's hand. "Well," Alan said. "If your problems are over and your life is just the way you want it, you should celebrate."

Alex gave him a questioning look. "Celebrate? How?"

"You taking those killer moves to the state competition. I lost a dancer, but to be honest, she wasn't that good anyway. Come on, Alex, make him eat crow and regret the day he let you get away."

Her mind flashed back to the conversation she and Wes had had over dinner.

"So, when is the contest? I want to see those moves."

"I'm not doing it."

"Why?"

"Because that's not who I am. I just dance for me."

"Oh, okay, so tell me you're afraid without telling me you're afraid."

"Listen, I'm not trying to embarrass myself on a statewide level."

"Your words, 'you're pretty good at it.'"

"I am."

"Then you need to compete."

"It's in two weeks, I'm pretty sure you're going to be gone by then."

"I'm the boss. I can stay as long as I want. You should enter the contest."

Shrugging, she looked at Alan. "Fine, I'll do it. What am I dancing?"

"With you in the contest, we can do the paso doble. Or maybe the tango." Alan clasped his hands together. "The choices are endless with your talent. Thank you, thank you for doing this!" Alan twirled across the floor.

"Color me surprised," Robin said. "You're going to let the world see Alexandria Richardson can do something else other than running a business?"

Alex tried to smile, but tears sprang into her eyes. "I'm only doing this because I let *him* move me out of my comfort zone. I believed it was my turn. You and Logan found your way back to each other, Yolanda found Chuck, Nina and Clinton are deliriously happy, hell, Daddy is engaged. Why can't I get my happy ending?"

"Alex," Robin said as she hugged her sister. "Are you sure you and Wes are through?"

"Let me know if you would stay with a man who sat on your bed telling another woman to send nudes. Or, even better, telling his ex that he'll never meet anyone like her. If he wanted to be with his ex, he should've made that clear. But he made this big, fake effort to come here and pretend that we meant something more to each other. He just wanted to come here and humiliate me."

"That's what I don't get. Why come here for you if his mind was elsewhere?"

"When I found out that he was doing the new wing, I should've left it alone. You can't mix business and sex."

"Alex, I know you're hurting, but maybe you misunderstood something. Are you going to at least have a conversation with him?"

"I've talked enough." Alex tossed her water bottle in the recycling bin. "Remember when we wanted to go on *Star Search*?"

"My God, yes. But we couldn't come up with an act."
The sisters stood in front of the mirrored wall and struck
a pose.

"We should've danced," Alex said.

"Clearly, you're the dancer."

Alex did a quick two-step, then a spin. "Yes, I am."

"But you can't dance your way out of your feelings for
Wes," Robin said.

Alex rolled her eyes. "What do the kids say? *Catch
flights not feelings*? I have nothing for that man. It's the
disrespect for me. You know I will not be disrespected by
anyone."

"Well, if that's how you feel, I guess it's *good-bye,
Wes*."

After a few more dance moves Robin decided she was
ready to have an adult conversation with Logan. "Maybe
I'm pushing too hard for adopting a baby," she said as she
and Alex left the studio.

"You're going to be fine. Just make sure your husband
wants to be a father as much as you think he does."

"You're sounding like Logan right now. I want my
own family and I thought I'd dealt with everything, but I
haven't. I just want to . . ." Robin started crying and Alex
hugged her tightly.

"Robin, have you talked to a therapist about how you
feel?"

She nodded as she wiped her eyes. "She asked me why
family was so important and I couldn't answer. I mean, I
have you guys, I have Logan, but I still feel this empti-
ness."

"Sis," Alex whispered. "I know you got a lot of love to
give. You have a sweet spirit and you want to be like

Mom. You already are. Robin, if you and Logan adopt or hire a surrogate or whatever you all decide to do, make sure you're doing it for the right reasons."

"What do you mean, *right reasons*?"

Alex sighed and took a step back from Robin. "Do you remember Mr. Eldridge?"

"Yeah, that old, snaggletooth man who would always tell Dad he didn't have a son to carry on the family name. What about his ugly ass?"

"I heard him say that, and part of my whole being has been to make sure I represent the Richardson name. I wanted to make sure Dad's legacy would live on forever because of sorry men like that. As the oldest daughters, we internalized a lot of things. Look at Nina and Yolanda— they have a freedom we didn't give ourselves."

"Okay, I get that, but what does that have to do with me?"

"Robin, you were so close to Mom, you wanted to be like her, have a family, and that's something you won't let go. But you have to figure out if it is truly what you want or what you think is expected of you."

Robin blinked and fixed her lips as if she was going to say something, but she just nodded. It wasn't lost on Alex that she needed to take her own advice.

CHAPTER TWENTY-FIVE

When Alex and Robin arrived at the bed-and-breakfast, Alex sucked her teeth when she saw Wes outside with his camera.

"Why did you have to park over here?" Alex gritted.

"Maybe this is a sign. You need to talk to him and there he is. Everyone is going to have adult conversations today." Robin leaned over and gave Alex a kiss on the cheek. "Be a grown-up."

When Robin got out of the car Wes waved at her. Alex rolled her eyes, wishing that she hadn't introduced him to her sister, that she'd never felt his kiss or seen the glory of his naked body.

That shit didn't matter now because he'd made his decision about who he wanted and showed Alex exactly who he was. She got out of the car and refused to look at him. To hell with being an adult. She didn't want to speak to this asshole.

"Alex," Wes called out as he jogged toward her. "What's going on?"

"Wes, why don't *you* tell *me*?"

"Are your sisters all right, because earlier you were . . ."

"No, earlier when you were in my bed, I heard you."

"Heard me?"

She folded her arms across her chest and sighed. "Yeah. *I'll never meet another woman like you. Go ahead and send me pictures.*" Alex wanted to slap him, punch him in his chest, but she wasn't trying to make a scene.

Then he laughed. "You didn't hear what you thought you heard."

"Whatever, Wesley. If you want to be a playboy and spread your dick all over, fine. Do that, but don't come here and pretend I mean something to you. And don't sit in my bed telling another woman to send you nudes. You can legitimately kiss my ass and never speak to me again."

Alex turned on her heels and stormed away. She didn't want to hear Wes's excuses and she didn't want him to see her crying.

Wes counted to five before taking off after Alex. She was halfway to the elevator in the lobby when he caught her. "Alex," he said, trying to keep his voice even. She whirled around and glared at him.

"Not doing this here." She stabbed the Up button on the elevator keypad as if it had stolen something from her.

"Just so you know, that phone call was work-related."

Alex laughed, and the sarcasm vibrated throughout the lobby. The desk clerk glanced at her boss for a quick second. When she noticed Alex's arched brow she returned to looking at the computer screen.

"I'm not sure if I got an invisible tattoo on my forehead that reads *stupid* or if we're on a hidden camera show because you have to be joking. I take business calls all day and they don't sound anything like that."

"So, this is about pictures?" Wes pulled out his phone and scrolled to Jasmine's text messages. "See for yourself."

"I don't . . ." Alex gasped when she saw the photos of a family standing in front of the bed-and-breakfast.

"My ex grew up in North Carolina and her family spent many summers here. When she told me about her visit here, I knew she had pictures. Jasmine keeps pictures of things that make her happy. These are the pictures I asked her for."

Alex pressed the phone in his hand. "Oh."

"That's all you have to say?"

"I got to go," she said, then stormed out of the lobby. Wes started to follow her, but it was his turn to be pissed off. If she had such a low opinion of him, what was this all about? Why did she think he'd be spending time getting to know her if he had feelings for his ex-wife. And that was a freaking laugh. Jasmine had a whole life in London. And that life never including him. Wes never lamented the end of his marriage or wanted a replay with Jazz. It was obvious they worked well together, but their romance was beyond over. He didn't feel like he needed to explain all that to Alex because it should've been clear that she was the only woman he had an interest in.

What am I even doing? Wes thought as he crossed the lobby, calling out Alex's name. She was halfway across the parking lot before he caught up with her. "You don't get to be loud and wrong, then walk away."

"Maybe walking away is the right thing to do," she said in a low voice.

"The right thing for who? Let's be clear: I'm not going anywhere. Alex, I want you, I need you in my life. I didn't come here to soak up Charleston history. I came here for you."

"Wes, I made a mistake and I apologize, but since we're working together, maybe we should just leave it at that."

He shook his head. "Can't do it."

Alex folded her arms across her chest. "This isn't up for discussion. I skipped out on a meeting with you today because I was in my feelings. That's not who I am. I don't like being that person. I've never been afraid of anything. I never took a step back because I didn't put my emotions into business, yet here we are."

"We don't have to be here. I need you to just be honest and deal with something you're ignoring."

"I'm not ignoring anything. I just laid out why . . ."

"How do you feel about me? Because I'm falling in love with you and I don't want to be in love alone."

Alex gasped. "You–we don't . . . Do you mean it?"

"I wouldn't say it if I didn't. Your dad approved my design for the new wing. This is usually when I board a flight. But I see I'm going to have to stick around."

She raised her right brow. "Don't skip your vacation for me."

"I'm not skipping anything because I'm leaving here with you. I'm going to make you mine. Heart, body, and soul."

"Wes . . ."

He stroked her cheek and brushed his lips against hers. "Let's take a walk on the beach later."

"That's not a good idea."

"We need to talk, and waves and stars seem to calm you down. Humor me. If I come out here in two hours and you're not here, then I'm gone."

She nodded. "I'm going inside. 'Bye."

Wes watched her walk away and wondered if he would see her again.

Alex slammed into her room and paced the floor. Why was this so hard? Why did he have to say he was falling in love with her? And why was she so upset about it? Alex stopped and looked in the mirror. The confused reflection looking back at her gave her pause. *This is not you. Why can't you just tell him how you feel?*

"Because I'm afraid," she breathed. Part of her wanted to just crawl under the blanket and hide from the truth.

She stripped out of her workout clothes and headed to the bathroom for a quick shower. As she stepped underneath the spray, Wes's words echoed in her head: *Because I'm falling in love with you and I don't want to be in love alone.*

Alex turned the water off, ready to make the decision to tell him that he wasn't alone. She dried off, then smoothed coconut oil on her skin and ran a bit of it through her hair. Next, she needed to figure out what to wear. Before she could decide on her outfit, there was a frantic knock at her door. "Hold on," she exclaimed as the knocking persisted. Grabbing her robe, she pulled it on and crossed over to the door. Nina stood there with tears pouring down her cheeks.

"Alex," she said in between sobs. "There's been an accident. D–Daddy's in the hospital and Lillian . . ."

Alex pulled her sister into the room. "Let me get dressed. What happened?"

"I–I don't know. Hurry up so we can get there. Alex, we're not going to lose him, are we?"

"Come on, you can't think like that. Daddy isn't going anywhere." But inside, Alex was on the verge of breaking down. "Where's Clinton?"

"Hilton Head."

"Have you told Robin and Yolanda?" Alex tugged her dress over her head.

"They're at the hospital, I–I'm too scared to drive over there."

"Is he at MUSC?"

Nina nodded. Alex took her sister's hand and kissed it. "I got us. I'll drive."

The women rushed out to the car, and as they drove to the hospital, Alex noticed that her phone hadn't connected to the car's Bluetooth. She shrugged it off, just concerned about finding out her father's condition.

Upon reaching the hospital, Nina and Alex leaned on each other as they walked in. Alex crossed over to the reception desk and asked where Sheldon Richardson was.

She typed his name in the computer, then looked up at Alex. "He's in the emergency room. If you go down the hall and take a left, the nurse will be able to help you."

"Thanks," Alex said, then turned to Nina. She held on

to her sister's hand as tears spilled down her cheeks. "Nina, you need a second?"

She wiped her eyes. "No, let's go."

When they reached the emergency department, Alex spotted Yolanda, Robin, and Logan standing in a corner, smiling. What the hell?

Alex crossed over to her family. "What's going on? Where's Daddy and Lillian?"

Robin placed her hand on Alex's shoulder. "Take a breath. Everything is fine."

Alex narrowed her eyes. "Everything is fine? But Nina said . . ."

"You know Nina is a storyteller," Yolanda said. "I called her and said Dad was in an accident, and she ran with it, making up her own details."

Nina wiped her teary eyes again. "Wait, what are you saying?"

Logan stood in the middle of his sisters-in-law. "Pops has a broken ankle. He's going to be fitted for a boot. Ms. Lillian is going to stay overnight for observation. She may have a concussion."

Alex waved her hands. "So, what actually happened?"

"Well, Pops and Ms. Lillian were T-boned by a drunk driver on Savannah Highway. His car is totaled and it looks a lot worse than their injuries. So, Nina, don't look at the pictures."

Nina shook her head. "You don't have to tell me twice."

"Wait, I'm confused," Alex said, then pointed at Nina. "This one was acting as if . . ."

Yolanda shook her head. "Robin, I told you we should've called Alex and not sent Nina over there."

"I'm sorry," Robin said.

"Can we see Daddy?" Alex asked.

Logan nodded and led the women to the small room where Sheldon was resting. "Ah, there are my girls. You all see I'm all right?"

Nina rushed to her father's side and gave him a tight hug. "Daddy, I was so scared. I thought . . ."

"Shh, shh. I'm going to be fine, baby girl." Sheldon stroked her back as Nina cried.

Alex moved over to her father and sister. "There are better ways to get our attention, Dad." She tugged on Nina's arm so she would move. When Nina finally did Alex took a seat on the edge of the bed.

"Good to see you, Alex. Why did you miss the meeting today? Wesley's designs were inspired."

"I'm sure they were. But that's not important. How are you feeling?"

"With these high-power drugs, I'm fine right now. Once I get moved to a room, I'll be fitted for a walking boot."

"But remember, you're going to have to be off your feet for two weeks," Logan said. "I spoke to your doctor because I know Richardsons are hardheaded."

"Watch your mouth, Son." Sheldon laughed.

"Y'all are hardheaded," Yolanda said as she crossed over to her father and kissed him on the cheek.

"So, did you change your name to pot or kettle?" Alex asked. Everyone in the room laughed, except Yolanda.

"I'm not the hardheaded one in this room," she snapped.

"Darling," Sheldon said. "You are the most hardheaded child I have. When I pray for my girls at night I have to say an extra prayer for you and Chuck."

The laughter continued, and this time Yolanda joined in. "Well," Nina said. "Hopefully Nora will be more like her namesake and not her mama."

Sheldon shook his head. "I don't know why each and every one of you don't know that those stubborn streaks y'all have came from your mother. When Nora wanted something she dug in and would not be moved." He looked at Yolanda. "When she made up her mind about something, unless you had a stack of evidence to prove her wrong, there was no coming back." He tilted his head toward Robin, and Logan hid his smile. "And don't tell her no or say she couldn't do something. Oh, Nora Caswell Richardson would make you eat your words. Sometimes with a side of hot sauce." He gave Alex a pointed look. "Or with a thick glob of honey that choked you." Nina and her dad locked eyes.

"And what did we get from you, Daddy?" Nina asked.

"Three of y'all got my height."

"Well, you know what they say," Yolanda began. "Big things come in small packages." She was the shortest of her sisters, standing at five foot five. Alex always said Yolanda was loud to make up for the inches she didn't grow into. That was a hill Alex would die on.

"All right now," Sheldon said. "Don't y'all start anything in the hospital."

Logan smiled. "I'm going to go check on your room."

"And let me know how Lillian is doing, too," Sheldon said. "If you can pull some strings to get our rooms close together . . ."

"Already working on it," Logan said as he slipped out of the room.

A few minutes later Sheldon's pain medication kicked

in and he was out like a light. Alex expelled a cleansing breath.

"I'm so glad his injuries are minor," she whispered to her sisters. They all mumbled *yes*.

"I'm sorry I overreacted," Nina said to Alex, then hugged her. "But Clinton wasn't here to calm me down, so that job reverted back to you."

"You are an annoying little girl, you know that?" Alex said, then kissed her sister on the forehead.

CHAPTER TWENTY-SIX

The wind from the ocean felt like a slap in the face to Wes as the time ticked away. Alex had been late before, but this time felt different. Maybe she'd made her decision and it didn't include him. He pulled out his cell phone and called Alex.

Voice mail. *Message received*, he thought as he ended the call. Gathering his blanket and the picnic basket he'd gotten the sweet people in the kitchen to prepare for him and Alex, Wes headed back to his room. It was time for him to go.

He didn't acknowledge anyone as he crossed the lobby. He was pissed. What happened to her guts? She could've told him to his face that she was done and wanted nothing to do with him. She'd had her mind made up when she'd told him that she would meet him.

Slamming into his room, he tossed the blanket on the

bed and set the basket on the desk. Part of him wanted to march over to the family wing of the B&B and make her tell him to his face that she was done, that she wanted anything but him.

Now you're acting like Liz. She doesn't owe you anything. You're the one who decided to tell her you were falling in love with her. You probably scared her away.

He pulled up the airline app on his phone and booked a flight to New York. He'd be flying out at ten in the morning. After getting his confirmation, Wes placed his phone on the charger, then headed for the bathroom to take a long shower.

"So, who's going to spend the night with Dad?" Yolanda asked as she and her sisters sat in the waiting room. Logan had told them that Sheldon was going to stay overnight because he hadn't wanted Lillian to be alone. Then he'd experienced an adverse reaction to the pain medication, so he was going to be monitored to ensure it was a minor issue.

The doctor and nurses were settling Sheldon in his room, setting up the monitors and getting him comfortable in his bed.

"I will," Nina said. "I don't want to leave him alone."

"I can stay," Alex said. "Won't Clinton be back tomorrow morning?"

Nina shrugged. "If he's coming back in the morning, he's probably going straight to work. And with Dad being here, won't you be needed in the office?"

"You're right. I wasn't thinking," Alex replied.

"Wow, we have entered the *Twilight Zone*. Alex wasn't thinking about business," Yolanda said with a smile.

"I'm not fooling with you this evening," Alex said. "Don't you need to get back to my niece and nephew?"

Yolanda nodded. "Robin, are you ready?"

"I'll ride home with Logan. He's not working tonight, he's just following up on Dad and Lillian so we won't worry," she said.

"Or harass the nurses on duty tonight," Logan said as he walked over to the sisters to update them on what was going on. Lillian was being monitored to make sure her head injury wasn't serious. She had been placed in the room next door to Sheldon's even though he had tried to convince his doctor to put her in the room with him.

"They are so cute," Nina said.

"Only you would say that," Alex said.

Nina placed her hand over her heart. "I'm a hopeless romantic. Love is all around us if you just open your eyes to it."

I'm falling in love with you and I don't want to be in love alone echoed in Alex's head. Wes! She was supposed to meet him. She was about to reach for her phone, then remembered she'd left it.

"Robin, let me borrow your phone," she said.

Robin pulled her phone out of her purse and handed it to Alex. "Yo-Yo is right, we are in an alternate reality. You're out here without your phone."

As she dialed the bed-and-breakfast main number, she nodded toward Nina. "When you have this one crying in your face, it's hard to concentrate."

"Richardson Bed and Breakfast, how may I serve you today?" the desk clerk said.

As impressed as Alex was with the greeting, she was going to focus on why she made the call. "Yes, may I have Wesley Prescott's room?"

"I'm sorry, but that guest has asked not to be disturbed this evening. Would you like to leave a message?"

"Um, no, thank you." Alex ended the call and handed the phone to Robin.

"Did you just set up a booty call?" Robin whispered.

"No." Alex ran her hand across her face. "I think I've stepped in it this time. Wes and I were supposed to meet on the beach, but when Nina told me about Dad . . ."

"I'm sure he'll understand."

Alex snorted. "What if he doesn't? I wasn't understanding with him earlier."

"You mean when he was talking to his ex?"

"Yeah, and asking her for pictures she and her grandparents took at the bed-and-breakfast when she was a kid. Not nudes."

"Oh, damn. Sis, you got a lot of crow to eat."

Alex nodded. "And that's not my forte because I'm usually never wrong."

Robin scoffed. "I think you and Yo-Yo drink from the same fountain of delusion."

"At least you and Logan seem to be getting along better."

Robin smiled. "We talked and agreed to slow down on the adoption process. We're going to talk to a therapist and do things the right way."

Alex hugged her sister. "I'm glad you came to that conclusion."

Nodding, Robin sighed. "Honestly, I never fully dealt with the cancer and losing the ability to have kids. I mean, that shit with Kamrie allowed me to mask my feelings."

"You all haven't heard from the psycho nurse, have you?"

"Hell no. She is someone else's problem. I mean, they are in my thoughts and prayers, but fuck that bitch."

Alex brought her hand to her mouth and pretended to be shocked. But Robin's anger was directed in the right place. When that woman claimed Logan was the father of her son, it nearly destroyed Robin.

"Anyway," Robin said. "Let's tell Daddy good night, then you can go make Mr. Prescott understand why you left him hanging."

I hope he listens, she thought as they walked into Sheldon's room.

When Alex drove back to the bed-and-breakfast she wished she'd had her phone so she could explain herself. What was she going to find when she got to his room? She parked in her marked spot and rushed inside.

She gave a brief wave to the evening clerk, then headed for the elevator. Alex pressed the button three times, even though she knew it wasn't going to make the car come any faster. After what felt like an hour the doors finally opened. Alex pressed the button for Wes's floor and took a deep breath. What if he didn't open the door when she knocked? What if he was with some hot chick he met on the beach while he was waiting for her?

Stop jumping to conclusions, she thought as the doors opened. Stepping off the elevator, she took the three steps to Wes's door. She knocked and held her breath. A couple of beats passed and nothing. She knocked again, this time a little harder.

She heard footsteps and prayed they were his. The door opened and a shirtless Wes greeted her. "Oh, I hope I wasn't . . . um, hi."

"What are you doing here?"

Despite herself, Alex's eyes roamed his damp body, stopping at his waist. "I didn't stand you up."

"Then what do you call it? You show up hours late after I poured my heart out to you. What kind of games are you playing?"

"I'm not playing a game at all. My father was in a car accident and . . ."

"You couldn't pick up the phone or answer any of my calls?"

"Because I left my phone when my sister came to me crying about our father's accident. At that moment he was the most important thing to me." Alex dropped her head and started crying. "I was so scared. I thought . . ."

"I'm sorry. Is Mr.—Sheldon all right?" He took Alex into his arms and hugged her tightly.

"Broken ankle and a few scrapes," she said once she caught her breath. Wes lifted her chin and wiped away her tears.

"I guess today is the day we both jumped to conclusions—the wrong ones."

"Let me say I'm sorry for thinking the worst about you. But if I'm honest, I don't have high expectations in matters of the heart. It seems like no matter what someone gets hurt. So, I've been hiding. Better to be alone than in pain."

"That's no way to live," Wes said quietly.

"I know, and if it wasn't for you cannonballing your way into my life, I would've been fine."

He hitched his brow at her. Alex shook her head. "You can't miss what you never had."

"But what happens now, since you've had a taste?" Wes asked.

Alex sighed. "Maybe I blew my chances to find out what to do next."

Wes winked at her, "You came really close." He led her over to the bed. "Let me put some boxers on. Do you want a drink or anything?"

Instead of sitting on the bed, Alex followed him to the dresser and wrapped her arm around his waist. "I do want something. And you don't need to waste a clean pair of underwear." She pulled off his towel and stroked his dick until he moaned in delight.

"If this is how you say you're sorry, please feel free to mess up every day."

"I was just getting started, but if all is forgiven, I can stop." She dropped her hand. Wes reached for it and placed it on top of his hard penis.

"Don't stop now," he said. Alex kept stroking him and then she licked the side of his neck, and Wes moaned. "You're not playing fair at all."

She brought her lips to his ear and licked his lobe before saying, "This isn't a game, sir."

Wes spun around and smiled. "Then let's take this to the bed."

She nodded. "Let's do it."

The couple walked to the bed and Alex stripped out of her clothes before curling up beside him. She brought her lips to his ear and kissed it slow, tracing his ear with her tongue. She nibbled his lobe and stroked his chest.

"I'm so sorry I doubted you." Not waiting for his reply, she kissed him slow and deep. Their tongues danced like they were in a ballroom. She pulled her mouth away from his and licked her lips. "And I'm sorry you thought I was just going to leave you hanging on the beach with no explanation." She brushed her lips against his chest, then flicked her tongue across his nipples, making him call out her name. Muttering it like a mantra as she eased down his body, using her tongue as a guide. When her mouth hovered over his penis, she said, "And this is the last *I'm sorry* you'll get from me for a while. Normally, I'm always right."

"If this is you wrong, I don't want you to ever be right."

She took him into her mouth, licking him slow, sucking him hard. Wes gritted his teeth and released a growl as she took him deeper. Her mouth was hot and wet and the more she sucked, the wetter she got everywhere. Her need and desire for Wes was about to explode like a volcano. But she'd have to wait until he was ready. After all, she was offering the apology. Lick. Suck. Lick.

"Stop, stop," he cried. "I don't want to come right now. I need you on top of me."

"Protection," she said as she tore her mouth away from his hardness.

He pointed to the nightstand. Alex opened the top drawer and found an unopened box of condoms. She wouldn't allow any negative thoughts to form in her mind. Why wouldn't he have condoms? He knew they'd have sex at some point during his visit. That was the nature of their relationship. She opened the box and took out one of the golden packets. Wes wanted to reach for it, but Alex had rendered him motionless. Lucky for him, she made quick work of opening the package, sliding the condom in place, and mounting him. She gripped his shoulders as she ground against him. Slow. Then fast. Wes gripped her waist, slowing her down to his rhythm.

Slow. They went slow, pressing their bodies against each other.

Alex nipped at his lip as her thighs began to tremble. He ran his index fingers down her inner thighs and she came hard and fast.

"Now, promise you won't do that again," he whispered before reaching his own climax. Alex tried to speak as her body spasmed from the most epic orgasm ever. After her breathing returned to normal and her heart rate slowed, she was able to say, "If this is what happens when I'm wrong, maybe I should do it more often."

"Only if this is the apology I'm always going to get. Or you could wrap yourself up in a nice little nurse's uniform, a pair of red heels, and fishnets," he said with a wink.

"You're a funny young man. Being a nurse isn't sexy. You know all the nurses I saw tonight had on scrubs and Crocs."

"I'm sure that would look good on you and even better balled up on the floor." He patted her hip. "I guess I need to change my plans for tomorrow morning."

"What did you have planned?"

"I was going back to Brooklyn and sending Kyle down here to finish the project."

Alex propped up on her elbow. "So, if I hadn't come here tonight, I wasn't going to see you again?"

"Maybe. I can't say that two or three months from now I wouldn't have booked a room here just to see the look on your face."

"Alone or with a guest?"

"Depends on how many of my texts you ignored. But I

wouldn't want to bring drama to your family's property, so I guess I would've come alone."

"How nice of you. Interesting that you thought it out."

"So, check this: I was in the shower and I was thinking that I wasn't mad at you. I was sad that you expected the worst out of life and that I hadn't showed you that I had nothing but the best intentions for you. Then I was mad at me because I failed."

"Come again?" She wrinkled her nose in confusion and tried not to notice that her pussy was throbbing with need or that his erection was growing. "How had you failed?" *Please don't touch my thigh*, she thought as he inched closer to her. And he put his hand on her knee. Then her thigh. *Damn it, how am I supposed to listen now? Just look into his eyes. Do that bs Nina says she does in the locker rooms.*

She tried it for about fifteen seconds. It didn't work. She was looking at his beautiful dick while he was pouring his heart out.

Wes whistled and pointed at his face. "Ma'am, eyes up here."

"I'm not ready to have this conversation with you until you put some shorts on at least."

"Fine," he said with a smile, then covered his nakedness with the blanket. "But hear me out for a second."

Alex took a deep breath, then pushed his hand away from her thigh. "Go for it."

"I should've shown you how much you mean to me so you would've never had to question my feelings."

Alex's eyes filled with tears, but she didn't say anything, fearing she'd be a blubbering mess. And Wes wasn't done.

"I'm not a fan of the South; this was going to be Kyle's project. But meeting you changed everything. You were the one thing I didn't know I needed, but I know now that you're the one thing I can't live without."

"Wes," she breathed.

"Don't make me live without you," he said. "Let's give it a try."

Alex stroked his cheek. "Okay," she said, nodding her head. "Just do me a favor and don't break my heart."

"I got you," he said, then gave her a piercing kiss that made her shiver. Maybe this love thing wasn't that bad.

CHAPTER TWENTY-SEVEN

Over the next few weeks Alex was in charge of operations at the bed-and-breakfast. Wes stayed on at the property, spending time with her and getting to know her sisters, who he thought were hilarious. Especially when they found out she had entered the dance competition.

That night everyone had gathered at Nina and Clinton's place in Summerville for dinner. As they lounged outside on the patio, Wes made an offhanded comment about dancing.

Yolanda broke into laughter as she rocked her son. "Who are you going to dance with, Wes?"

"Um, Alex. Your sister has some moves."

"He's right," Robin chimed in.

"You guys can stop talking about me as if I'm not here," Alex said as she leaned on Wes's shoulder. She noticed Nina was staring at her, smiling as if she was watching a movie or something.

"You didn't tell them about next week, did you?" Wes asked.

Alex shook her head. "You see how they are."

"What's happening next week?" Nina asked. "A wedding?"

Robin shook her head and pointed her thumb at Nina. "Clinton, no more wine for this one."

"Right," Alex said.

"But for real, what's going on next week?" Yolanda asked. Robin smiled, but the cold glare from Alex told her that she should keep her mouth shut.

"Okay, fine," Alex began. "I'm representing the Alice Davis Dance Studio in the statewide competition."

Yolanda gasped and Nina nearly dropped her half-empty wineglass. "You're a dancer now?" Yolanda exclaimed.

"Y'all, Alex is good at it," Robin revealed. "I saw her moves and she'd win *Dancing with the Stars*."

"This one?" Nina asked, pointing her thumb at Alex.

"Yes," Wes said. "Seeing her dance is like watching honey flowing over sugar cubes."

Yolanda rolled her eyes as she handed Chuck Bradford and he handed her Nora. "Baby girl, your auntie has been holding out on us. I need visual proof."

Alex looked around at her sisters and brothers-in-law. "You're a jerk, Yo-Yo. Charles, you're a saint for sticking with her. But we don't accept returns, so she's yours for the rest of your life."

"I wouldn't have it any other way," he said as he winked at his wife.

Alex turned to Clinton. "Do you have any Coltrane?"

"Of course." He called out his smart speaker's name. "Play *A Love Supreme*."

Alex stood up and started swaying to the music. Then she did a quick step, a twist, a kick, and an elongated dip. Nina and Yolanda were speechless as everyone else clapped. Wes stood up and pulled Alex into his arms. Bringing his lips to her ear, he smiled. "With moves like that, you're going to win. But I know one thing, we should get out of here because I need to see that again."

Alex grinned. "With or without clothes?"

"All right, guys," Wes said. "We're out."

"No, no, no," Yolanda said. "Alex, where and when did you learn those moves. I mean, damn."

"I started dancing ten years ago to relieve stress. Lord knows I should thank you and Nina for me being this good. Y'all were stress monsters."

"So, what you mean is *thank you*?" Nina quipped.

Alex turned to Wes. "You see why I don't like them?"

"Okay, so why did you keep this hidden?" Nina asked. "You could've been all over the state using your moves to promote the B&B."

"Yeah, no. I did this for myself. Another workout so I didn't strangle my younger sisters or Randall Birmingham."

"Oh, you should've strangled that sack of shit," Clinton snapped.

"Ouch," Wes said. "Guess that guy isn't a Richardson favorite."

"Hell no," Nina said. "He had my husband arrested, tried to make Alex think Clinton was trying to steal the company and using me. He's trash. The absolute worst."

"Anyway," Alex said. "Alan thinks we're going to win because I'm dancing the paso doble."

"That's a hard dance," Robin said.

"But it's my favorite," Alex replied with a shrug.

"And we're going to go practice," Wes said. "See y'all later." Alex laughed as he ushered her to the car.

"You're too much," she said as she unlocked the car and they got in.

"No, you don't know what you do to me. Every time I see you dance, I think about that night on the cruise and how much I wanted you."

"Now you have me," she said as she started the car.

"That's right, and I want you again and again."

"Can I show you something?" she asked as they started driving.

"Sure."

Alex drove to a small park off the main road. She pulled into the small driveway and Wes looked around, feeling a bit confused. "This is usually where the bad things happen in the horror movies."

"You trust me, right?"

"That's usually the second sign something bad is going to happen," he replied with a laugh.

"Listen, you're ruining what can be a beautiful moment." She put the car in Park and they got out. Alex linked her arm with his and led him to the reflecting pool. Two benches surrounded the silver pond.

"Wow, it's beautiful," he said. "Sorry for the jokes. It reminds me of our visit to the spring on the island."

"I thought about that when we were on the way to Clinton and Nina's. I used to pass this place without a second thought, but I'm starting to see the beauty in nature and I wanted to kiss you by this pool."

"Um, say less," Wes said as he caressed her cheek. Their lips met in what felt like an electrifying kiss. Alex melted against his chest as his hands roamed up her back. They broke the kiss and stared into each other's eyes.

"Dance with me," she said as she stood up.

"Yes," he replied. Wes stood and took her into his arms. As they swayed together, Alex really felt as if she and Wes had something real, something strong. And she was ready to admit that she was in love with this man. She was happy. There wasn't a cloud hanging over her head.

"You know, when you win this competition, we're going to have to celebrate with two trips," Wes said.

"Two trips?"

He nodded. "First, you got to see Brooklyn. Then we're getting on a jet and heading to Alaska."

"Wait. What?"

"That's if you win first place. Second place, we're off to the Bahamas."

"Oh no, that's too much pressure," she said. "Thank you."

"For what?"

"For being everything you said you were. And thank you for making me fall in love with you."

Wes brushed his lips against hers. "I'd say *you're welcome*, but I have to thank you, too. I never thought I'd meet someone who would take my breath away the way you did."

She kissed him soft, slow, and deep. "We should probably go because I want to make love to you for the rest of the night."

"Sounds like a plan to me."

They rushed to the car like two teenagers who just found out there were no parents at home.

*   *   *

Wes woke up with a start. His arms were empty and he knew he'd fallen asleep with Alex in them. He heard the shower going and smiled. Just as he was about to join her in the bathroom, his phone rang. He was surprised to hear it was Johnathan.

"What's up, J?" he asked.

"Just checking to see if you're still among the living down there in the South. Is there a problem at the bed-and-breakfast or something?"

"Not a problem at all," he said as the bathroom door opened and Alex walked out. A pink towel hugged her damp body and he wanted to tug off the towel and get a repeat of last night. "This is an important project and I'm more hands-on with it." He winked at Alex as she picked out her underwear. "What's going on, Johnathan?"

"We have some proposals we need to go over and I thought you would've been back weeks ago. You sure you're not on another vacation?"

"Yeah. You know, you can send me the documents and I can go over everything without being in the office."

Alex dropped her towel and Wes nearly dropped his phone. "E-mail me everything, and yeah, I'll get back to you." He hung up the phone before his brother could reply. Wes stood up and crossed over to Alex.

"If you wanted me to get off the phone, you could've just said that," he said, wrapping his arms around her waist.

"Slow down, cowboy. Remember, we're having break-fast with my dad, then I have rehearsal."

"Alex, as good as you are, you can skip rehearsal today and we can hit the beach. I found this nice, secluded spot where . . ." There was a loud knock at the door. Alex groaned.

"Go away, Yolanda!" Alex called out.

"No, you have to let me in! I have your dance costume."

"This can't wait?"

"Just because Wes is in there with you, it doesn't mean I'm going away."

Wes smiled and shrugged. "I guess you better let her in." He grabbed Alex's robe and handed it to her before he ducked into the bathroom. Even though Yolanda knew he was there didn't mean she needed to see him in his boxers.

He heard Alex open the door and how exuberant Yolanda was about her costume design. "Put it on, put it on. I was up all night making this."

"Just neglecting my niece and nephew, huh?"

"You know, when they come in the studio with me, they just watch me like I'm creating magic. Chuck didn't believe it at first, but he tried to take them out when I was working one night and they cried; he brought them back and complete silence."

"Wow and wow. This is . . . Are you sure about these colors?"

Wes's curiosity was piqued. Now dressed in his jeans and a tank top, he walked out of the bathroom to see Yolanda's creation.

"My God," he said as he drank in Alex's image in an emerald green, pink and gold gown. It was fitted with a flared skirt. The bodice was made like a halter top, the back cut out right above her hip. She looked like the supermodel he assumed she was when they met on the cruise.

"He likes it—you have to wear it," Yolanda said with a smile.

"But can I dance in it? No doubt this is beautiful, but I have to make sure I can move in it. Can I take it to rehearsal this afternoon?"

"Yes, if I can come and video it for Instagram."

Wes laughed. "I have to see this," he said.

"Whatever, but if I pop out of this, you better not post it," Alex said as she studied her reflection in the mirror. "It is a really great design, Yo-Yo."

"Just FYI, I do wedding dresses, too," she said, then dipped out of the room.

After Yolanda left the room Alex didn't know if she should acknowledge her sister's remark or just get ready for breakfast. She wasn't thinking about marriage and she didn't want Wes to think she was trying to pressure him into anything.

She slipped out of the gown, then laid it across the bed.

"If you don't put on some regular clothes, we're not going to make it to breakfast," Wes said as he drank in her naked body.

"Down, boy," she quipped. Alex dressed quickly in a cropped top, blue leggings, and white sneakers. "Regular enough for you?"

"Nope, still too sexy," he said as he pulled her into his arms and kissed her.

She smacked him playfully on the shoulder. "Let's go," she said. As they walked to the main building, Alex turned to him and said, "I hope my sister didn't put you off with her wedding-dress comment."

"Why would that put me off? I see the kind of relationship you guys have and I know she was messing with you."

Alex couldn't explain why she felt some kind of way about his answer. She was just settling into the idea of being in a relationship and now she was upset because he didn't want to get married. *Stop tripping.* Once they got to the dining room Alex was surprised to see so many people in there. Many were staff members, some she didn't recognize, and her sisters and brothers-in-law were there.

"I didn't know this was a party," Alex said when Robin and Logan crossed over to them.

"Me either," Robin said, then turned to Wes. "Good morning, Wes."

"Morning," he replied as he and Logan shook hands.

"Is this about the new wing?" Logan asked him.

"Not that I'm aware of. I know Sheldon wanted to wait a month before construction started."

Alex nodded. "We're trying not to interfere with the busy season."

Robin touched Wes's shoulder. "Daddy is so excited about your designs."

He glanced at Alex. "This place is magical. I found a lot of inspiration."

Alex tried to hide her smile, but Robin noticed. "I bet you did," Robin said. "Yolanda and Nina are saving our seats. And you don't know what this is all about."

"I don't," Alex said as they walked to the table.

Nina stood up and hugged Alex and Wes. "Good morning, guys," she said. "Yolanda told me about your ball gown and that we're going to watch you practice in it."

"Really? My rehearsal is going to be y'all's field trip?"

Yolanda shrugged. "Listen, this dancing thing is new and it's not fair that Robin has seen the full effect of it. And he danced with you."

Chuck shook his head. "Baby, I'm going to turn away if Alex decides to do something to you."

"Wow. You're lucky I love you," she said, then kissed him on the cheek. "Besides, Alexandria the Great knows I'm her biggest fan."

"Oh do I?" Alex jibed. "We're going to have to talk about you having a fashion show here soon."

"Wait. What?"

"You're a brilliant designer and I want to see you have all the success in the world. I know what you lost, closing your shop in Richmond."

Yolanda shivered. "I don't even want to think about that." Chuck wrapped his strong arms around his wife's shoulders.

"It's okay, darling. We're over that and you're safe," he said.

"I know. All thanks to you," Yolanda replied.

"Excuse me?" Nina snapped. "As I recall, I was blamed for introducing Chuck Morris into your life. Where is my thank you?"

Alex cleared her throat. "Do I need to tell Daddy you two are showing off in public?"

Robin laughed as Yolanda and Nina rolled their eyes at Alex. Seconds later, Sheldon, who was just in the walking boot now, no longer needing crutches, and Lillian walked into the dining room. Everyone got quiet when Sheldon held up his hand.

"Thank y'all for being here this morning," he said. "Life will take you through many twists and turns. Lil and I can attest to that. We were making plans for a big party to celebrate our love. And had tasted some of the Southern Cake Queen's most delicious slices and then here comes that car." He looked down at his walking boot.

"So," Lillian said. "We made a decision. We didn't need a big party to prove how much we love each other. But we do need the most important people in our lives to share in this moment with us and have some cake."

"We got married this morning," Sheldon exclaimed. Everyone broke into applause, except for Alex and Robin.

Shock didn't begin to describe how Alex felt. She had accepted that her father loved a woman other than her mother, but to get married so quickly?

"You don't look happy," Wes whispered.

"I'm at a loss."

Robin locked eyes with Alex. *What the fuck?* she mouthed.

Yolanda looked at her older sisters. "Problem, ladies?"

"Oh, shut up," Robin said. "You know this is out of left field."

"Guys," Nina said. "Dad isn't getting any younger, and a car accident has a way of changing your outlook on life. Do not ruin this for them."

Alex sighed. Nina may have been right and she didn't want to spoil her father's happiness. She looked up at him and Lillian as they kissed. If anyone deserved happiness, it was Sheldon. He'd spent his life taking care of his daughters, making sure each one of them was happy. It was their turn to celebrate him. Alex stood up and ran toward the couple. Sheldon gave her a questioning look. "May I say something?" she asked.

Sheldon looked at Lillian, then turned to Alex. "All right," he said with a warning implied.

"This is the surprise that I needed this morning. You have always loved us, your daughters, your staff, and now Ms. Lillian. Your love gave us wings, and now I get to see my Dad happy again. Thank you, Ms. Lillian. I think I speak for all my sisters when I say welcome to the family and thank you for putting that brilliant smile on our father's face."

Sheldon and Lillian hugged Alex. Then the other sisters joined them up front and they all hugged the happy couple. Sheldon pulled Alex to the side as Lillian showed off her ring and accepted well wishes from Robin, Nina, and Yolanda.

"Thank you," he said. "Because I know you meant every word you said. That's going to go a long way with your sisters."

"You know, we're not babies anymore. We can't have wonderful lives and expect all your joy to only come from golf." Alex kissed his cheek. "I love you, Daddy."

"I love you too. Now, what's this I hear about a dance competition in Columbia?"

Alex laughed. "I'm trying something new. Stepping out of my comfort zone."

"Guess I should thank Wes for pushing you in the right direction. But that's going to have to wait until after the honeymoon. Make sure you keep that young man around."

"Will do. Now, where's that cake?"

Sheldon and Alex returned to Lillian and the Richardson sisters.

EPILOGUE

A lex stood backstage at the Colonial Life Arena, shaking her arms, trying to stay loose before her performance. She closed her eyes and took a deep breath. She knew she looked perfect. Her gown was flawless, her gold pumps were comfortable, and thanks to Robin hiring a makeup artist, her face looked phenomenal.

But she was nervous as hell. *Why did I agree to do this? What if I fall?*

"All right, Miss Alex, are you ready?" Alan asked.

"I better be, right?" Alex walked to the edge of the curtain. Of course the arena was packed. And . . . she was going to kill Yolanda. Her sister, sitting in the front row, had an "Alexandria the Great" sign. As soon as the twins were three, she was going to give them a pound of cotton candy, then take them to their mama in the middle of the night. That thought made her smile.

"And now, from the Alice Davis Dance Studio of Charleston, dancing the paso doble, Alexandria and Alan."

The curtain opened and Alex stood at the ready. She heard Yolanda scream and tried to keep a straight face. Five beats passed, then the music started. Alex threw her hands in the air and snapped her fingers as she took two quick steps toward her partner. Alan held out his hand to her and she took it, then spun around and kicked her right leg up. They spun, then stood face-to-face and quick two-stepped across the stage. Alan dipped her, then brought her back to standing. Now it was time for Alex's solo. She flung her skirt, cross-stepped, kicked her leg up, and dropped down in a split. Then, as if her spine was made of rhythmic springs, she sprang up, did a two-step, spun around, and ended up beside Alan. They stepped across the stage, hips rolling in concert. Then they turned, taking each other's hands, and floated across the stage with their fancy footwork. For the finale of the dance, Alex shimmied down Alan's body and ended the dance with a flourish.

The entire audience was on its feet, clapping and whistling. Alex wanted to cry. She'd done it. Would she do it again? Probably not. But damn, that felt good.

Once they were backstage, Alan and Alex embraced. "That was amazing! I need a cigarette," Alan said as he bounced up and down.

Alex exhaled. "Oh my God, that was exhilarating."

"And you were beautiful," Wes said as he walked over to her.

"How did you get back here?" she asked as he took her into his arms.

"In the words of the great poet Method Man, 'Cash Rules Everything Around Me.' I needed to kiss the best dancer in the state of South Carolina before she got the crown and forgot all about me."

She ran her hand across his cheek. "Wesley Prescott, you know you're unforgettable. I would've never done this had you not blown up my comfort zone. Thank you."

Wes brushed his lips across hers. "I better not mess up your makeup."

"Do it anyway," she said, then kissed him slow and deep. Wes's hands roamed her bare back as their kiss deepened.

He broke the kiss, then stared into her eyes. "Hey," he said. "Where do you want to get married? At the beach or New Year's Eve in Juneau?"

"What are you talking about?"

Before he could answer, the contest host called for all the contestants to return to the stage. Alan tugged at Alex's arm. "Sorry, handsome, we have to go get our trophy."

Alex shrugged and joined the other dancers on the stage to get their scores.

Wes watched as the dancers waited for the announcement of the winners. Didn't matter to him what the judges said, Alex was the winner. Looking at her as they called her name, he wondered what her answer would be when he got the words out. Wes knew there wasn't a life for him if Alex wasn't in it. She'd made him realize love was more than a four-letter word; it was the warm feeling he got every time he saw her, thought about her, kissed her, and made love to her.

He wanted her to be his forever love. All he could do right now was pray that she wanted the same thing.

"And the winner for best overall, Alexandria and Alan

from the Alice Davis Dance Studio!" Thunderous applause erupted from the audience. Alex and Alan took a bow, then accepted the trophy. Then the photographers started taking pictures, and of course Alex and Alan had to be in all of them.

Yolanda, Nina, and Robin rushed backstage. "Oh my God, Alex was amazing," Nina said.

"And she looked great, if I do say so myself," Yolanda said.

Robin shook her head and waved at Wes. "Did she dance with you like that when you guys were on vacation?"

He laughed. "There was more leg when we danced."

Finally, picture time was over and Alex rushed backstage. Her sisters enveloped her in hugs. "You really are Alexandria the Great and now you have the hardware to prove it," Yolanda said.

"Your sign was a bit much," Alex said. "But thank you all for cheering me on."

Wes cleared his throat and reached into his jacket pocket. "I think I asked you the wrong question earlier," he said.

Alex tilted her head to the side. "Something about Juneau, right?"

"No, how about I ask you this: Will you spend the rest of your life with me?" He pulled a green velvet box out of his pocket and opened it.

Alex's mouth dropped open as she looked at the pear-shaped diamond ring. "Are you serious?"

He nodded. "Are you going to be my vacation partner for the rest of our lives?"

"More importantly, can I design the wedding dress?" Yolanda asked.

Robin elbowed her sister. "Hush."

Alex brought her hand to her mouth. "Wes."

"Alex," he said.

"Yes, yes. And I want Juneau on New Year's Eve."

Wes grabbed Alex and kissed her as if they were the only two in the world. "I love you so much," he said when they broke the kiss.

**Don't miss the previous installment in the
Richardson Sisters series . . .**

OPEN YOUR HEART

**Their family's historic bed-and-breakfast in
Charleston, South Carolina, is a legacy the four very
different Richardson sisters are determined to protect at all costs. But sudden passion is a seductive—
and dangerous—complication . . .**

For fashion boutique owner Yolanda Richardson,
coming home is a matter of life and death. Witness to a
brutal crime, she's terrified to put her family's B&B in
the crosshairs after she starts receiving death threats. Her
only refuge is the protection of her reserved hired body-
guard, Charles Morris. But Charles is anything but safe.
His icy cool-under-fire—and hidden intensity—is too explosive for Yolanda to resist . . .

Love always equals loss—Charles knows that hard
equation all too well. Controlling his emotions keeps his
clients from harm—and his heart safe. Yolanda's beauty
and headstrong spirit have him wanting her in all kinds of
ways. But for her own protection, he has to do his best to
keep her at arm's length. Until unexpected danger and
lethal misunderstandings put their survival—and any
chance at a future together—on the knife-edge . . .

PROLOGUE

It was a warm May night and Yolanda Richardson had spent more time in her Richmond boutique than she'd planned. But the summer dresses and suits that had just come in were beyond beautiful. The yellow, pink, and purple outfits just popped. When she opened the shipment, she knew she wouldn't rest until she put those items on display.

And that was what set her fashion boutique apart from every other store in the city. Yolanda dealt in one-of-a-kind items from up-and-coming designers. Her plan was to add some of her own designs to the fold at some point. But believe it or not, the outspoken wild card of the Richardson family was fearful to share her work with the world. Her youngest sister, Nina, had seen a few of her sketches, but Yolanda hadn't shared them with anyone else.

There was something about your baby sister telling

you that the work was good that eased Yolanda's ego for a while. She looked up at her display window and smiled. She had the mannequins dressed in the amazing sundresses and had sunflowers surrounding them. It looked like one of those fields that people stopped at on the side of the road to take pictures. But instead of a sun lamp, she had a spinning disco ball in the corner, just to add a little quirk to the scene. And because she'd accidentally ordered the silver ball two years ago and had no idea what to do with it.

Now it had found a home that would call attention to the store. She was proud of her work, even if it was super late and she still hadn't eaten dinner. Her stomach growled, echoing the point that she needed to eat.

Just as she was about to take a picture of the display for her Instagram feed, Yolanda heard a couple of loud pops. She thought it was fireworks at first, but it was May. There were no celebrations going on in the middle of the night.

Then there were more pops. Louder this time and Yolanda realized they were gunshots. She took off from the sidewalk in front of the shop and ducked behind the trash cans on the side of the building and watched a car speed into the alleyway. She closed her eyes and prayed this was a bad dream.

Yolanda was frozen in place as the door to the white Chrysler 300 opened and a man was pushed out of the back of the vehicle.

Another two men hopped out of the front seat, both holding guns. Their faces filled with anger and malice burned in her brain and she prayed they didn't notice her quivering in the corner.

"You think you can steal from me?" the tallest man

growled. "There is always a consequence for every fucking action."

The man cowering on the ground threw his hands up. "Danny, man, you got it all wrong. I'll get you the money. Things are hard right now, but I'm trying."

Danny took a step closer to the begging man and all Yolanda noticed were his shoes. Patent leather church shoes. Who wears their Sunday best to threaten someone? She held her breath and tried not to move as she watched the drama unfolding in front of her.

"Don't do this, man. I'll get you the money."

"Too fucking late. You probably can't even come up with the interest." Danny pointed the gun at the man's head and fired three shots. Yolanda covered her mouth with her hand. Seeing death in person was nothing like the movies. Blood oozed into the street; parts of that man's skull littered the road. The smell of gunpowder filled the air and her nostrils.

"Pick him up," Danny ordered the other man as he crossed over to the car and popped the trunk. The other man, who was medium height but built like a muscular bulldog, picked up the dead man as if he were a pile of trash and tossed him in the trunk.

When Yolanda saw brain matter ease out of the man's head, her knee quivered and bumped the plastic trash can. Since it was empty and the street was silent, the thump echoed.

Danny and the bulldog turned toward the trash cans and Yolanda closed her eyes as she curled up into a ball. Did they see her? Was she going to join that man in the trunk with several bullets in her head? She held her breath.

"You think someone is out here?" the bulldog asked.

"Let's move," Danny said as they got into the car. Yolanda waited until she heard the car pull out of the alleyway before she dashed into the boutique. She was too shaken to call the police. So she hid in her office until the sun came up. To say she was afraid would be the understatement of the year.

As Yolanda left that morning, she kept looking over her shoulder for the mysterious Danny and that bulldog-looking man. Perhaps she was being unfair to bulldogs. That man looked more like the devil than an animal or a human. If she was lucky, those men hadn't seen her and knew nothing about who she was.

Now she regretted ignoring the security warnings the Business Neighborhood Association had sent out over the last few months. But she'd told herself that she was too busy getting ready for the summer season to pay attention to scare tactics. Crime wasn't a problem in downtown Richmond these days. Well, until last night. Yolanda took the long way home, trying to wash the memories of murder out of her head. But she kept seeing that man's brains oozing out of his head after he begged for his life. What would happen to her if she reported this to the police? The killers already knew where her shop was. It would only take a simple Google search to find out who owned it.

Doesn't mean they would know you were there last night. Yolanda might have known going to the police was the right thing to do, but she couldn't do that today. All she wanted to do was go home and try to forget with the help of a bottle or two of wine.

Once she got home, Yolanda called her boutique manager, Kelly Coe, and told her that she wasn't feeling well and wouldn't be in today.

"You've been working too hard, boss lady. Do you

need me to call Uber Eats and have some food sent over to you?"

"No, no. I have some soup and crackers here. Just take care of the orders for me, and if my sisters call, don't tell them I'm sick," Yolanda said, trying to keep her voice light.

"All right. Hope you feel better."

Yolanda told her good-bye, then curled up in her bed. She tried to close her eyes, but the images of last night's brutality played in her mind over and over again.

Yolanda tossed and turned until about noon. When her stomach growled and she knew she wasn't going to get any sleep, she headed for the kitchen and made a tuna salad sandwich, poured herself a glass of wine, and headed for the den to watch the news. Before she could take a bite of her sandwich, she saw his face on the TV screen.

"A local businessman was found dead in the James River." The man's face popped up on the screen and Yolanda dropped her wine glass. It was him. She listened intently as the newscaster finished the story.

"Affectionately known as Bobby G., Robert Gills owned a few restaurants and a couple of clothing stores in Regency Square. Police say he suffered multiple gunshot wounds before being dumped into the river. Two fishermen found the body this morning and called the police."

Yolanda shut the TV off and headed for the kitchen to grab a mop, broom and dustpan. This was becoming all too real. This man's death wasn't going to go away and those killers weren't going to disappear. She said a silent prayer that they'd never connect her to what they had done. Yolanda was still too afraid to talk to the police about what she'd seen, even if she knew it was the right thing to do. Her lawyer sister, Robin, would be ashamed of her inaction. And her father, Sheldon Richardson, would tell her that she needed to do the right thing.

She had no idea who Danny and the bulldog were, but they didn't look like the kind of people you'd testify against in court. She tried to reason that the police would find the killers without her help. Yolanda had seen enough *Law & Order* and true-crime shows to know that police solved murders all the time without an eyewitness.

At some point, you're going to have to do the right thing, her voice of reason said. Yolanda closed her eyes and wondered why her voice of reason always sounded like her older sister Alex.

After sweeping up the broken glass in her den and mopping up the wine, Yolanda had lost her appetite and decided to check in on her youngest sister, Nina. She hadn't talked to her globetrotting sister in a couple of weeks and Nina, who was a freelance sportswriter, always had something going on.

But what Yolanda really needed was someone to hold her and tell her everything was going to be fine, or better yet, wake up and find out that last night had simply been a nightmare. She grabbed her phone and started to call her sister when the phone rang. It was her boutique. She had already told Kelly in no uncertain terms not to bother her. If you can't play sick at the company you own, then what is the point? Yolanda reluctantly answered the phone.

"Hello?"

"Yolanda," Kelly said. "I know you're not feeling well and I didn't want to bother you, but I noticed a couple of our security cameras were off-line and then I saw something disturbing from last night."

Yolanda inhaled sharply. "What did you see?" She knew she should've deleted the video. Unlike Yolanda, Kelly paid attention to the business neighborhood watch newsletters. Made sense that she checked the security camera feed every day.

"Two men shooting someone in the alley. Should I take this to the police?"

"N-no," Yolanda stammered. "We're just going to keep this on the hard drive and not say a word about it."

"But, Yolanda, don't you think. . ."

"Kelly," she said quietly, "I was there and I'm afraid they're going to come back. If no one asks for the video, then we don't say anything about it." *And maybe all of this will go away*, she added silently.

"You were there? Oh my goodness, Yolanda! Did anyone see you?"

"I don't know and I don't want to discuss it further."

"All right. Well, if you need anything call me."

Yolanda ended the call and tossed her cell phone across the room. What was she going to do now? Since someone else knew what happened, Yolanda knew she had to do the right thing and go to the police. But first, she needed a little liquid courage.

A bottle and a half of chardonnay later, Yolanda was asleep on her sofa. The right thing was just going to have to wait.

The ringing of her cell phone woke her up a few hours later. She smiled when she saw the face on the screen: a great distraction, Harrison Moore, her off-and-on boy toy, who could cook. If he wanted to come over today, she would definitely let him spend the night. Just so she wouldn't be alone.

CHAPTER ONE

Two weeks had passed since the murder outside Yolanda's shop and she hadn't been back. She'd given Kelly all the excuses she could muster, from being sick to going out to do some meetings with designers. All she'd really done was hide out in her house and talk herself out of going to the police about what she'd seen. Yolanda had called the Crime Stoppers hotline, but when she was put on hold three times, she'd lost her nerve.

Today, she made the decision to head back to the shop. Kelly had taken on a lot of responsibility for the summer sale and the end-of-the-day reports proved that she'd been working hard. Yolanda couldn't keep leaning on her store manager like this. As she drove to downtown Richmond, she felt as if every car was following her. Then when she saw a Chrysler 300, she yelped. Thankfully, there was an older man driving and not giving her a second look. Arriving at work, she parked in the garage across the street and headed into her boutique.

"Aww, the prodigal owner returns," Kelly said as she folded shirts for a display in the middle of the shop.

"I'm here and you can go home for the day."

"Are you sure?"

Yolanda nodded. "I can't thank you enough for holding this place together over the last two weeks."

"It's been my pleasure. And that display window has brought so many people in. I think it's the disco ball."

Yolanda shuddered inwardly. That damned window had been why she couldn't sleep at night. But since the story had left the headlines and the evening news, maybe the killers didn't care who saw them.

That made her feel a little better about not calling the police. Though she'd never tell another person that she'd seen the killing. It was bad enough that Kelly knew.

"Hey, Yolanda," Kelly said before she headed out the door. "I meant to tell you, the neighborhood watch leader, Walton Kennerly, came by and said the detectives on the Bobby G. killing want the videos from the security cameras."

Yolanda's breath caught in her chest. "Um, what did you do?"

"I told Walton he'd have to talk to you." Kelly took a deep breath. "I think you should just give it to them. There are a lot of people who want to know what happened to Bobby G."

"Let me ask you something," Yolanda said. "If I give Walton the video, is there anything on it that identifies our shop?" She closed her eyes and watched the scene in the alley play out in her head all over again.

"I don't think so, it just has the time stamp and the alley. Have you been all right, being that you . . ."

The bell above the door rang, indicating that they had a customer. Yolanda was about to smile until she saw it was Walton.

Walton was the kind of guy who had gotten passed over for hall monitor in middle school and used his adult life to make up for that slight. She shook her head as she watched him walk in, dressed in dad jeans and golf shirt. His bald head glistened with sweat as he crossed over to Yolanda. He always looked as if he had tasted sour milk.

"Yolanda, glad to see that you're here," he said, then wiped his mouth with the back of his hand.

"What's going on, Walton?" she asked as she folded her arms across her chest.

"We're trying to help the police solve Bobby G.'s murder and I heard you all might have some video of what happened that night."

Yolanda shot Kelly a cold look. There went her bonus. Kelly turned away from her and looked down at her feet.

"Yeah, possibly," she said.

"I'm collecting the videos to give to the police, so, what do you have?"

"Give me a second to download the security video," Yolanda said as she started toward her office. "You can keep him company, Kelly."

"But I thought," she started. Yolanda rolled her eyes and headed for her office. She grabbed one of the USB drives she kept in her desk and downloaded the video. Watching it again made her stomach lurch. Maybe this was enough. Walton could be the hero and no one would know that she'd been in the alley.

Moments later, she returned to the showroom, where Kelly was helping a few customers. The two girls from Virginia Union University whom she'd hired as clerks and Instagram influencers were on the floor as well. Fine, Kelly could leave. "All right, Walton, here you go."

"Thanks. You never noticed the things that happened on this video before Kelly told you about it?"

"I don't check the feed every day."

Walton expelled a frustrated breath. "I asked all of the businesses here to do that in the last three newsletters that I sent out. Does the safety of the district not mean anything to you?"

Yolanda closed her eyes and squeezed the bridge of her nose. "I don't need your attitude right now. You have the video, now please leave."

"I'm sorry, I wasn't trying to give you 'attitude,' as you say, but it's scary to know that someone was murdered here."

Who the hell are you telling? she thought as she offered him a plastic smile. "Well, Walton, I have customers."

"Just a quick reminder, the next neighborhood watch meeting is Friday. Diamont's will be providing the refreshments."

Yolanda was tempted to go to the meeting to sample the new bakery's goods, but listening to Walton go on and on for hours was enough to make her decide to skip the meeting. Then again, Yolanda figured she needed to see if any other business owners knew about the murder. In her heart, she hoped someone else had seen Danny and the bulldog, then called the police. The more time passed, the more her conscience gnawed at her.

Bobby had a family and she knew she'd be devastated if someone killed . . . She wouldn't allow the thought to fester in her mind.

"I'll be there," she finally said. Her response was enough to get Walton to leave. Yolanda greeted her customers before heading back to her office. Sitting at her desk, she glanced at the phone and thought about calling the police. Fear paralyzed her as she placed her hand on the phone. Her name would be public record, her address and her phone number. What if they came after her?

And who was this Danny person? How dangerous was he? Yolanda wasn't willing to find out. She figured if she kept quiet, she could stay alive. So far it had worked, and if it wasn't broken, she wasn't going to fix it.